Weeding Out Lies

Weeding Out Lies

A
Texas Flower Farmer
Cozy Mystery

Jackie Layton

LeVel
BEST BOOKS

Author Photo Credit: Kellianne Layton

First edition

ISBN: 978-1-68512-387-1

Cover art by Level Best Designs

This book was professionally typeset on Reedsy.
Find out more at reedsy.com

Dedicated to my family. Tim, Mom, Dad, Bill, Amanda, Brooke, Allie, Cameron, Scott, Kellianne, Zane, Evie, Reagan, Chris, Carol, Kelli, Eric, Jessica, Sadie, Lainey, Joe, and Logan, I love you all! Thanks for supporting my dream of writing.

Praise for Jackie Layton's Books

"Completely charming and exactly what a cozy mystery should be."—Hank Phillippi Ryan (for *Bite the Dust*)

"Kept me guessing till the end. Andi Grace is an excellent amateur sleuth … and *Caught and Collared* is an engrossing and enjoyable cozy mystery."—The Book Decoder, Best Books of 2022

"Andi Grace is adorable, resilient, and has a doggedly curious need to solve a murder. A pleasure to read."—C. Hope Clark, award-winning author of *Edisto Tidings*

Chapter One

The aroma of coffee greeted me as I entered Anytime Coffee House on the square in Lutz, Texas. I adjusted the flat-bottomed bag of flowers on my shoulder while standing in line.

The stranger behind the counter stood taller than my five-foot-nine inches. He was lean with neat dark blond wavy hair and a cowlick that fell over his forehead. Muscles bulged in the sleeves of his green polo. It wasn't Brett Tirabasi, the owner, and my friend.

The lady in front of me shuffled away with her order.

"Good morning. Would you like to order our daily special?" The mysterious barista smiled.

I blinked because staring would be rude. "Where's Brett?" My voice squeaked, and my face grew warm from his intense gaze.

"He's taking off for a few days. I'm Jake Hunter, and I'm perfectly capable of handling your order."

"Nice to meet you, Jake. I'm Emma Justice." I riffled through my jute tote bag stuffed with a variety of spring flowers.

The bell dinged on the shop's door. Another customer entered the coffee shop, and I needed to place my order. Would the new guy be as accommodating as Brett?

"I don't mean to hold your line up, and I'm sure your brew-of-the-day is lovely, but I'd like a green tea with local honey."

He reached for a dark blue mug. "Do you ever drink coffee?"

"Sometimes, but I prefer tea. Please." My hand touched the cold metal travel mug in my bag. I dug it out and passed it to the barista. "Brett always

1

uses my personal cup to help save the environment."

Brett knew my regular morning beverage, and today I needed local honey to help with my allergies. I readjusted the turquoise and white polka dot flat-bottom bag on my shoulder. It matched my turquoise ring and had inspired my purchase.

"It's important to protect our planet." He set my travel mug to the side and winked. Then he proceeded to pour coffee into the blue mug and added a dollop of cream and a squirt of something, probably sweetener. "Humor me and try this while I prepare your tea."

I took the mug from him and couldn't deny his brew smelled appealing. Nutty notes drifted up from the half-full mug.

A young woman appeared and elbowed the irritating barista out of the way, then stepped in front of the register. "You may as well drink it. It's his Texas pecan morning brew. Coffee's on the house, especially since you're humoring Jake. Let me ring up your order."

"I'm confused about Brett's disappearance. And how did he find two strangers to run his business? No offense." If he'd planned to leave town, why not hire a local to take care of the coffee shop?

The dark-haired woman smiled. "None taken. We're old friends. Brett and Jake are almost like brothers."

"Okay." But was it? What was so wrong with Brett that he needed to bring outsiders into Lutz? I paid for my tea and stuffed the change into the tip jar before moving to a vacant table. I settled my bags on the empty chair beside me before I sipped the coffee. My taste buds sang at the deliciousness. Part of me wanted to dive into the coffee, while another part of me wanted to savor it. I took a second sip and leaned back, watching Jake recreate the delicious drink for the next customer in line.

His moves were smooth and natural. It wasn't his first time working as a barista, especially not if he could concoct his own Texas pecan coffee. Why was he here, though?

If Brett had been in an accident, the news would've been all over town. Lutz, Texas, was small, and secrets were as rare as an ice cube in the Sahara.

Jake appeared and placed my tumbler on the table. "One green tea with local honey for the lady." He slung a white towel over his shoulder.

"Thank you." I smiled. "The coffee's marvelous, though."

Again, he winked at me. "Regret not taking my advice?"

"Maybe, but I need this for my allergies." I met his gaze.

"Whatcha doing with all them flowers?"

"I'm a flower farmer and deliver flowers to some of the local businesses in the mornings."

"Do you suppose that's what's causing your allergies to flare up?" His eyebrows rose, challenging me.

What a smarty pants. "The flowers could be part of my allergy issues, but it's my job." I'd spent over fifteen years working as a pharmacy tech while raising my daughter. There wasn't a day I hadn't dreamed of working with flowers. When Abby started college a couple of months earlier, she'd inherited her daddy's life insurance. I quit my job and followed my dream, but this stranger didn't need to know my history.

"Hmm. Maybe I should buy some for this place."

"I'll fix you up after I finish my tea." I reached for my travel mug, then paused. "Is Brett really okay? I don't remember him taking a day off since the shop opened."

Jake shrugged. "He needed a few days for personal reasons. It just so happens I'm waiting to hear back from a job interview. So, I offered to fill in and even brought my sister to help."

"Is she also between jobs?" I held the insulated mug of tea tight, hoping some warmth would seep into my cool hands. For some reason, my hands and feet were almost always cold. Despite the warm morning, today wasn't any different.

"As a matter of fact, Celia took the week off in order to spend time with her big brother. She's also got a soft spot for Brett." He shook his head. "Go figure."

"Sounds like she loves both of you if she sacrificed vacation days to work at a coffee shop."

He glanced at his sister. "She's the best, but I better get back to it. You need anything else?"

"I'm good. Thanks."

He walked away with a spring in his step.

Why hadn't Brett confided in me about taking time off? We'd been friends for years, but maybe the relationship wasn't as deep as I imagined. Oh, well. I'd talk to him another time.

I took a sip of the tea then pulled the tablet out of my tote and reviewed my morning schedule. I'd already dropped flowers off at the library and the nursing home. I'd leave flowers here, then head to Heart of Texas Bed-and-Breakfast and Paige's Turn Bookshop. Afterward, I'd go home to check my email and work in the gardens behind my house.

I finished my hot tea and glanced around the clean coffee shop. Two women sat at a round table with a Bible open between them. Old men sat on stools at the counter, discussing college basketball and March Madness. A young mother with circles under her eyes jiggled a stroller while sipping her drink. I remembered the days of being a young mom and surviving on coffee and very little sleep.

"Sure, you don't want to get a cup of coffee to go?" Jake asked from his spot behind the counter. His brown eyes twinkled as if daring me. At least he hadn't winked again. The big flirt.

"If you promise my heart won't explode right out of my chest from so much caffeine, I'll buy a cup of your special coffee and take it with me."

"Give me your travel mug, and I'll wash it for you."

I walked across the chunky tile terrazzo floor. "Here you go."

Jake took my flowery travel mug and backed away. "Coming right up in an eco-friendly cup."

"Nice. Are you a poet or songwriter?"

"Not hardly. Today, I'm a barista, and I'll doctor your coffee the same as before."

I pulled ten dollars from my purse, then studied the flower selection in my bags. Carrying extras had become a way of life for me, and this day was no different.

Cosmos would work in Anytime Coffee House. "Hey, Jake, do you have a glass milk jug or something I can use as a vase?"

4

"Hold on." He disappeared into the back and returned soon. "Will this do?" He handed me a short, clear milk bottle.

"Perfect." I arranged white and pink cosmos in the vase even though I usually only delivered flowers. Money in one hand and the flower arrangement in the other, I approached Jake at the register. "Ta-da."

"Very nice." He took the vase and placed it on the glass shelf over the pastries. "How much do I owe you?"

"Consider it a gift welcoming you to Lutz."

He tilted his head to the side. "Thanks, Emma. Here's your coffee."

I placed the money by the register.

He pushed it back to me. "Consider it a gift for giving in to my pushiness."

He'd thrown my words back at me.

"Well played." I laughed and accepted his gesture. "How long are you in town for?"

Jake shrugged. "It depends on Brett and my potential new job. With a little luck, Lutz will be my new home."

"All right then. I'll see you tomorrow morning. You and Celia have a good day." I picked up my bags and headed for the door.

A man wearing a hoodie jostled me, making me glad Jake had secured the lid on my mug.

I glanced at the rude person. His shoulders were hunched, and he had dark blond hair and a scruffy beard. Those were the only details I could make out. Nobody I recognized, so I continued on my way. Three strangers on a Friday was an unusual occurrence. Many weeks I only saw visitors on Saturdays. People flocked to Lutz on weekends for retail therapy. We were known for antique and vintage shops as well as art galleries and eclectic shops. We also held plenty of festivals to draw more people to our little town.

It was a short walk to the bed and breakfast. I only needed to walk around two segments of the town square, then three blocks up Main Street.

I knocked and entered the establishment. "Faith?" She and her husband Zig had owned the place for a few years and placed orders with me at least twice a week. Great customers and better friends made for a perfect

5

combination.

The slim blond woman appeared. Her shoulder-length hair touched the top of her red polka dot blouse. "Hi, Emma. I'm excited to see what you brought."

"I've got a lot of bluebonnets and dianthus with some forsythia and marigolds. Lots of color for you this week."

"I love it. Would you help me arrange them in vases? Mine never look as pretty as yours."

"I'd be happy to help. It'll give us time to catch up."

"Let's work in the kitchen. I've already lined up some vases."

"Don't forget different things can be used as vases. Milk glass, tea cups, mason jars, a pitcher, or even a teapot. Look around this place and get creative."

Zig was sitting in the kitchen watching the morning updates on a sports station. "Morning, Emma." Zig was taller than most men. He'd retired from acting when it put a strain on his marriage, and the bed-and-breakfast had become a business for the couple to manage together.

"Good morning." I took a sip of my pecan coffee.

"Looks like I best mosey along and let you two enjoy your visit." He walked over and kissed his wife. His black skin made a stark contrast with Faith's paleness. They were a beautiful couple.

After he disappeared, we chatted about anything, everything, and nothing at all.

I stood back and studied our handiwork. "What do you think?"

"These arrangements will look amazing on the tables. Maybe one day I'll get the hang of it."

"Of course, you will." I gathered my belongings and strolled to the front door with Faith.

She said, "The weather is growing warmer, and we'll be full this weekend."

I understood her hidden message and nodded. "I'm working in the garden later, and I'll cut some flowers perfect for little vases in the guest rooms."

"Sounds great. I'm much better at small flower arranging." She smiled and raised her slender shoulders. "See you then."

"Bye." I clutched my bags and strolled to the bookstore while continuing to finish the pecan coffee. I retraced my steps to the square but turned onto Maple Street. Lutz was small enough I could walk most places.

I studied the front window of Paige's Turn Bookshop. New mysteries and classic whodunits were displayed with a magnifying glass and microscope. Paige was in her early fifties and had opened the bookstore when she retired from teaching. She and I shared in common following our dreams later in life, although I was only thirty-eight. We had each started businesses involving our passions.

Fridays were Paige's day off. At least she didn't interact with customers. She worked in the back of the store, ran, and got caught up on life in general. Willow Moore, the banker's wife, worked every Friday and part-time some of the other days. Willow and I got along fine, but the woman tended to hang out with other wealthy women. Until she decided to file for divorce a few months earlier, she'd only done volunteer work for her many social organizations, the school, and our church. She hadn't worked for a paycheck from the day her first child was born.

Willow and I mostly crossed paths at the high school. My daughter was a year older than Willow's daughter Christine, but they had been involved in some of the same after-school activities, like choir and volleyball. Our conversations mostly revolved around the kids, the weather, and local events.

I finished my coffee and entered the store. "Willow? It's me, Emma."

I set my bags near the register and unwrapped vases from tissue paper. With a careful touch, I lifted sunflowers, purple hyacinth, verbena, and seasonal foliage from my polka dot bag. Using my Swiss Army Knife, I trimmed the stems and arranged flowers in the two large white ceramic vases I'd bought specifically for Paige.

Celia entered the store, and a bell tinkled over the door. She met my gaze and paused. "Hi there. I'm sorry, but I didn't catch your name earlier."

"Emma Justice. It's good to see you again so soon. Are you off for the rest of the day?"

"I'm taking a break, and there was no way I could resist exploring the bookstore. You don't find many independents around these days."

"That's true."

"It looks like the owner carries some fun things as well as books."

"Yeah, Paige tries to have something for everyone who enters the store." I opened a packet of plant food and dumped some into each vase. "Willow works for Paige on Fridays. She must be in back. I'm only here to provide some ambience." I pointed to the arrangements. "Why don't you look around? I'll get water for the flowers and check on Willow."

"Maybe she hasn't officially opened yet." Celia glanced right and left.

I shook my head, and a red strand of hair fell forward. I pushed it behind my ear. "It's mid-morning, and the door was unlocked." The lights were on, and soft music played on the sound system.

Emma nodded. "That makes sense. Okay, I'll be in the mystery section."

The door to the back room was open, and I walked through the doorway confident Celia wouldn't steal anything. "Willow, you've got a customer."

Whoa. Something was wrong. Books were scattered on the counter, stool, and floor. Boxes had been tipped over. Various tools had fallen to the floor from a vintage red Craftsman toolbox that had been knocked over. Whenever I'd been back here in the past, the area had been neat and organized. Chills marched up my arms to my neck.

"Willow?" My voice cracked. "Where are you?" I inched toward the workstation, where I'd helped Paige open packages in the past.

On the back wall was a table with non-book displays. There was a hanging jewelry organizer with a display of gold daisy necklaces. Next to it was a jewelry stand with daisy bangles and a wooden display rack of earrings.

A shiny red flat slingback lay on the floor, freezing me in my tracks. Willow loved to wear red shoes, and I doubted Paige had started selling shoes. So, where was Willow?

I turned on my toe and fled to the front of the store. "Celia, I think something's happened to Willow. Will you help me find her?" Terror spurred me to ask a stranger for help.

"Sure." The brunette placed her stack of books on a table and crossed the store to join me. "Does she have health problems? Seizures or maybe a history of strokes? I know CPR, if that helps."

"I don't know her health history, but I've got a bad feeling." I latched onto her arm, feeling stronger, knowing I wasn't alone. With a little luck, I hoped we'd be laughing about my fears soon. It wouldn't be the first time I'd overreacted. "One of her shoes is lying on the floor."

"If there's one thing my brother taught me, it's facing our fears makes us brave." She smiled, but her lips wobbled.

Her youthful appearance made me feel like a jerk for involving her. "You know what? I shouldn't put you in the middle of this. Why don't you go back to the coffee shop? Or wait on the street. I'll come out and tell you when the coast is clear. If I don't appear in fifteen minutes, call the cops."

"No, ma'am. We'll stick together. That's another thing my brother taught me."

"Okay, thanks." I re-entered the back room with Celia at my side. "Earlier, I called Willow's name, but she didn't answer." We walked past the flat red leather slingback and the center worktable. "The bathrooms are back here."

"I'll check this one." She flipped on the light in the men's room, and I moved to the women's restroom. "Empty."

"This one's empty too. I guess we should look out in the back alley." I moved to the metal door. The wood bar used as an extra barricade leaned against the wall, so I reached for the knob.

"Wait, I'm going to call my brother." Celia's voice shook.

"Why?" Then again, what could it hurt? "Fine, but I'm going to see what's out here."

"Give him time to come over." She tapped on her phone.

I'd stalled long enough, and it really would be embarrassing if my imagination had galloped out of control. My shaky hand returned to the knob, and I turned it. Should I wait? No. I wasn't a baby. If my friend had tripped and hurt herself, moments could make a difference in her recovery. I pushed open the heavy door.

Willow Moore's body lay on the blacktop. Her sightless eyes looked to the sky. "No!" I stumbled past her to the tall chain-link fence separating the alley from homes on the next street. I clung tight to the steel mesh before I fell to the ground beside the banker's wife. A dark wet stain pooled near her head and shoulder.

My stomach churned, but I reached out with a shaky hand to check for a pulse, because that's what you were supposed to do. At least on TV shows, the person who found the body checked for proof of life. Placing my index and middle fingers on Willow's wrist, I lightly pressed against the pale skin. Nothing. I felt no pulse.

Celia screamed, and I fell back.

Footsteps pounded on the asphalt. Jake ran toward us from the far end of the alley.

I wiped tears off my face with my shirttail, stood, and moved to Celia. Poor thing appeared worse off than me. "Don't look." I touched her shoulder and asserted pressure, trying to lead her back inside.

"She's dead." Celia pointed at the body but stood rooted to the spot.

Jake reached us. "Aw, man. What happened?"

Celia ran to her brother and threw her arms around him. "It's horrible. That woman is dead. You must've suffered so much in Afghanistan and all the other places you went. No wonder you've been worried about Brett. Oh, Jake, this is dreadful." She sobbed.

"Shh, shh, shh. Let's get you inside." He succeeded in moving his sister away from the ghastly scene.

I closed my eyes and leaned against the brick building. It seemed cruel to leave Willow alone. Time passed. Seconds or minutes. Who knew? The fast pounding of footsteps forced me to open my eyes.

Jake reappeared. There was no smirk or flirty wink. He wore the expression of a man aware of the serious nature of the situation. "Emma, come inside with us. I've called the police."

I jumped at his nearness, then met his dark-eyed gaze. "She shouldn't be alone."

"She's in a better place than this. Come on." He didn't touch me, but his words captured my attention. "You can't help her now."

My pulse pounded on the side of my head. If I'd gotten to the store earlier, would Willow still be alive? Or would the killer have murdered both of us? My throat tightened, and I looked around the alley, not seeing a soul. Had the killer fled, or was he watching from the shadows? I turned and bolted past Jake Hunter and into the bookstore as fast as my shaky legs allowed.

Chapter Two

While "Don't Mess With Texas" was created as an anti-littering campaign, the sentiment applied to our beloved police chief too. At the crime scene, Chief Matt Young bossed people around like there was no tomorrow, and I had no intention of interfering with his investigation. He sent Jake, Celia, and me to sit down in the front corner of the store until he could question us. The chief was in his element and gave me hope the killer would be caught.

The brother-and-sister duo settled onto the denim-covered love seat catty-corner to the blue checkerboard pattern armchair I'd claimed. Celia's face remained pale, and she bounced her leg. Jake rubbed his earlobe. He stared at the display of books written by local authors and propped one sneaker-clad foot on the pine coffee table, but I doubted any of it registered with him. Jake appeared to be lost in his thoughts.

I gripped the arms of my chair and studied the growing crowd in front of the bookstore. People watched from the sidewalks on both sides of the street. The cops had flipped the window sign to Closed, but the emergency vehicles parked in front had caused a stir. Was the killer watching? Chills zipped up my spine. It kinda made sense. Arsonists were known for watching their fires, so maybe the same could be said for killers.

I whipped out my phone and took pictures. I stood to get a better view and kept pressing the button.

"What are you doing?" Jake rose to his feet and towered over me. At my height, I didn't often look up at a man. He was probably six-two or three.

"Taking pictures."

"Why?" He propped his hands on his hips.

I lowered my voice and leaned closer. "The murderer could be out there. Watching. You know what I mean?"

He ran a hand over his face and sighed. "Do you work for the police department?"

For the love of daffodils. Moments earlier, I'd decided to stay out of Matt's way, and now I was looking for the killer. "Well, no, but Willow was a friend. What if the cops are so focused on the alley that nobody's watching the front? My pictures might help find the killer."

"You're a flower seller—"

I raised my hand to stop him. "Flower farmer."

Jake quirked an eyebrow. "Sorry, but you have no experience solving crimes."

"I'm not an idiot. Find clues and follow them." I turned my back on Jake and returned to snapping pictures. I'd read lots of mysteries and had a vague notion of what to do. To be fair, I had no formal training. Still, it couldn't hurt to take pictures.

Chief Young appeared. "Do either of you know where Paige Booker is?"

"Not a clue." Jake moved away and sat beside his sister.

Was there tension between Jake and Matt? I slid my phone into my pocket and faced the police chief. "She usually runs on Friday mornings."

"Any chance you know her route?" The chief motioned for one of his men to come over and join the conversation.

"Uh, she usually goes around the square. I've seen her run down my street, so maybe she takes one of the paths around the lake. I'm sure she'll show up at some point. Most Fridays, Willow handles customers, and Paige works on inventory and other stuff." I stared at him. "She'll be devastated when she hears the news."

Chief Young cut his gaze from mine, then pointed to one of the officers. "Find Paige Booker, and bring her here."

It made sense Paige needed to know about the murder as soon as possible. After all, the crime had been committed at her store. Intensity rolled off the two cops. I'd rather be working on my flowers or curled up with a good book. Instead, I was at a murder scene. Poor Willow. My heart broke for her family.

When the officer left the store, Chief Young stared at me. "Quit taking pictures, Emma. I'll be back and question the three of you soon. Until then, don't discuss the case amongst yourselves." He strode to the back of the store.

My face grew hot. "I'll text them to you. There might be a clue in one of them."

"No more pictures, Emma." The chief's voice boomed.

It'd be a lie to tell him I was sorry. I made eye contact with Jake.

"Busted." Jake shook his head. "I tried to warn you."

"At least he didn't make me erase the photos."

"He seems awful familiar with you. Are you two in a relationship?" He raised his eyebrows.

"You really don't understand how small our town is. We all know each other. The police chief and I are only friends." I returned to my seat and began to look at the photos I'd taken with my phone. In the first picture, I saw Benjamin and Zoe Garcia, the owners of Amalfi's Pizzeria. It made sense they'd be curious because their business was next to the bookstore. The Nelle sisters sat on a bench. Nothing suspicious about the senior citizens. Maybe it had been a silly idea to imagine the killer would be standing in the crowd.

The door flew open, and Paige Booker entered her shop with keys jingling. "What's happening?"

I stuffed my phone into my pocket and hurried to Paige's side. I touched her arm. "Come sit down, and I'll tell you."

"No." My fifty-something friend shook me off. "Tell me now."

I swallowed hard. Why'd I have to be the one to inform Paige about the tragedy?

"Come on, Emma. What's going on?"

"Willow's dead. Somebody killed her behind the store." I couldn't be blunter than that.

Paige's keys fell from her hand. She moved past us and collapsed into the chair where I'd been sitting. "No. Willow can't be dead." She rocked forward, resting her arms on her thighs.

I knelt beside Paige, rubbing her back. "Did you see Willow today?"

"Yes. I met Nick here early to do his pest control thing. Monday is his normal day, but I'd asked him to treat the upstairs apartment. I'm considering renting it out." Paige tugged her wedding ring off, then pushed it on, staring out the window. "He was up there when Willow arrived. I trusted she could handle Nick, and I left for my morning run. Fridays are my only day to sleep in and run later." She pointed to her jogging shorts and a T-shirt with a picture of Agatha Christie on it.

"Yeah, the whole town watches to see which author T-shirt you're going to wear every Friday."

Paige whispered, "I can't believe Willow's dead. Do you think the police will accuse me of killing her?"

"That's silly. You can't possibly have a motive." Yet, Chief Young had been insistent on finding Paige. Of course, there was also the matter of a loan.

"I was mad at Willow, but not mad enough to hurt her." She ran her hands up and down her arms. "If they arrest me, will you help prove I'm innocent?"

"Me?" My voice squeaked.

"Yes, you're one of the smartest people I know. You're good at analyzing situations. I need your help. Please."

Jake tapped my shoulder before I could form an answer. "You best wait for the cops to question her."

Paige widened her eyes like she hadn't noticed Jake before. She lifted her chin but didn't stand. "I'm Paige, and this is my shop. Who are you?"

I gasped at Paige's rude tone.

Jake frowned, and there was no sign of the flirt from earlier.

I jumped in to answer Paige's question before Jake replied. Last thing we needed was for the police to hear a testy discussion. "This is Jake Hunter and his sister, Celia." I pointed to the young woman on the loveseat. "They're in town to help Brett at the coffee shop. Celia was with me when I found the body. She called Jake when we realized something might be wrong, and he came to help."

15

Paige nodded. "Pleased to meetcha. Sorry for being rude. You just caught me off guard. What a horrible thing for you to have to deal with."

"Ain't my first rodeo, but I'd feel better if I could get my sister outta here." Jake turned his attention to Celia.

I studied the three of them. We were all hurting, and it wasn't fair for Chief Young to keep us waiting like we'd done something wrong. "I'll be back." I marched away.

Jake caught up to me by a table of jewelry created by a young Texas designer. "If you disturb the crime scene, Chief Young's not gonna be too happy. There's a chain of command, and he'll get to us when he can."

"Ex-military?" I pretty much had figured out what his answer would be.

"Once a Marine, always a Marine. Oorah." His perfect posture and stance reflected his training.

"As I stated earlier, Chief Young is a friend, and he won't mind if I interrupt him." My hands shook. If I went outside to speak to him, there'd be no avoiding seeing Willow's body again. I touched the table to steady myself.

"You okay?" Jake reached out and gripped my shoulders.

Tremors overtook my body. Tears leaked out of my eyes and down my face. Willow had been a friend. She was older than me, and we lived different lives. Money had never been a problem for her, and I'd scrimped for every penny my entire adult life. Still, I'd always liked Willow. How could she be dead?

I swayed toward Jake, the Marine. Courageous. Warrior. The opposite of me. The thought of seeing Willow again terrified me.

"Aw, now." His voice softened.

"Who would've killed Willow?" I leaned against his chest and into his strength.

"It's going to be okay. Let's sit down until Chief Young is ready to talk." He patted my back.

Embarrassment washed over me. I was supposed to be a strong, self-sufficient woman. When my husband died close to twenty years ago, I'd raised my daughter alone. Never had I leaned on a man, but this situation was far different than anything I'd ever experienced.

I'd give myself grace for the moment, then I'd go back to facing the world. Who would've hated Willow enough to kill her? I shivered, and Jake held me tighter. Our little town had always felt safe. People looked out for each other. We supported each other when times were tough. Except for my decision to marry Bo Justice years earlier, I'd always been a good judge of character.

Who would've killed Willow? And why? If we had a murderer living amongst us, and if it was a friend, it'd be hard to learn to trust again.

I stepped away from Jake. He was new in town and possibly only passing through. Could it be a coincidence he arrived in Lutz right before Willow's murder? Surely not. Brett trusted him to run the coffee shop. "Sorry about that. I'm not prone to outbursts."

"I would've been concerned if you didn't react to your friend's death." He gave me a lopsided smile.

While I didn't know Jake Hunter, he was Brett's friend. I trusted Brett, and for now, I wouldn't accuse his Marine buddy of anything other than being a flirt.

Chapter Three

C hief Young reappeared, and it was obvious the moment he realized Paige was in the bookstore with us. His step faltered, and his eyes widened. "Ms. Booker, we've been looking for you."

"I came as soon as I saw the commotion in front of my store." Again, she fiddled with her wedding ring. She was a widow who had never quit wearing her ring because she'd had a happy marriage.

"Where have you been?" He spread his feet apart and crossed his arms.

I gulped. What a relief that he wasn't staring me down, but poor Paige.

"I was on my morning run." Her voice cracked.

"I have some questions for you. Why don't we talk in the back of the store?"

"If it's all the same to you, I'd rather answer your questions here." She patted the empty chair.

"We could always go down to the station. There's an interrogation room where you can make yourself comfortable."

Paige's complexion paled. "How about I follow you to the back of the store?" She stood and walked past us and the book displays.

Chief Young clenched his fists and followed her. "Do you have a change of clothes? We're going to need the ones you're wearing to test for gunshot residue."

"Yeah, I have a change in back, but is it really necessary?"

"I'm afraid so."

Jake said, "I guess we're to stay here."

I flapped my hands for him to hush. "Shh. Maybe we can hear what they say."

Jake swiped a hand over his mouth, but he didn't argue.

I squeezed between Jake and the end of the loveseat and better positioned myself to hear the chief and Paige.

"Excuse us." Jake moved closer to Celia, giving me more space.

I held a finger over my lips and leaned on the arm of the loveseat. If I'd been really brave, I would've tiptoed closer to the back to hear better.

"Where were you this morning before your run?" Chief Young's tenor voice was always easy to identify.

"I opened the store early for the pest control man. You know him. It's Nick Jones. Anyhow, when Willow arrived, I left."

"Nick Jones was still here?"

"Yes."

"Did you and the victim have a fight?"

"No." Paige's voice softened so much I couldn't distinguish the next words she uttered.

"Do you expect me to buy that?" The chief's tone sounded as disbelieving as his words.

Yikes.

"I'm telling you the truth. We didn't argue today. No doubt you've heard the story about my request for Willow to help me with the bank. When Willow refused to push the bank to give me a loan, I was upset. Deep down, I understood, though. My financial woes were not her fault." Paige raised her voice and sounded a bit hysterical.

The officer who'd been sent to find Paige entered the store.

I glanced his way and repositioned myself in hopes he wouldn't think I'd been spying. "Paige is back there with Chief Young."

"Thanks." Perspiration beaded his forehead, and he swiped it away with his arm as he headed back to his boss. The door slammed behind him.

I dropped my head back onto the cushion. "I think Paige is right about being a suspect."

Jake sighed. "She may have been the last person to see Willow alive, so it makes sense they'd question her."

I turned my head and gave him a fixed look. "What about the bug man? Nick Jones."

"I'm sure the police will question him. If he's any good, he treated both the inside and outside of the store, especially if she's wanting the upstairs apartment to be rented."

I snapped my fingers. "Which means he would've seen Willow whether she was dead or alive."

Celia leapt off the loveseat. "I'm going to be sick."

"Come on." I stood and patted her back. "You know where the restroom is."

"Yeah, in back where Paige is being questioned." She moaned.

"I'm sure the chief will let you through."

Jake stood. "There could be evidence in the restroom. The coffee shop is close."

"I'm not going to make it." Celia bent over.

I darted to the cash register and pulled out the plastic-lined trash can. "This is better than nothing."

Celia grabbed it and lost her breakfast.

My gag reflex kicked in, and I ran to the back room. "Matt, Celia's sick, and I'm about to hurl. Please let us go for now." In my panic, I'd called the police chief by his first name. I'd apologize another time.

"Fine, but first, one of my people needs to do a presumptive swab test and a more detailed test for gunshot residue. Then I'll meet you at the station in an hour." He narrowed his eyes. "One hour. Got it?"

"Yes, sir. Are you saying Willow was murdered with a gun?"

"I'm not making any public announcements, and neither are you." He stalked away.

I glanced at Jake. "Why is he testing the three of us? Willow was dead when I got here, and y'all never even met Willow."

Jake said, "I'm sure it's procedure. When the case goes to trial, Chief Young can confirm he tested the three of us. Don't worry about it."

Don't worry? Easier said than done.

The officer who'd been searching for Paige appeared with three kits. He dabbed, swabbed, and processed Celia first. Jake was next, and then me. After my turn, I walked home, intending to splash cold water on my face and wrists.

What had poor Willow done while trying to survive the attack? Her shoe had been in the building, but her body was in the alley. She must've tried to run. Maybe she'd thrown something at the gunman before exiting the building. Tears welled up.

I took a deep breath. It was time to regain my composure before the police questioned me.

Exactly one hour later, Jake, Celia, and I met at the police station. We stood in the bland reception area, waiting.

Celia's pale complexion brought out my motherly instincts, and I patted her arm. "How are you holding up?"

She shook her head. "Not good."

Jake said, "You need to rest when this is over."

"No." Strands of her dark hair had escaped from the messy bun. "We need to get back to the coffee shop. Tyler can't continue to handle the place by himself."

Jake slid an arm around his sister's shoulders. "Shh. Don't worry about Tyler. I told him to close up if things got too wild."

Chief Young appeared. "Come on back. All y'all passed the presumptive test for GSR."

"That's good because I didn't shoot Willow." My hands shook on the way to the little interrogation rooms. Each one appeared to contain three chairs and a table. We were each sent to a different room, and Chief Young questioned us separately.

I'd pulled myself together. Sorta. I replayed the scene over and over again to provide answers to the chief's questions. It wasn't the best way to recover from finding Willow's body, but I hoped it'd help him catch the killer.

After answering the questions, I drove home to work in the gardens. My home sat on a five-acre lot right across the train tracks from downtown. This was my first year as a flower farmer, and I'd done my research. Others had started their flower-growing businesses in their backyards, and I followed

21

their pattern. My plan was to expand a little every year.

Pulling weeds had always relieved my stress in the past. I removed the ring Granny Fair had left me in her will. She'd understood me like my parents never had. I placed it in a little ring bowl and turned my attention to a picture of Granny Fair. Man, I missed her, but it was time to get busy. I changed clothes and put on my straw cowboy hat. Red hair and fair skin had led to many sunburns in the past. I walked down a gravel path to the dahlia boxes and plucked weeds.

Flowers were the perfect companion in times of joy and in times of sorrow. You planted them in the soil, then you watered and fed them, and one day they grew. Then they died. People died too, but Willow's sudden demise had caught me off guard. I shouldered tears off my face. Never before had I watered my garden with tears.

Willow hadn't even died with both shoes on, and she'd been obsessed with footwear. Whenever she traveled to Dallas, Atlanta, and even New York City, Willow returned with at least one new pair of shoes. Women around Lutz dreamed about looking in her closet because Willow's clothes were almost as spectacular as her shoes.

I ripped the faded blue bandanna from around my neck and blew my nose on it. Crying over my friend wouldn't solve anything. Paige was in serious trouble, and she was also a friend. I needed to find clues and help the police track down the real killer.

I clipped flowers for Faith to use at the bed-and-breakfast, then trudged to the house.

My reflection in the backdoor window stopped me in my tracks. Water-proof mascara hadn't stood up to the challenge of my day. I headed to the bathroom and showered. Afterward, I felt better.

With a glass of water in hand, I got comfy in my slip-covered chair and propped my feet on the matching ottoman. How would I prove Paige hadn't murdered Willow? Doubts assailed me. Who was I kidding? I wasn't trained to catch a killer. However, Paige had asked for my help. She believed in me. The least I could do was try. Yes, I'd give it my best shot.

Where to begin? I was part of a mystery book club and had learned a thing or two about crimes. Working in a pharmacy, I'd acquired certain detection skills when dubious characters lied to me. Today I'd found Willow's dead body, and it seemed as if I owed her something. If I'd delivered the flowers earlier, she might possibly still be alive. Could I have prevented her attack? A shiver ripped up my spine. More likely, I would've been killed too.

My thoughts drifted as I tried to devise a plan of action. Sitting here in the safety of my gathering room wasn't solving the murder. Faith and Willow had been friends, and she seemed like the best person to start questioning.

I jumped up and got ready to visit Faith. I carried small vases of cosmos and coreopsis in a woven wood basket my grandmother had used to deliver meals to friends. The bed-and-breakfast was less than a mile from my home, and the weather was delightful. Warm but not hot on this sunny Friday morning in March. Hard to believe it was still morning.

From my home, I walked up Main Street, over the train tracks, around the town square, and continued on Main to the bed-and-breakfast. I paused at the police station on the corner of First Street. Were the cops looking into Willow's background? Did they know she was about to divorce her husband? The trial was imminent. Rumors predicted it'd be ugly too.

Jake stepped out of the station and trotted down the steps. Deep furrows on his forehead marred his handsome features. He drew to a stop in front of me, and his expression cleared. "Emma, whatcha doing here?"

"I'm heading to Heart of Texas Bed-and-Breakfast to deliver these." I pointed to my basket of flowers. "What are *you* doing?"

"I applied for a job earlier this week and decided to come back and check on the status."

"You're a cop?" My voice squeaked.

"I'm not employed yet." He put on his military-style Oakley sunglasses and pushed them up with a tan finger. "Come on, I'll walk you over."

"It's not that far." Three blocks, to be specific.

"My sister and I are staying there, and I want to check on her. It's the first time she's been part of a murder investigation."

Me, too, but I was older and supposedly more mature. Although, was there any age when a person wouldn't react to murder? "How's she holding up?"

He pointed toward the b-and-b, and we walked. "You'll like this, flower lady. I gave her a cup of chamomile tea, and she's resting." He gave me a half-smile.

"Tea. Nice touch to soothe her raw nerves." Shaky legs made it a struggle to walk as fast as normal, but Jake didn't rush me.

"I thought you'd approve."

"If Celia has trouble sleeping, I can give you some lavender. Both dried and fresh stalks have calming properties." I dug into my bag and removed a fresh stalk. "Here, give this to your sister."

"Thanks."

"How old is Celia?"

"She's twenty-six, but I bet you thought she was younger."

"Yeah. She has a youthful quality about her. Do you mind if I ask how old you are?"

He laughed. "Why? Because I don't look that young? You'd be right. I'm thirty-eight."

"Hunh. Me, too."

We finished our walk in silence. When we reached our destination, Jake opened the front door and held it for me.

Faith met us in the foyer. "Jake, your sister fell asleep in the TV room. I closed the door so no guests would disturb her."

"That's right nice of you. I appreciate it, and if you don't mind, I'll check on her." His lips flattened, and he left us alone.

I did my best to smile. "Faith, I've got your flowers for the guest rooms."

She wrapped her arm around my shoulders in a motherly fashion. "Let's go to the kitchen and have a cup of tea."

I followed her lead. "More caffeine is the last thing I need right now, but thanks."

"I love these little vases. Thanks for taking care of them for me." She took the basket from my grip and pointed to a barstool at the island. "Sit. I've got a new herbal red tea. No caffeine."

"Perfect." I ran my hands over the marble countertop. "You and Willow were good friends, so it seems like I should be taking care of you."

Faith filled her electric tea kettle with water and pushed the button for it to boil. "I don't think the truth has really hit me yet, but you saw the body and are probably still in shock." She removed cups and saucers from a cabinet and scooped tea leaves from a ceramic canister, and dropped them into a stainless-steel infuser. She set it into a teapot, then reached for a bowl of various sweeteners, including honey.

It was time to look for clues and smush down my grief. "Faith, who do you think killed Willow?"

She flipped her blond hair over her shoulder and avoided eye contact.

"I know Willow and Vince were in the process of getting divorced."

Her shoulders drooped. "They were due in court next week. It was going to be messy. So very messy."

"I heard Vince was having an affair."

"Multiple affairs over the years, but please don't spread it around. This past year, Vince often disappeared for a day here and there. Willow found receipts from various hotels in Dallas, Austin, and Houston. She didn't know if he had multiple women or traveled the state with one. When she questioned him about his trips, he was evasive. So she concluded the obvious."

The electric kettle clicked. Faith reached for it and poured hot water over the infuser.

"Is that why it was going to be so bad?"

Faith stared at the counter and swiped at invisible crumbs before answering. "Yes. She planned to make the affair public in court this week. The bank won't put up with infidelity from any of the employees, and the board would be forced to fire him."

"No more respectable bank president. Why didn't Vince just divorce Willow, then date the woman?"

She poured tea into cups and passed one to me.

I added a drizzle of honey and stirred, giving her time to answer.

"Willow's family started the bank. When the older generation died off, Willow bought the cousins out of their shares of the business. Although many of the family members are on the board. Even Willow's brother, Cal Hoffman, is on the board. They allowed Vince to be president when Willow had her first baby, because she wanted to stay home with her children. A divorce would end Vince's career."

"Hence the affair." I sipped the tea. "This is good."

Faith's face relaxed, and she came around the counter and sat beside me. "It's my new favorite."

I smiled. "I understand why."

She ran her finger around the rim of her cup. "The four of us hung out together when we first moved here, but then the tension between Willow and Vince got to be more than we were comfortable with. Zig and I knew their marriage was in trouble, but we didn't wade into their dustup. I was always available to listen to Willow when she needed to share though. Vince and Zig played golf with some other businessmen, but the two of them rarely hung out together."

"Any chance Zig learned anything from Vince about their problems?"

Faith stared at her tea. "Not really. Vince always flirted with the girls going around the course with refreshments, but he never flat-out admitted he was having an affair to the men when Zig was around. Willow also hired a forensic accountant to go through their finances. Vince didn't try very hard to hide the money he spent on other women. There was also evidence he might have embezzled money. Willow figured when she took control of the bank, she'd pay auditors to get to the bottom of Vince's business shenanigans."

"That's a shame." And pretty stupid, but it'd be ugly to say that out loud.

Jake stepped into the room. "What's a shame?"

"Willow's murder." I drank my herbal tea and avoided sharing what I'd learned.

Faith hopped up and offered to fix a cup for Jake, but he declined her offer. They discussed Celia instead. Maybe she'd been protected throughout her life. I didn't know. Finding the body had shocked me, and it was possible I'd fall apart later. At the moment I was angry.

Jake crossed his muscular arms. "I wonder if Celia would do better if she spent time with Brett's service dog."

"We've never allowed dogs to stay here because so many people have allergies to animals. Can your sister visit the dog at Brett's place?"

"No worries." Jake smiled. "I'll figure something out, but I need to get back to the coffee shop."

Faith patted his arm. "I'll be around all afternoon if your sister needs anything. In fact, I'll join her and read a book or something." She shot me an indecipherable look.

I hopped up and placed the dirty dishes in the farmhouse sink. "I'll head out too. Don't worry about my basket. I'll collect it next time I come by. You might add more water to the vases. Thanks for the tea."

"See you later." She all but shooed us out of the kitchen and onto the sidewalk.

"Wow, I guess Faith really wanted her quiet time to read." I laughed.

"Seems like it." He walked in the direction of the town square.

I fell into step beside him. "It sounds like you're really concerned about your sister."

"She's shook up, but I think she'll be all right." He glanced at me. "How are you doing?"

"I'm fine."

"Fine's not necessarily good." Jake shook his head. "Where are you headed?"

Good question. "Home, I guess. Who do you think killed Willow?"

He rubbed his chin. "The spouse is always the most likely suspect, but these people are strangers to me. They may have been deeply in love with no marital problems."

"Marital bliss wasn't their story. Divorce proceedings are scheduled to begin next week, but I guess that's off the docket now. If you hear any relevant gossip at the coffee shop, will you let me know?"

Jake rounded on me. "Don't get involved, Emma. I'd hate for you to get hurt."

I straightened my shoulders. "Lutz is my town. Willow was a friend, and Paige is an even closer friend. You heard Paige ask me to help prove she's innocent."

"Yeah, I did." He ran a hand through his hair. "It was an unfair request. I don't care how smart you are, it could still put you in harm's way. Not to mention, the authorities won't want you to interfere in their investigation."

"If I find a lead, I'll alert Chief Young." Unfair or not, I couldn't walk away from a friend.

"Again, mind your own business. The cops don't need to solve a second murder."

Of all the nerve. I reached for a lavender stalk and inhaled. "You're not on our police force, and I don't answer to you. In fact, I suspect you're looking for clues yourself."

He yanked off his sunglasses and glared at me. "I've been a Marine, and I graduated from the police academy. Something tells me you haven't done either."

Where was a snappy comeback when I needed one? "Uh, no."

Jake ran a hand over his face. "I didn't mean to insult you, but there's a killer running around your town. Emma, you need to be careful." His apologetic tone matched his words. Raised eyebrows and widened eyes convinced me of his sincerity.

"You're right." I'd be careful, but I wouldn't give up. If I'd gotten to the bookstore earlier, maybe Willow would still be alive. It was too late to help her now, but Paige was another story. I wouldn't lose two friends in one day. Willow to death and Paige to jail. No, I'd find a way to prove Paige was innocent.

A look of uncertainty passed over Jake's face. He pushed his sunglasses back on, and we continued on our walk. "All right then. How about I treat you to an iced tea at Anytime Coffee?"

"No, thanks. I had tea with Faith. Say, do you remember a stranger coming into the coffee shop after I left?" We walked toward the town square.

Jake laughed. "Honey, you're all strangers to me."

"Guess that makes sense."

"Who did you have in mind? I've got a pretty good memory."

"I know most of the locals, but a man entered the shop, and I can't place him. He had dirty blond hair and a beard."

"Looked like a boxer. Maybe five-ten? Gray hoodie with faded letters advertising the Dallas Cowboys?"

"Whoa." The pieces of information clicked into place. "That's him exactly. Do you know the guy?"

"Nope." His pace increased. "Drinks his coffee black. He ordered two extra-large cups to go."

"How do you remember so many details?" I upped my speed to match his.

"It's what I've been trained to do." He smirked. "Might even be in my DNA."

"I used to be a pharmacy tech, and we spotted our fair share of drug dealers and called the cops. So, you might say I've had a bit of training myself."

Jake laughed. "Good to know."

We reached the coffee shop on the square. "I'll see you later."

"Is that a promise or a threat?" He flashed me his crooked smile.

"Ha, ha. Very funny." I took the long way home to give myself time to sort through the questions bombarding me.

How long would Jake be in town? Where was Brett? Who killed Willow? Her husband? Would Vince stoop to such behavior to keep control of the bank? What about the stranger at the coffee shop? Why did he appear the exact day Willow was killed? Probably a coincidence. Who'd like to see Willow dead? I refused to believe Paige was guilty. So, if my friend was innocent, who was the culprit?

Chapter Four

My best friend Sophie Becker showed up at my place around suppertime with deli sandwiches and Apfelkuchen, otherwise known as German apple cake. Sophie owned the town bakery, and I could easily pack on extra pounds just smelling her delicacies. It was a good thing I spent so much time outside working with flowers.

"Are you hungry?" Sophie stepped into my gathering room.

"After the day I've had, I want to dive into the cake and skip the rest." I took the plate of sandwiches and carried it to the kitchen table. Country music played on the local radio station soft enough we'd be able to talk while we ate.

Sophie laughed. "But you won't. I'm trying a new dressing with goat cheese in it. I think it's a good combination with the pickles and fresh veggies on our sandwiches."

I pulled out a pitcher of fruity water and a bowl of grapes to go with our sandwiches. "Sounds like I'm your guinea pig before you serve it to customers."

She placed the glass cake stand with a pretty dome on the counter and gave me a one-armed hug. "That's what friends are for, and when you get your herb garden going, I'll be your best customer."

I set the table with sweat-resistant tumblers and mismatched china I'd bought at yard sales. "I hope they grow as well as my flowers."

Sophie and I sat across from each other, and she said, "A green thumb should work for anything. I've got faith in ya."

I unwrapped my sandwich from the wax paper and studied the ingredients.

30

Cucumbers, peppers, carrots, alfalfa sprouts, and lettuce on homemade sourdough bread. "Looks yummy."

Sophie said a quick blessing, and I bit into the thick sandwich. The creamy dressing had a nutty flavor. "Yum, this is going to be your next big hit. I don't see any nuts, but it tastes like it should have them."

"I used a bit of walnut oil. Of course, I'll need to warn customers in case they have nut allergies."

"Yeah, you sure don't want to get sued." I took another bite.

Sophie plucked a green grape from the stem and rolled it between her thumb and forefinger. "I heard about Willow."

The bite in my mouth lost all flavor, and I reached for my water and drank deeply. "This ranks as one of the worst things to ever happen to me, and I am aware that sounds incredibly selfish. She had so much to live for."

"My guess is what you're experiencing is normal. Have you talked to Abby? Lizzy? What about Wyatt?"

I hadn't called my daughter, sister, or brother. "No."

"Then you need to discuss it with me. What happened this morning?" She popped the grape into her mouth.

"I'm sure you've heard the story multiple times today."

"True, but you need to process what happened. Tell me about the woman who was with you." Sophie had taken psych classes in college and may have missed her calling.

"Celia Hunter. She and her brother Jake are working at Brett's place for a few days. What's going on with him?"

Sophie patted my hand and shook her head in tempo with the slow love song playing on the radio. "I don't know about Brett. Did you and Celia discuss how you felt afterward?"

"No, but I ran into Jake later, and we talked." I took another bite of the veggie sandwich. "Oh, and I discussed it with Faith when I took flowers over for the guest rooms." The food in my mouth muffled my words.

"Interesting." She lifted her dark eyebrows.

"Sometimes it's easier to talk to a stranger than a friend."

"Let's pretend that doesn't offend me. Tell me about Jake."

"If I'd told you right away about Willow's murder, I would've been a blubbery mess. You know how it is. You're my best friend. My safe person. I don't have to pretend to be strong around you."

Sophie nodded. "I get it. So, Jake?"

My neck grew warm. My declaration I could share anything with Sophie had come back to bite me. Ouch. I pictured Jake Hunter. Tall, neat dark blond hair with a cowlick, brown eyes, and his crooked smile. "Swoonworthy sums the man up."

"Ya don't say?" Sophie chuckled.

"Kinda, but he's also infuriating. He told me not to look for the killer because I'm not equipped. He's a Marine. He also attended police academy and thinks he's more qualified than me to look for the killer."

Sophie's eyes widened. "It sounds like he's definitely more qualified. What are you thinking? You have no business trying to solve a murder."

"If I'd been a few minutes earlier, Willow might still be alive. For instance, if I'd skipped the coffee shop and gotten to the bookstore earlier. Plus, Paige is worried the police will think she killed Willow because they'd argued about a bank loan. She asked me to help prove she's innocent."

"Your first reason is crazy. You might've gotten yourself murdered too. As for Paige, she needs to trust the police to catch the real killer. Those guys are in the bakery often, and they're smart. Also, they don't order donuts all the time. They make healthy choices, like muesli, for breakfast. They are the men and women Paige should trust to catch the killer."

I lifted my hands in surrender. "She's really scared."

"I'm scared for your safety." My friend shook her head. "I know that look. There's going to be no stopping you."

"Hey, determination is a respectable quality. If it wasn't for a good amount of drive, I'd still be working at the pharmacy."

Sophie nodded. "I know, and you've always encouraged me with my business. You've got my support on your investigation, at least up to a point. You are my dearest friend, and I don't want anything bad to happen to you."

Her words eased the tension from my shoulders. "Thanks for not trying to dissuade me."

"I can't let you try to solve the murder by yourself. How about we take a sympathy cake to Vince after we eat?"

My stomach dropped. "I suppose you mean the apple cake."

"Exactly. Flowers for the funeral and food tonight."

"As much as I hate to give up dessert, you're a genius. We'll pay our condolences, and maybe we'll stumble upon a clue." I wasn't close to Willow's husband, but part of the beauty of small-town life was how the community stuck by you. "I won't grill him for answers about his relationships with Willow and possibly other women. I'll be tactful and respectful of the family's pain."

My friend smiled. "I've never known you to be anything other than respectful. I'll drive us over to the Moore mansion, and you can practice what you're going to say."

I gave a long glance toward the apflekuchen. My mouth watered in anticipation. Too bad it was more important to find clues and catch the killer.

Twenty minutes later, we pulled up to the front of the house, and Sophie braked. "Somebody's standing in the driveway, so I'll park on the street."

I looked. "It's Rita Flores, Vince's assistant. I guess it makes sense for her to be here. She's probably not heartbroken, though."

"I agree." Sophie parallel parked in front of the Moore house. "She's had a huge crush on the man for a long time."

"Yeah. It's the worst-kept secret in Lutz." I hopped out and veered toward the woman. "Hi, Rita. How are you doing?"

"What do you mean?" She teetered on her black stilettos.

"I know you're close to the Moore family. You must be hurting too."

She blew her long dark bangs out of her eyes and nodded. "It's a terrible shock, and I stopped by to pay my respects."

Sophie joined us, carrying the cake. "We wanted to do the same, and we decided to bring something sweet."

Rita nodded. "If you baked it, they'll enjoy it for sure. I need to go." She walked to a black sports car and waved before leaving.

Sophie nudged me. "I always felt kinda sorry for Rita. Do you think Vince will notice her now that Willow's gone?"

"According to Faith, Vince was having an affair. Who knows? It could've been her."

"Then it seems like she'd stay longer with the grieving family. Unless she's leaving to keep up appearances."

"Come on, let's check on the family. Later we can think about Rita." I led the way to the front door and rang the bell.

The white brick Tudor house with stone and wood trim made an impressive statement. The immaculate yard and landscaping added to the declaration of wealth and good taste.

The door opened, and a man wearing a navy suit, short curly black hair with strands of gray, and a neatly trimmed beard with more gray opened the door. Not Vince Moore. I ran my hands over my jeans. "Hi, I'm Emma Justice, and this is Sophie Becker. We were friends of Willow's. We wanted to stop by and tell you how sorry we are for your loss."

The man blinked rapidly but didn't utter a word.

Sophie lifted the glass cake plate. "We brought food. I made it myself, and I'm a baker. You can eat it for dessert or even breakfast if you're so inclined."

"Where are my manners? Please, come in. It's been a terrible shock for all of us." He motioned for Sophie and me to enter. The man took a few steps before turning back to face us. "I am Daniel Moore, Vince's father. Like I said, we're all in shock."

We followed Mr. Moore to a large living room. He stopped beside an older woman who stood near a wall, looking at a collection of family pictures. "Darling, these are some of Willow's friends."

The introductions were swift and awkward, but when Vince's mother offered for us to take seats, we did. Mr. Moore disappeared with the cake.

Sophie and I chose the long gray couch, and Mrs. Moore sat in a chair the color of vanilla. It was situated across the ornate glass-and-metal oval coffee table from us, as if she needed a protective barrier. She massaged the pearl necklace around her neck.

I leaned forward. My initial plan had been to find a clue to Willow's death, but Vince's parents looked pained by the loss. "How can we help your family?"

Mrs. Moore dabbed at her eyes with a cotton handkerchief. "We don't know much about this area, and our son is grief-stricken. One of Willow's old boyfriends showed up and offered to hold the service at a reduced price because they'd been friends. His mortuary is in Dallas. Does that seem too far away for people to drive for a funeral service?"

Sophie said, "It'd be much easier, and better attended, to have the funeral and burial here in Lutz. If the funeral home's not big enough, there's the community church. They often host big funerals."

Vince's dad returned and sat in the other vanilla chair. "I heard your suggestion, and I agree. A local funeral is best. The kids' friends will be able to come by and offer comfort to Christine and Blake. Dallas doesn't make sense."

I shrugged. It didn't make sense to me, either. "We have a local florist, and I'm a flower farmer. There's also Sophie's Bakery, and the church ladies will host a luncheon for your family after the burial. I mean, if you'd like them to. Not everyone likes that kind of thing."

Mrs. Moore narrowed her eyes. "We'll discuss the options with Vince tonight."

"Where do y'all live?" My gaze ping-ponged from one Moore to the other.

At last, Mr. Moore cleared his throat. "Baltimore. I'm a professor at a small liberal arts college, and Mary used to teach piano at a private high school."

A door slammed so hard my heart lurched. Footsteps pounded, then the unmistakable whoosh of a refrigerator door opened and closed with glass bottles rattling.

Mrs. Moore tapped her chest in a nervous way. "That must be Vince."

Unsure what to expect, I held my breath.

Vince entered the room carrying a bottle of water. He dropped his suit jacket on the nearby dining room table and dragged a chair over to where the four of us sat. He stopped to kiss his mother's cheek before sitting. "Thanks for the cake, Sophie. I'm sure it'll be the first thing to disappear."

"You're welcome. We don't mean to intrude, but we wanted to express our condolences."

So many questions jumped from my brain to my mouth, but I pressed my lips together.

"Thank you. Willow will be missed greatly. I'm more concerned about the kids than myself." Vince's neutral expression confused me.

"Was Willow living here at the house?" So much for keeping quiet.

He narrowed his eyes. "Of course, she lived here. Why?"

Time to shift gears. "Oh, you know, I thought we might help pick out her burial clothes. She was always the height of fashion, and it'd be one less thing for you to deal with."

Mrs. Moore stood. "Vince, I never understood Willow's Texas style, and it'll be too hard on Christine. Why don't you let the girls help me pick out something special?"

"Fine."

Sophie and I followed the woman up the grand staircase and to the main bedroom. I glanced around the room and tried to decipher if Vince had been living here with Willow. The room was immaculate with antique cherry furniture. No dirty socks on the floor. One nightstand had a Bible and journal on top, but there was only a lamp on the other. There were no pictures on the walls or dressers of a loving couple, although there was an empty picture hook between large photos of the kids.

"This is Willow's closet." Vince's mom opened two doors with a flourish. "Mercy, it's big enough to hold anything you might need. I guess it's true that everything is bigger in Texas."

"Grandma, what's going on?" A young feminine voice surprised me.

I made eye contact with the teen and stepped closer to her. "Hi, Christine. I'm so sorry about your mother."

"Thanks." She flattened her lips.

Mrs. Moore turned on her toe. "Christine, I didn't hear you come in. We need to pick out a dress for your mother to wear."

"What does it matter? She's dead. Gone forever. Who cares what she wears?" The teenager's face fell, and she burst into tears.

Vince's mom said, "Oh, darling. I'm here now. We'll get through this together." She led her granddaughter away and left us alone in the bedroom.

"Pick something red. I'm going to look for clues." I shut the door and turned the lock.

"Have you lost your mind?" Sophie hissed.

"No." I stepped into the bathroom and gathered a few toiletries for the mortician. There were no signs of shaving cream, aftershave, or other obvious manly products. Back in the bedroom, I opened drawers and found Willow's belongings but nothing of Vince's. I tried the only other door in the room. It was a smaller walk-in closet filled with women's coats. I entered the space, looking for something. Too bad I didn't know what. I stumbled on the carpet. Odd. In this extravagant house, how could there be a flaw in the flooring? It didn't make sense.

I knelt and felt around the floor, then turned on my phone's flashlight app for a better look. It wasn't a flaw but a square patch. I lifted a corner of the blue medallion area rug and found a safe. A hidden safe. What was in it? I tried the handle. Nothing.

Sophie joined me. "What are you doing?"

"Hold it down. I found a safe, but it won't open."

"You're going to get caught." Her panicked tone didn't help my nerves.

I replaced the rug. "What did you find?"

"I chose this dress. It's the perfect piece for a business meeting or a social event in the evenings. Willow told me the swirly pleats always made her feel pretty, and the bright red is definitely an eye-catcher."

The bedroom door rattled, and I hurried to answer it.

Thank goodness Sophie closed the closet door, so nobody would suspect I'd been snooping.

Vince glared at me. "Why is the door locked?"

I waved him into the bedroom. "Shh, Christine was upset. Your mother is with her now, but I thought it'd be easier this way."

Sophie stepped forward. "I chose this dress and her red pumps."

Vince put fists on his hips. "Don't you think she should wear black?"

"No." Sophie shook her head. "Red was Willow's favorite color. How about her chunky silver necklace? You can remove it before they bury her."

Vince frowned. "The police say she was shot and lost a lot of blood. It seems inappropriate to dress her in red."

"Give me a minute." Sophie stepped back into the enormous closet.

I moved closer to Vince. "Do the cops have any leads?"

"Not yet." He leaned against the bathroom doorframe, trying to look nonchalant. The move looked more stilted than casual.

I lowered my voice. "Who do you think killed Willow?"

He didn't hesitate to ponder my question. "Paige Booker."

Maybe Paige had good reasons to be worried. "Why?"

"She wanted a loan. The woman went so far as to ask Willow to convince me to give it to her. Willow refused, then Paige approached me anyway."

"I don't get it. Willow worked for Paige, and they were friends." My hands grew damp. "Why wouldn't she agree to speak to you?"

"We weren't doing a lot of speaking the past month."

Sophie reappeared. "How about the regatta blue sheath dress?"

I nodded. "The silver jewelry will look nice with it too."

"Fine." Vince crossed the room, whipped open the bedroom door, and stepped into the hall. "I think my family needs to be alone right now."

I made eye contact with Sophie, and we draped the outfit on the bed next to the makeup pouch. "We can see ourselves out. I'm sorry for your loss, Vince."

"I lost Willow months ago." He headed down the stairs and opened the front door. "Thanks for the cake and helping pick a dress for Willow to be buried in."

"You're welcome." Sophie stepped outside first.

"Vince, please let us know if there's anything we can do to help."

"Thank you." He paused for me to exit, then shut the heavy front door.

On the way home, I took notes on my phone. I didn't believe Paige murdered Willow, and I'd do my best to help prove her innocence. Deep down, I believed Vince was behind his wife's death. Proving it would be the challenge. Vince was smart and cunning. He'd fooled Willow for years about his affairs, but I'd keep my eyes open and hopefully not fall prey to his evil ways.

Chapter Five

arly Saturday morning, I loaded flowers into my Silverado. I'd named my truck Ms. Daisy so I could tell friends I was driving Ms. Daisy. I reviewed my list. Check, check, and check. "Farmers' market, here I come."

The place opened at nine, and it was so close to my place, it was ridiculous. It barely took three minutes to drive there and park. If I wasn't hauling flowers to sell, it would be an easy walk. Wayne Johns managed the market. He made sure tents and tables were set up, giving the event an organized and uniform appearance.

In January, Mr. Johns had approached me to run a booth to give more variety to the market. Once I assured him there'd be an ample assortment of flowers and plenty to get through a day, he signed me on. Win-win.

I carried some supplies to my designated area near the entrance. I erected the metal rack that would hold nine galvanized buckets. It took me thirty minutes to get plants from my truck to the booth, and I was perspiring by the time nine o'clock rolled around. My cooler with wheels held more flowers to replenish what sold. I pulled a pink bandanna from the pocket of my denim shorts overalls and blotted the sweat around my hairline. It was a typical Texas Saturday morning in March.

After displaying arrangements on the table and single stems in buckets of water, I examined my bag of supplies for probably the hundredth time. Heavy-duty wrapping paper, tissue paper, clear tape, scissors, ribbon, credit card reader, and a calculator. There was even a first-aid kit because my middle name wasn't Grace.

"You look ready for business." A familiar tenor stopped my rooting around in the bag.

I straightened and met a brown-eyed gaze. "Hi, Jake. Shouldn't you be at the coffee shop?"

"Not this morning. Here's your green tea with honey." He handed me a steamy cup and pointed his thumb toward the space between parking and vendors. "Celia's running Anytime Coffee, and I'm experimenting with a food truck."

I recognized the Tex-Mex, the Greek, and the Bar-B-Q trucks that usually parked to the side. A turquoise and white VW van was unexpected, and I laughed. "The van? Does Brett know?"

"I'll let you in on a little secret." Jake looked both ways as if ensuring nobody would hear the big reveal. "I'm Brett's silent partner, and he knows about my trial run here."

I wrapped my cool fingers around the paper cup. "Brett doesn't have a partner. I'd know if he did." Wouldn't I?

Jake's crooked grin appeared. "Hate to burst your bubble, sweetheart, but I'm not kidding. I helped Brett get his start."

"Why haven't we seen you before?"

"Hence the name, silent partner." He turned. "I best get back to it."

If his words were true, I didn't know as much as I thought. "Hey, Jake. Thanks for the tea."

"Yes, ma'am." He strolled away wearing a red-and-black checked shirt, faded denims, and well-worn cowboy boots.

Maybe he wasn't as obnoxious as I'd thought yesterday. I sipped my tea and watched other vendors finish preparing for customers. Soaps, hand-woven scarves, goat cheese, wine, spices, muffins, and one stand had peaches, spinach, and kale. Impressive for March.

"Good morning, Ms. Justice. How do you feel about your first morning at the market?"

I lifted my chin and smiled at Mr. Johns. "I took your suggestions, made a list, and got organized last night. It helped me not be so anxious this morning." Even though I had a raging case of nervous energy.

He leaned forward and examined the flowers. "Look fresh."

"Yes, sir, Mr. Johns. They were cut this morning." I grew uneasy at his inspection.

"Call me Wayne." He stepped back. "Call or text me if you need anything. I'll be around all day."

"Great, and thanks for setting up my booth."

He nodded. "I discovered that things flow better when vendors only focus on their products. Have a good day, Emma."

"You too, Wayne."

The tall man walked away with a bow-legged gait. He reminded me of the cowboy movie star John Wayne, but it could've been the similar names.

Puppies barked, pulling my thoughts from the market's operations manager. The noise grew louder.

"Free puppies! Come get your new best friend." Two young girls, who I guessed were about ten, appeared with a red wagon full of adorable black yapping puppies. One girl pulled the wagon, and the other made sure none of the dogs escaped. Both giggled so much, I couldn't help but laugh.

A man approached me and pointed to one of the large vases of flowers. It was full of bluebonnets, autumn sage, periwinkle and appropriate foliage as filler. "How much for that one?"

I smiled at the older gentleman. "I like a customer who knows what he likes."

"It's my anniversary." He gave me a fifty. "Keep the change. I told my wife to sleep in, and I want to surprise her with a spectacular breakfast."

"Thanks. Anytime Coffee House is set up in the Volkswagen van, and they have an amazing pecan coffee."

He grabbed the vase. "Great. Have a nice day."

"Happy anniversary."

He waved, and I suspected his mind was on celebrating his marriage.

Why couldn't that have happened for Willow and Vince? Had their divorce been brewing for years? Did they ever love each other? Or had Vince fooled Willow into believing he loved her? Had he married her for the money and prestige of running the bank?

A young couple approached, holding hands.

Katie Paxson and Tyler Legend. They'd grown up in Lutz, and they were a year older than my daughter, Abby. "Good morning. It's so good to see y'all. How are you?"

Katie's wide smile was all the answer I needed. "We're home from college for a long weekend. Actually, we got home Thursday night. Life couldn't be any better. How's Abby? I heard she started college early."

"That's right. She started in January and loves living in Waco. She's made a lot of friends and likes her classes."

"Awesome." The word came out in three musical notes. Katie always had a dramatic flair.

I walked around the table and hugged both kids. "What can I do for y'all today?"

Tyler was biracial and had been bullied before a growth spurt in the eighth grade. I knew because I'd helped his parents bandage him up more than once. He held a special spot in my heart. He worked for Brett whenever he was in town. I suspected Brett had hired him more to encourage the kid than anything else. It'd been a good thing he'd been available to help out at the coffee shop yesterday when Jake had come to help Celia and me.

Tyler said, "I want to buy a bouquet."

I reached for a medium-sized bunch of flowers tied with a pretty ribbon. Sunflowers in the middle anchored the bouquet. Coreopsis and cosmos added interest and dimension. "What do you think of this?"

Katie sighed. "Sunflowers are my favorite."

"That's the one I want, then." Tyler's eyes shone.

I smiled at both of them. "This is my treat. I'm so proud of you two."

"No, I need to pay you." Tyler pulled a wallet out of his khaki shorts.

"Don't take away my joy. Why don't you buy coffee or something from the food trucks?" He opened his mouth as if to argue, and I shook my head. "Go on. Next time I'll let you pay."

Tyler gave me a quick hug. "Thanks, Ms. Emma."

Yeah, the kid was special, and doing something nice for him truly gave me joy. He'd never be like my deceased husband or Vince Moore. Tyler would make somebody a good husband one day.

I turned my attention to three ladies walking my way. They'd been friends with Willow. All had been members of the garden club. None of them worked outside of the home, but they were involved in community charities.

"Hi, ladies." They weren't much older than me, but they appreciated respect. At least, I thought they did.

The women talked amongst themselves and sorted through various flowers displayed in my galvanized buckets. I spread out paper to wrap their selections and wrote down the prices.

The flower combinations they selected didn't work, but I kept my mouth shut. If anybody understood that the customer was always right, it was me. I bundled each group of flowers securely in tissue paper and tied every parcel with a pretty pink ribbon. By the time we finished, I hesitated to tell them their total was over three hundred dollars. The shortest woman gave me her credit card with a tight-lipped smile. After the transaction processed, the three carried their purchases toward the parking lot.

The next few hours flew by. Mason jars with small arrangements turned out to be my best seller.

Jake reappeared and handed me a Yeti tumbler. "Thanks for sending business my way. Sweet tea."

My face warmed. "Sweetie?"

"Sweet. Tea. In the Yeti. For you to drink." His smirk added to my embarrassment.

"I appreciate it. How was your day?" With a little luck, I could bluff my way through the conversation. Hopefully, he'd forget about my embarrassing moment.

"It's been good. Actually, the morning went better than expected."

"I'm glad to hear it. Do you plan to set up here again?"

"It all depends. The owner of the van loaned it to me today for a trial run. I think it's a keeper. Well worth the investment, and I'll discuss it with my partner, Brett." He looked at the last few arrangements on my table. "I believe one of these will pick up Celia's spirits."

I handed him the prettiest arrangement. "Here you go. On the house, and

I'll return your Yeti later."

"Stop!" A child's scream and laughter caught my attention. It was one of the girls from earlier, chasing after a fluffy black puppy.

"Move." I ran around Jake and darted toward the bundle of fur.

The puppy scurried right, then left. I pivoted on the toe of my pink tennis shoes, reached down, and snagged the sweet critter. The little animal had curly black fur, making me believe he was a poodle.

"Yay!" The little girl squealed.

Jake nudged me. "I think he picked you."

"Think again, Marine. I'm starting a new business and don't have extra time to train a puppy." I handed the adorable dog to the little girl.

"Thanks, lady." She ran off with the pup. "Mommy!"

Jake lifted his sunglasses. "Yet you seem to have time to solve a murder."

"Just when we were getting along so well, and you had to go and ruin it." I headed back to my booth.

"Does this mean you don't want to know what I overheard earlier?" He raised his eyebrows.

I latched onto his arm and tugged him to the shade of my tent. "Of course I do. Please tell me what you learned."

He glanced around us and shook his head. "Too many people around right now."

I couldn't argue with him, but I was dying to find out. "Please?"

He leaned toward me and whispered. "Here's a little appetizer. Offshore bank account."

Chills popped out on my neck. "I bet Willow knew about the account. If she didn't figure it out on her own, the forensic accountant probably discovered it."

"My thoughts exactly." He reached for the little vase. "I'll be at the coffee shop if you want to talk."

Yeah, I wanted to talk to somebody about Willow's murder, but was Jake the right person? He was a new acquaintance to me, but Brett trusted him enough to be his business partner. That should tell me something.

Chapter Six

I went home and unloaded my supplies. I took a good amount of time checking the rows of flowers behind my house for bugs. When I bought my property, I committed to never use fertilizers, fungicides, or synthetic chemical pesticides. I also made sure the gardens didn't need watering. Satisfied, I took a quick shower and dressed before walking out the front door of my Craftsman bungalow. I walked up Main Street, scooted around the square, away from the coffee shop, and headed up Maple.

As much as I wanted to hear what Jake had learned at the farmers' market, I didn't really want to spend more time with the man. His presence made my stomach swirl in a good way, and that was bad. My track record with men was almost non-existent, and my marriage had been disastrous. I needed to keep my focus on work and catching Willow's murderer, not on the tall drink of water known as Jake Hunter.

A breeze swept through my ponytail and cooled my sunburned skin. No matter how much I stayed in the shade, my fair skin managed to freckle or burn. The curse of being a redhead.

In an effort to sidestep facing Jake right away, I headed to Paige's Turn Bookshop to check on my friend. Avoidance was the best modus operandi for the moment.

Once inside the bookstore, I could barely move through the throng of people. Customers crowded around Paige asking questions about the murder, and I'd never seen the place so busy. Bless her heart. She needed help. My red midi skirt with white flowers was appropriate attire to work, and I'd worked here when Paige had been in a pinch in the past. One of the great things about small-town merchants was our desire to help each other succeed.

I wiggled through the people. Most had the decency to have an item to purchase in their hands instead of only showing up for the gossip. I stuffed my red crossover purse under the counter. "Hi, Paige. Need some assistance?"

Paige's frown lessened. "Boy, and how."

"I'll run the register, and you can field questions." The next three people in line were the Nelle sisters. Each octogenarian sister had a style all her own, and they were almost always seen together.

Ms. Ruby handed me a steamy romance and cash, but she focused her attention on Paige and asked about the murder. I finished the sale and dropped the change into the paper sack. Ms. Gaby bought a devotional book and an Easter mug, and we followed the same pattern.

Ms. Rosalita took time to speak to me. "How are you, dear? I heard you found the body."

"Yes, ma'am. Honestly, it was quite a shock." My throat closed so tight I couldn't speak. I reached for the cozy mystery written by a local author and rang up Ms. Rosalita's purchase.

"I'll add you to the church prayer chain." She passed me a credit card.

"Thanks." I inserted the chip then showed her where to sign.

After she walked away, I continued to work the register until we'd served each customer. Paige walked the pastor and his children to the door and locked it once they exited. "Goodness gracious. If you hadn't stopped by, I'm not sure I would've survived. Thanks so much, Emma."

"You're welcome." I'd gotten up early and hadn't stopped all day. Exhaustion rushed through me, and I plopped onto one of the loveseats.

Paige sat across from me. "Most everybody wanted to ask about Willow's death."

"What'd you say?"

"There wasn't much to tell really." She yawned.

I leaned forward and a spasm zipped across my back. Changing positions, I leaned back and rested my tired feet on the coffee table. "Do you think

Nick Jones could've killed Willow?"

"Nick is mean enough, but I don't believe he's got a real motive." Paige met my gaze. "He'd more likely murder me than Willow. If I turn up missing, be sure the cops question Nick."

"Why you?" I had already figured out one motive for him to harm Paige, but I wanted to see if there were more reasons. Maybe he really had meant to kill Paige and got Willow instead.

"He's asked me out numerous times, and I've always turned him down. Between the two of us, Nick's first wife died mysteriously. He works with chemicals to kill bugs, so it's not a huge leap for me to believe he could kill a person with his work chemicals." She shivered. "He makes me uncomfortable, and I mentioned his name to the cops. That probably won't bode well for me."

Our logic matched, except I hadn't know about the dating angle. "Why do you use him for pest control?"

"Most of the people in town use Nick, and it's easier not to rock the boat." She shrugged. "It's a no-win situation."

My stomach growled. "Do you know if Nick and Willow got along?"

"No idea." She scooted a basket of chocolate candy my way.

"Thanks." I took a miniature bar. "Do you want to go out to eat with me?"

Paige stood. "No, I need to restock. Despite the murder, or because of it, this was my busiest day ever."

"Be careful who you say that to, or it'll look like you have two motives. We sure don't want the police to question you again."

"Great day. Two motives would keep me at the top of Chief Young's suspect list." She paused. "Are you still willing to help prove I'm innocent?"

"Yeah, but you shouldn't get your hopes up too high. Is there anything else I need to know?"

Paige crossed her arms. "Can you keep a secret?"

I gulped. "It depends."

"That's fair. There may be some unkind text messages on Willow's phone from me. Blame it on hormones or fear of losing my store, but I was really upset."

My stomach dropped. "How bad?"

"Pretty bad. I apologized in person the next day, and I knew it was wrong to blame her for not being able to get a loan. She forgave me. In fact, our little disagreement opened my eyes to other methods of getting money. I decided to rent out the apartment over the store. If that doesn't work, I'll sell my house and move in here."

"It might be a good idea to confess this to Chief Young before he finds it on Willow's phone or in the cloud or however that works."

"I'll think about it. Go get some supper." She opened the door for me. "Book club Monday night?"

"Yes. I'll see you then."

I wandered up the street and wasn't surprised to see most of the stores closed. Saturdays brought in a surge of business from tourists and other out-of-towners wanting a day to shop for antiques, vintage items, and all kinds of unique treasures. By evening many of the locals headed out to honkytonks and other restaurants on the outskirts of town.

Sophie's Prius was parked on the square. I peeked in the front window of her store and tapped, but there was no sign of my best friend. The sight of her car probably meant she was taking inventory or something in the back room and couldn't hear me. I walked to the merchants' alley between the square and First Street.

The sound of my footsteps bounced off the buildings.

Rusty Ramirez jumped away from Sophie's dumpster. "Howdy, Ms. Emma."

My heart lurched. "Rusty, you liked to have scared me to death."

He clutched a white paper bag in his dirty hands. His thick brown hair needed a good wash and cut. "Sorry. I best move along."

"No, stay here. I'll be right back." I glanced at him before I knocked on Sophie's back door. Rusty was the town criminal, but it was usually petty theft or a crime related to drugs. He'd been raised by an alcoholic mother, and his dad had worked on oil rigs. Mr. Ramirez had done all he could for his son in spite of the mother, but some of the locals said Rusty had broke bad. The real shame was his mother cleaned up her act after her son turned to drugs.

The deadbolt clicked, and the door opened. Sophie smiled. "Hi, Emma. Come in."

"Hey, girl. Do you have anything for me to give Rusty? He looks like he might could use a good meal."

She nodded. "One Hawaiian sandwich, coming right up."

"Thanks. I'll stay here and talk to him." I paused. "Go ahead and lock the door, though. No need to take any chances after the murder."

"Now that you mention it, you should come in here where it's safe."

"Rusty won't hurt me." At least, I didn't think he would. "It's not his modus operandi."

"I'll hurry." Sophie closed the door, and the lock clicked.

I held my red crossover purse tight against my side. "Rusty, Sophie's going to fix a sandwich for you."

He backed away. "I can't pay for it."

"It's my treat. Are you working anywhere these days?"

"Wayne Johns pays me cash to help set up the farmers' market every week."

Interesting. What had Rusty done with the money? Although, it probably hadn't been much. "If you want to help me with my garden, I'll pay you. The only condition is, you must be sober. No drugs and no booze when you're on my property." Being a pharmacy tech had taught me to be stern on those issues.

He avoided eye contact. "Okay."

"Rusty, do you know anything about Willow Moore's death?"

His head jerked up. The wide-eyed gaze prompted me to believe he knew something. "I didn't have nothing to do with her death. I don't kill people."

"I'm not accusing you of murder, but did you see anything unusual yesterday?" Dumpster diving wasn't a new thing for him.

He shook his head. "Nothing worth talking about."

Sophie called out, "Emma, here's the sandwich."

"Rusty, please don't leave." I hurried over to Sophie.

She handed me a fresh white paper bag with Sophie's Bakery logo on the front. "There are gingerbread cookies too."

"Thanks." I walked back to Rusty. "Here you go."

"Thanks. Tell Ms. Sophie I appreciate her kindness."

"Listen, if you saw something, the killer might come after you next. You need to tell the police what you know."

"I got nothing to say."

My shoulders drooped. "All right then. You be careful."

"Yes, ma'am."

I returned to Sophie and followed her into the bakery. "He knows something about Willow's murder."

"Then he needs to talk to the cops." She locked up behind me.

"That's what I said. He's scared, and who can blame him? He's been arrested so many times; he may fear they'll pin the murder on him."

Sophie crossed her arms. "I always thought getting arrested was his way of getting free food and a shower."

"Your theory may be right." Rusty broke my heart, and I often had wondered what kind of person he might have grown into if his dad had been around more or if his mom had been clean during his most impressionable years.

"What are you doing here?"

"I'd thought about ordering a pizza or something for supper. Do you want to eat together?"

"The church placed a big order for tomorrow morning, which means an early day for me. I'm getting organized tonight, then going straight to bed."

"Ah, the life of an excellent baker. I'll let you get back to work." I turned toward the door.

Sophie grabbed my arm. "No way. I'll let you out the front where it's safer."

I followed her through the building and gave her a quick hug. "See you later."

Outside I stared at Anytime Coffee House. It'd be simple to head home and eat yogurt and fruit for supper and try to forget about the murder. Wait. I wanted to help solve Willow's murder, even if it meant rocking my equilibrium by spending time with Jake. With slow steps, I meandered toward the coffee shop.

I crossed Maple Street on my way around the square and ran smack into Jake Hunter carrying a large fragrant pizza in a brown Amalfi's cardboard box.

"Hi, Jake." My stomach let out a tremendous growl. It was downright embarrassing.

He laughed. "Hungry?"

My face warmed. "A gentleman wouldn't say that to my face, but if you must know, yes."

"I never claimed to be a gentleman. My sister ditched me for Brett, and she was very clear they didn't want me around. Would you like to share my pizza?"

Another stomach growl made it impossible to deny my hunger. "Sure."

"We can eat in the coffee shop. Come on."

I hesitated for a moment. Jake was still a stranger, but he and Brett were friends. I looked each way, but the square was virtually devoid of people.

How bad did I want to know what he'd learned about Willow's murder? A tomato-y, basil, and dough fragrance drifted up from the box. I was starved, and the pizza smelled amazing. If Jake was some kind of thug, and I disappeared, nobody would suspect him. Surely, I was smart enough not to put myself in obvious danger. Wasn't I?

Chapter Seven

"If it'll make you feel better, why don't you tell one of your friends where you are." He pulled a keyring from the pocket of his jeans. "You know, safety and all that."

"Good idea." I tugged my phone out of my purse and texted Sophie. **I'm at Anytime Coffee House with Jake. I'll text you when I get home.** No, she might go to bed before I left. **Never mind. I'll tell somebody else.**

I didn't want to worry my daughter or Paige, so I sent a text to my sister. **Lizzy, I'm at Anytime Coffee House and need to talk to you later. I'm with Jake Hunter.**

I shoved the phone in the outer pocket of my purse with a sense of relief. I honestly trusted Jake, but after Willow's murder, it didn't hurt to be extra cautious. "Done."

Jake held open the door. "After you."

We collected forks, plates, and napkins, then Jake made two glasses of shaken sweet tea. "Honey and herbal. No caffeine." He set the glasses on the table and took the seat across from me.

"Very thoughtful to avoid caffeine. I would've been awake all night."

"I figured as much and decided I don't need another strike against me." He winked.

I laughed. "It's not like I'm keeping baseball stats. The only person to blame for drinking a caffeinated beverage this late would've been me."

He opened the box. "Hope you don't mind vegetarian. Celia's trying to convert me."

Mushrooms, green peppers, cherry tomatoes, green olives, and pieces of artichoke mixed with deep golden spots of cheese. Yum. I reached for a slice. "Good for her. I try to avoid meat as much as possible."

"I don't understand why Texas women avoid meat." He took a slice of pizza and closed the box before stuffing half the slice in his mouth.

"Don't mess with Texas women, buddy. We may cut back on meat, but there are plenty of farmers who grow vegetables and appreciate our decision."

"Hold up. I didn't mean to offend you. Is there a reason you prefer vegetables?"

"Forty is closing in on me, and I try to make healthy choices. Barbecue is my weakness, though." I took my first bite. Thick crust, spicy marina, veggies, and plenty of mozzarella made my taste buds dance. "Umm, delicious."

Jake took his phone, tapped a few buttons, and music filled the room. George Strait crooned. "Is country okay?" He took another huge bite.

I nodded. "I like all music. Can we talk about the offshore bank accounts you mentioned earlier?"

He finished chewing, then wiped his mouth. "Sure. Three snobbish women came over and ordered very specific coffees."

I lifted my hands in defense. "Not my fault. I only sent over nice people, but I have a feeling I know who you're talking about." At least, I thought that was true.

"Thank ya kindly. Nevertheless, they came." He pulled out another slice and studied it. "I'm still getting used to artichokes." He plucked off large chunks and scooted them to the side of his plate.

"And?" I speared the discarded artichoke pieces with my fork and added them to my slice.

"While they waited for their drinks, I overheard them discussing Willow and Vince's divorce. They were not kind."

His revelation didn't surprise me in the least. "What'd they say?"

"I didn't hear everything, but the gist of it is Vince had more than one affair during their marriage, and Willow must've been an idiot not to realize it. Those women didn't even consider she could've been a kind and loving wife." A clump of hair danced over his forehead. He needed a haircut, but the length didn't detract from his good looks.

"Are you married, Jake?" I didn't want to make an assumption just because he'd flirted with me.

"My wife died of ovarian cancer. Jennifer was amazing. She hid the truth from me at first, thinking the distraction would be dangerous while I was in Afghanistan. I was torn between being angry that she didn't tell me and loving her more for wanting to protect me." He took a deep breath and let it out slowly. "Before that, I was engaged to a girl by the name of Susie Rawlings. During my first tour of duty, Susie decided she'd be better off with my buddy from high school. Celia spotted them at the theater one day. She was just a kid, but she left her friends and confronted Susie. Celia called her a meanie and ran home crying. My parents broke the news to me."

"That must've been so hard, but I think you dodged a bullet with Susie."

"You're exactly right. I don't believe love is in the cards for me. One relationship was a lie, and the other ended tragically in death."

I reached over and patted his clenched fist. "I'm so sorry about both relationships, but I imagine the unfaithful one really tore you up."

He pulled his hand away. "Yep. I doubt you can understand how that shades your opinion of the opposite sex."

"You're wrong. You may've heard my husband died. The secret is he was also a liar and cheat. I discovered the lies after we were married, but I was pregnant and thought the baby would change him. It didn't. Bo didn't even come to the hospital the day Abby was born. On my twenty-first birthday, he showed up at my apartment stoned. We had a fight because I wouldn't let him hold Abby. I told him I wanted a divorce, and he left."

Jake tilted his head. "So you're divorced?"

I ran my finger along the bumpy pizza crust. "No. He died of an overdose a couple of weeks later. Neither of us had filed for divorce. I got two good things from Bo Justice."

"What were the two things?" He turned his hand so he was holding mine.

"Abby and a trust fund that is paying for her college education." I'd never come right out and told the story of my relationship with Bo to anyone.

Sophie and my sister knew because they'd lived through it with me. Together, they'd been my support system. My brother had been consumed with his own life, but he knew about my disastrous relationship with Bo.

Jake sighed. "Have you dated much since then?"

I shook my head. "Not a bit. I threw all my time and attention on Abby, and now I'm focused on my new business. What about you?"

"I've dated a lot of women without ever getting into a relationship." He released my hand and took another bite of his pizza.

Message received. Even if I wanted to think of Jake in a romantic way, it'd be a waste of time.

Jake gulped his tea. "Why don't you date now? Seems like you can work and date at the same time."

My relationship with Bo had left me with trust issues when it came to the opposite sex. "My husband's death didn't give me the opportunity to get child support. Don't get me wrong, I'm grateful for the college money, but Abby and I had a lot of lean years. She started college in January at seventeen. She's smart and got a nice scholarship. For the first time in years, I'm not consumed with how I'll pay my bills. Life will be easier if I don't have to deal with a man. No offense." Besides feeling helpless, Bo had left me feeling unworthy of love. "For some reason, God blessed me with the most wonderful daughter. Why rock the boat?"

"I hear ya."

We finished eating to the strains of Keith Urban and Thomas Rhett.

I wadded up the paper napkin and leaned back in the wooden chair. "We got way off track. What else did you hear regarding Willow?"

"The three ladies believe Vince has been hiding money in offshore bank accounts. Caymans and maybe Belize, but I could be wrong there. They definitely said the Cayman Islands, though."

I dug into my purse, pulled out my phone, and took notes on what I'd learned. My tablet and phone were connected by the cloud, and I could combine them later.

"Um, whatcha doing there?" Jake stretched his long legs out to the side of our table.

"Taking notes on the murder. Who do you think killed Willow?"

"I don't know enough people around here to have a clue." One eyebrow quirked. "Who is on your list?"

Interesting question. "Why do you care?"

"Two heads are better than one." He crossed his arms. "Don't forget I shared what I heard."

Sugar. He made a good point, and fair was fair. "Vince Moore is at the top of my list. Paige thinks the cops are looking at her, but I don't believe she could kill Willow. There's also the pest control man Nick Jones. He's a creep."

"That doesn't mean he killed Willow."

I leaned forward and propped my arms on the table. "True, but he was at the bookstore Friday morning. That gives him the opportunity. Now we need to figure out a motive."

"Why do you believe the cops are focused on Paige?"

"She asked Willow to help her get a loan for the store. Sophie, Paige, and I have bonded over the challenges of being a female small business owner in Texas. Paige has been struggling for a while." I drummed my fingers on the table. "Willow wouldn't agree to speak to Vince about a loan for Paige."

Jake gathered our trash and took it to the garbage can behind the counter. "Can I get you more tea?"

"No, thanks. What are your thoughts on Paige?"

"Money is often a motive for murder." He returned to the table and sat. "Love and power are two other possibilities. Do you have the five Ws in your notes?"

"Not sure what you mean."

"What, why, who, where, and when. You already know who and where."

I typed the words into my app. "Vince might have at least two motives. When the divorce was final, he'd lose his job as bank president, which means no income from the bank. Power, check. Money, check."

"What about his most recent girlfriend? One of the women thought she was from Austin and an art dealer."

"I don't have a clue who it is, but I met Vince's parents Friday evening.

They were very nice." I studied the man across from me. "If we're working together, there's one more thing I discovered."

"Go ahead." He pointed to me as if it was my turn.

"Vince and Willow hadn't been living together. You know how some couples refuse to leave until the bitter end, not to lose the house?" I paused until Jake nodded. "That wasn't the case with the Moores."

"He told you?"

"No, but Sophie and I searched the main bedroom. Vince's clothes and toiletries weren't there." I smiled, proud of my announcement.

"I don't want to know how you got into his bedroom, but maybe he's sleeping in the guest room."

And there went my thunder. I powered off my phone and paced.

"Emma, you okay?"

"Yeah, just disappointed. I should go. Thanks for supper."

"You're welcome." He hopped up. "I'll walk you to your car."

"I didn't drive."

"Then I'll walk you home. Until the murderer is caught, you need to be extra careful."

"Jake Hunter, I'll have you know I've been taking care of myself for years." I shook my finger at him.

"Yeah, but was a killer running around town all those years?"

I opened my mouth to reply, and he placed his fingers on my lips. My heart flipped.

"Emma, you've been asking questions about Willow's murder, and you were the first to find her. What if the killer was lurking in the shadows? I doubt you want your daughter to be an orphan."

I took a deep breath. It was hard to argue with his logic.

"Emma, may I walk you home?" His gaze met mine. "Please?"

I lifted my chin. "Well, since you asked so nicely. Yes."

I stood on the sidewalk while Jake locked the coffee shop. We walked toward the corner.

A loud clang froze me in place.

Jake grabbed my hand. "Let's get you to safety."

"I live this way." We took off at a dead run.

Chapter Eight

Jake and I darted past the alley. A scrape followed by a muted howl came from the shadows. I slowed, but Jake tugged at my arm. "Hurry."

"No, wait." I pulled away from his grip. "I think it's an animal."

Jake groaned but followed me into the alley.

Woof. Woof.

I headed toward the sound. "It's a dog. Let's check on him. He might be hurt."

Jake's hand shot out, halting my steps. He moved in front of me. "It could be dangerous."

The tense set of Jake's shoulders warned me not to argue again. I didn't know what he'd experienced in Afghanistan, or anywhere else, for that matter. I'd gotten my way to check on the creature. The least I could do was allow Jake to take the lead if it made him feel better.

Woof. More scraping followed the pitiful bark.

The soft sounds of a honky-tonk song drifted into the alley.

Jake turned on his phone's flashlight app and walked toward the distressed dog.

I followed with my own light.

Next to a ramp leading into the pizza restaurant, a dog had his head stuck in a small metal bucket. Poor thing thrashed around trying to get out of the container, but the handle had become lodged behind the pooch's front leg.

"Okay, boy. Aren't you just a piddlee'o thang? Stay calm." Jake knelt beside the struggling mutt. "It's okay."

Woof, woof, woof. The cry echoed in the bucket, and he backed away from

Jake.

"Let me try." I knelt beside Jake. "I have a way with animals."

"By all means. Have at it."

The dog backed himself into a corner between the ramp and building. With his front paw, he continued to lose his battle with the bucket.

"Hi, boy. I bet you're scared, and I understand what that's like." I kept my voice soft like when I used to read bedtime stories to Abby. "My name's Emma, and this is Jake."

The dog's frantic motions calmed.

"We want to help you get free. How'd you like that? Will you let us come closer?"

He growled.

I looked toward Jake. "Should I keep talking?"

"Yeah, try a little longer. I'd hate to call the animal control people."

"I don't want that to happen." I told the dog about my day. "This was the first time I've been a part of the farmers' market, and it was so much fun. I bet you would've liked to play with the puppies I saw there. They were poodles." I inched closer and talked about how much Abby had begged me for a pet when she was growing up. I'd never been able to afford one. "If you let us free you, we'll check your tags. I'll make sure you're safe." I reached a tentative hand out and stroked the dog's back. A briar scratched my fingers, but the dog didn't draw away.

Jake crawled to the dog. "Keep talking and petting him, and I'll try to remove this contraption. Actually, if you could wrap your arms around him, it might offer more comfort."

"Sure thing." I took my time and continued to speak in a soothing voice. At last, my arms circled his scrawny body. "He's so skinny. I can feel his ribs."

Jake touched the bucket, and the dog growled.

I switched from talking to singing songs I'd taught children in church. I touched the dog's front leg, which appeared to be caught in the handle. Once I assisted the helpless creature bend his leg out of the way, Jake lifted the bucket off his head and tossed it to the side with a clang.

The dog barked, but this time it sounded happier, maybe even relieved. "He's got burrs in his fur."

Jake chuckled. "Maybe you can turn that into a song."

"Okay, Mr. Smarty-pants. I think he needs to be seen by a veterinarian." I held the dog close. "He doesn't have tags or a collar."

Jake stroked the dog. "You're right, since we don't have information on his owner, we need to get him to a vet. Do you know one?"

"Well, yeah, I know names of vets from working at the pharmacy, but I've never used a one."

"I'll text Brett and see who he uses for his dog Rufus."

Achoo.

I glanced at Jake. "Bless you. Are you allergic to animals?"

"That wasn't me. Stay here with the dog." Jake stood and walked deeper into the alley. "Who's there?"

A rumble began in the dog's chest.

"Shh, it's going to be okay. At least, I think it is." I rubbed his bony side with one hand and dialed 9-1-1 with the other.

Jake's commanding voice shouted out, "Come out where we can see you."

"Nine-one-one, what's your emergency?"

I turned my attention to the dispatcher while keeping an eye on the alley. "This is Emma Justice. We're in the alley behind Paige's Turn Bookstore and Amalfi's Pizzeria. We need help."

"A unit is on the way. Are you in danger?"

"Maybe. Jake Hunter is with me. And a dog. There's also at least one other person hiding somewhere in the alley. Don't shoot us."

A siren blipped, and Chief Young ran toward me. "Emma, are you okay?"

"Yeah." I nodded. "That's Jake Hunter, but we heard somebody sneeze. This is where Willow was killed. Do you think it's the murderer?"

"I'll find out." He hustled toward Jake, and the two men spoke in quiet tones.

The dog panted and looked at me with soulful dark eyes.

"I don't know if we should move or stay."

Jake jogged toward me. "Chief wants us out of here."

There was my answer. "What about the dog? We can't leave him."

"Precisely." Jake scooped up the runt and held him against his chest. "Lead the way, but keep your head down."

Not exactly words of comfort. I hunched my shoulders and took off with Jake on my heels. We escaped from the alley, jogged down the street a bit, and stopped at a bench on the sidewalk. We were far enough away to be out of danger but close enough for the officers to find us to ask questions. We sat without speaking. The dog panted in Jake's arms, and we took turns holding him.

The next couple of hours were a blur. More officers arrived, and by the sounds of the scuffle, someone was captured. The only problem was nobody would tell me who.

Jake and I answered Matt's questions, then we took the dog to Brett's veterinarian. After a quick exam, the vet asked to keep him overnight for observation. He also planned to give the little mutt a good physical with lab work. Brett had assured us Dr. Bushy Erb was the best, and while I hadn't known the pitiful dog long, I wanted to protect him.

On the way home from the veterinarian's office, I slowed Ms. Daisy near the police station.

Jake chuckled. "It's killing you not to know if they caught the killer."

I eased into an empty parking spot on Main Street. "I'm as curious as all git out. Aren't you?"

"It can't hurt for us to go inside." He hopped out of the passenger seat.

I shut off the engine and joined Jake in the empty street. "Do you want me to do the talking?"

"Either way." His easy stride annoyed me.

Why was I so nervous? I hadn't done anything wrong. I hurried to keep up, but Jake beat me to the door and held it open for me. "Your parents taught you good manners."

He tilted his head. "Might be the nicest thing you ever said to me."

Well, shame on me, then. I'd do my best to treat Jake better. In the meantime, we had a killer to catch, if the cops didn't already have him in jail.

Chapter Nine

Jake and I sat across the desk from Chief Matt Young. Because the man and I had been friends for years, before now, I'd always been comfortable around him. He was at least five years older than me. I'd also known his wife before they divorced, and she took off to Waco. Matt had a son and daughter, but they lived with their mom. Our daughters had taken dance classes together at church when they were young, and Matt's son was a high school football star.

I crossed and uncrossed my legs. "Chief, we were curious if you caught Willow's killer tonight. It sounded like you apprehended somebody in the alley. Was it the killer or a homeless person? Somebody else, maybe?"

He folded his hands together on his desk. "Emma, we were friends before my promotion, and you can still call me Matt."

His words eased my nerves. "Thanks, Matt."

"As for your question, there were two men in the alley where you rescued the dog. One was Rusty Ramirez. He's been a lawbreaker for years, but I don't think he killed Willow. There was another person in the alley, but he escaped. Rusty won't tell me who the man was, but we found a knife under the steps going into Amalfi's. I think the other person threatened Rusty."

"I gave him food earlier when I caught him dumpster diving behind the bakery. What do you think he was doing in the alley?"

"His favorite pastime. Getting high." Matt ran a hand through his short brown hair. "I'm glad you gave him food and not money."

"He told me he had cash from the farmers' market, and I wondered what he'd done with it." I crossed my legs again. "There must be some way to help

Rusty."

Jake drummed his fingers on the arms of his wooden chair. "That's the problem. He's got to want to get better."

Matt nodded. "Your friend's right."

Jake's hands stilled. "Is it possible Rusty knows something about the murder? Was the man with him tonight involved in Willow's death?"

I'd wondered the same thing. "I asked him earlier if he knew anything. You know he sticks to the shadows."

Matt looked from me to Jake and back to me. "You questioned Rusty about Willow's death?"

"Kinda."

Matt's nostrils flared. "Emma Justice, what on earth were you thinking?"

"Like I said, Rusty lurks in the back streets and alleys. That's where he was both times when I found him tonight. It's possible he saw something but is scared to report it." I took a deep breath.

"Let me handle the investigation. I don't want to lose another friend." Matt turned his attention to Jake. "You're not on the force, yet, but if you can keep Emma out of my investigation, it'll go a long way to your getting hired."

Jake coughed. "We only met yesterday, but from what little I know about Emma, when she makes up her mind, there's no stopping her."

I raised my hand. "Hey, I'm sitting right here."

Matt smiled. "I didn't say it'd be easy."

Jake stood. "Emma, would you please come with me?"

"I can see myself home, Jake Hunter." I brushed past him and left the two men in Chief Young's office. If that's how Matt treated his friends, I didn't want to be his enemy.

If Rusty had been arrested, I'd have to wait before asking him any more questions. Not that I believed he killed Willow, but I agreed with the police chief and Jake. Rusty knew more than he was telling.

I drove home by myself and called Abby. It was past time to update her on the happenings in Lutz.

Chapter Ten

My doorbell rang before nine on Monday morning. Wearing threadbare jeans, my straw cowboy hat, and a lightweight cotton shirt to weed the garden, I walked from the kitchen to the front door, yawning along the way. Since the murder, nightmares had disturbed my sleep.

Jake stood on the covered porch, holding an insulated mug. "Morning, Emma."

"Hold on a minute." I hurried to the kitchen and grabbed the Yeti he'd loaned me Saturday. When I opened the door this time, I handed him the tumbler. "Here you go. Nice and clean."

He lifted one side of his mouth. "Thank you. I brought you green tea and local honey."

"Why?" Oops, my tone sounded rude. Texas was called The Friendly State for a reason. "I mean, how nice."

"Let's call it a peace offering." He passed the hot drink to me.

"Thanks, but shouldn't you be working?"

"Brett said he's bored of lying around and taking it easy. He opened the store and told me to go for a walk or something."

"I thought he was taking some personal days off. Now it sounds like he's been sick. What's going on, Jake?" I took a sip of the tea. Perfect temperature and delicious.

"It's not my story to share. Sorry."

I leaned against the doorframe and propped one foot on the other. "Are you sticking around town now that Brett's back at work?"

His eyes widened, and he turned the Yeti in circles in his hands. "That's the plan."

"What if Matt doesn't hire you to work for the police department?" I eased the lid off and took a drink of tea.

"I've got a lead on another job with a construction company focused on restoring old houses."

"Interesting. I pictured you more as a rambling man."

"You would've been right in the past. I've been running wide open most of my adult life, and Texas is plenty big enough to do that these past few years, but it's time to settle down."

My cell phone rang. "I need to get that. It could be an order. You can come in, if you like." I strode through the gathering room and hooked a right into the kitchen and breakfast nook that filled the back corner of my bungalow. "Hello."

"Ms. Justice?"

"Yes, this is Emma."

"This is Dr. Erb's office. We're ready for you to pick up your dog." The woman's high voice was too peppy for a Monday morning.

I set the cup on the counter and gripped the phone with a damp palm. "He's not my dog. Dr. Erb was going to find his owner."

"Cowboy's owner died, and the extended family doesn't want him. Believe me, I spent my Sunday afternoon practically begging his relatives to adopt the sweet pooch. It's up to you, or he'll end up in the pound." Her voice had turned serious. "And you know what happens there."

I gulped. "He'll die?"

"You didn't hear that from me. Listen, Dr. Erb said you can foster Cowboy for a few weeks. See if it works out. We've got a crate full of goodies for you and Cowboy. Can you come over before lunch?" She sounded way more cheerful now.

What choice did I have? "I'm on the way." I ended the call.

"Everything okay?" Jake's expression showed concern.

"I don't know. Cowboy, the dog we found, is now mine." I snatched my keys from their spot in my ceramic flower bowl. My purse hung on the decorative metal spiral sun with hooks. I turned and met Jake's gaze. "I know nothing about taking care of a dog. Zip. Zilch. Nada."

He raised both hands. "I get the picture. Would you like me to go with you to pick up Cowboy?"

His words calmed my nerves. "Yes. Thanks. You know this is a huge responsibility."

"True, but you raised a daughter. You've got this." He pointed to the counter where my cup of tea sat beside his empty tumbler. "Don't forget your drink."

I reached out with a shaky hand. More caffeine might not be the wisest decision, but I needed it.

"Hey, Emma." His hand touched my shoulder. "It's going to be okay."

"Really? I don't even know for sure what kind of dog Cowboy is."

"Golden retriever is my guess." He gave me a crooked smile. "I believe you'll do a great job taking care of Cowboy. Now, let's go."

I tossed the keys to Jake and picked up my tea, wrapping my hands around its warmth. "Do you mind to drive? I need to corral my scattered thoughts." I had my day planned. Spend most of my time working in the garden, take pictures, then work on social media to promote my business.

"I don't mind. Let's Roll."

As we drove around the square, I sipped my tea and hummed along to a Brett Eldredge tune on the radio. I was doing my best to relax. The dog would probably respond better if I wasn't uptight.

Willow's three supposed friends entered the yoga studio with water bottles and rolled-up mats. Two men stood at the corner waiting for the walk signal. They appeared to be talking but didn't look at each other. The taller man was a stranger to me, but the shorter guy triggered a memory. I pointed. "Jake, do you know either of them?"

He stopped and allowed a car to pull in front of us, then looked toward the men. "The dude in jogging shorts was in the coffee shop Friday."

Friday. The day Willow was murdered. Chills broke out on my arms. "Ah, that's it. He was wearing jeans and a hoodie then." Same straggly hair and stubbly beard.

"Right. He ordered two black coffees."

"How do you remember that?"

"I play a little game where I try to guess what a customer will order. I pegged him to be a black coffee kind of guy, and it was nice to be right."

"Will you drive around the square again? Let's see where those guys are going."

Jake glanced my way. "Won't it look suspicious?"

"People do it all the time to get a good parking place. I need to get a better look at them."

"Your friend, the chief of police, asked you to leave Willow's death alone."

I huffed. "What makes you think this has anything to do with Willow?"

He changed lanes to keep circling instead of going directly to the vet clinic. "I've got your number, lady. You won't let this go."

I turned in my seat to keep an eye on the men. "Lutz attracts people who like to collect old things. We host festivals and antique sales. Those don't look like our normal tourists, plus Saturday is the day folks visit our town. Not Mondays. Shoot, some of the stores are closed on Mondays to recover from the weekend."

"Not normal. Gotcha." Jake stopped for a pedestrian. "It's always good to be aware of your surroundings. I'm impressed you noticed the strangers."

"Hey, I learned that working in a pharmacy. I guess it's even more important when you're fighting in a foreign country."

"You have no idea." His jaw tightened.

"I'm sorry for whatever horrors you experienced. Thanks for your service." I started to touch his arm. His frown warned me not to try and break down his walls.

"Yes, ma'am." His gravelly voice confirmed my suspicion.

The men crossed the street and paused in front of the bank. Lone Star Cattleman Bank of Texas. The very bank Willow's dad and uncles had started before she was born. "You don't think they're planning to rob it, do you?"

Jake whipped my truck into an empty parking space with a slight squeal of tires. "Not on my watch." He shut off the engine but left the keys in the ignition.

I gripped his arm. "What are you doing? Take it easy with Ms. Daisy."

"Ms. Daisy?"

"Yeah, my truck."

"Sorry." He glanced at my hand on his arm. "Man, your fingers are ice cold."

I let go of his arm. "They're always cold."

"Do you have Reynaud's syndrome?"

I shrugged. "I doubt it."

"It's a condition where you often have cold feet and hands." He rubbed his jaw. "You really should take better care of yourself."

"I eat healthy food and exercise." I sipped my still-warm tea and avoided eye contact.

"Fine, but have you asked a doctor about your hands? Also, have you ever been tested for allergies? I've noticed that you sneeze around flowers."

"That's none of your business. You don't need to fix me." Movement outside the bank distracted me from our debate. "Wait. Look." I pointed.

A woman walked outside wearing a gray blouse, a black pencil skirt, and stiletto heels. She spoke briefly to the men, and it appeared that they knew each other. "That's Rita Flores."

"Remind me who she is."

"Vince's assistant. She orders flowers from me and food from Sophie when they're celebrating birthdays at the bank or hosting retirement parties and such. Why would she be speaking to the strangers?"

"Because they're not strangers to her. You don't walk out of your job with no purse and get in a conversation on the sidewalk for no reason."

"Keen sense of observation." I pointed to the three of them. "Look, the taller guy reached out and touched her arm. It was practically a caress."

"Another thing you don't normally do to a stranger. You got a ball cap in here?"

I reached into the backseat and retrieved a gray hat with sunflowers on the front. "It's not very masculine."

"It'll do. Wait here." Jake adjusted the plastic band in back before tugging on the hat. He jumped out of my truck and jay-walked to reach the group.

He spoke to them, and they pointed to the coffee shop, then the three of them dispersed in different directions. Jake sauntered back my way with a smug look on his face.

Instead of returning to me though, he shot into Anytime Coffee.

Now what? I took another drink and drummed my fingers. Weeds needed pulling, a dog needed picking up, and a killer needed capturing. Although, to be fair, it'd been my fault Jake circled the square.

My phone vibrated, and Brett's name appeared.

"Hi, Brett. What's Jake doing?"

"No how are you? No I missed you, Brett? Nothing about me?" Brett had always teased me like I'd imagined a normal brother would pick on a sister.

I slumped into the seat. "I'm sorry. I really have missed you. How could you leave me to deal with Jake?"

A laugh barked out of my friend. "I get that. Jake would like you to pick him up in five minutes at the bed-and-breakfast. Something about not tipping his hat to the two guys y'all saw on the street. Does that make sense?"

I sighed. "Yeah, it does. Five minutes, huh? Let's discuss your love life. Any sparks between you and Celia?"

"Girl, dontcha be grinding my coffee beans. Talk to ya later." He hung up.

I laughed. Brett's avoidance told me more than a simple yes. What had he been waiting for? Was it some kind of Marine code preventing him from dating his buddy's sister? The age difference? There was possibly eight years between them. Maybe it was the long-distance aspect, or his PTSD could be a barrier. Brett did a great job of hiding his emotional wounds, but I knew what meds he took from my days as a pharmacy tech.

I settled my tea in a cup holder, vaulted the console, then slid behind the wheel. I started the truck and drove to the bed-and-breakfast. I couldn't wait to hear what Jake had learned, but drawing attention to myself wouldn't be wise. I drove the short distance like a little old lady who couldn't see over the steering wheel. Nice and slow.

Jake waved to me from the front porch where he stood talking to Faith. I parallel parked across the street and waited until he hopped into the passenger seat.

"What'd you learn?"

"Buckle up, both literally and metaphorically. I'll tell you on the way."

I had already buckled my seatbelt but didn't waste time arguing the point. I pulled away so he'd spill the news faster. "So?"

"Rita called the scruffy guy Kevin. You know the one we saw at the coffee shop Friday?"

"Yeah. Half a name is better than nothing, but is that all?" I glanced at him.

"Nope." He grinned. "I think we should officially work together to find Willow's killer."

My foot went to the brake before I realized it, and I'd stopped in the middle of the street. A car honked, and I stepped on the gas. "Are you serious? Why?"

"You know the people in Lutz, and I have training and experience. We were also two of the first three people to find Willow. What do you say? Shall we make it official?"

"You bet I want to work on this mystery with you." It'd be way easier if he wasn't trying to tell me to back off every step of the way. I pulled into the parking lot of the vet clinic. My hands trembled, which had nothing to do with allergies or Reynaud's disease. I didn't know if the shakiness was because I was about to adopt Cowboy or because I'd be investigating Willow's murder with Jake. Whatever the cause, I refused to back down.

Chapter Eleven

"Cowboy?" I looked around my backyard. It'd be easy to hide in the flowers. "Come, boy."

Cowboy was six months old and a golden retriever, according to Dr. Erb. He'd been rescued once from the animal shelter, and I was his second rescuer. Poor thing hadn't had much stability in his short life. Cowboy had been groomed at the vet's office, and all the burrs had been removed, leaving a few bare spots in his short beige coat.

"Cowboy!" I ripped off the yellow garden gloves and washed my hands with the hose. If I lost the dog on the first day, I'd be the worst pet owner ever. The pitiful pup deserved so much better, especially after his previous owner died. Shaking water from my hands, I ran to the open gate. The thing had never closed well, but I'd not once worried about it before owning a dog. Cowboy probably hadn't worked hard to escape, and if I found him—no, when I found him—I'd fix it. "Cowboy!"

"Hey, lady. Did ya lose your dog?" Jake and Cowboy walked on the sidewalk in front of my house, calm as could be.

Of all the people to find my dog, it had to be him. He probably thought I was the biggest joke in town. "Yeah, he must've jiggled the gate open. Where'd you find him?" I knelt by the dog and rubbed his head.

"On the square. I was about to go into Anytime Coffee House and relieve Brett when I spotted your dog wandering around."

"Dr. Erb didn't tell us how long Cowboy has been left to fend for himself. I hope he hasn't gotten used to a life of roaming." I peered into the dog's sad eyes and stroked his back. "I'll keep you safe. You don't need to run away again."

Jake cleared his throat. "I'll shove off."

I stood. "Thanks for rescuing my dog. I'll get the gate fixed. The chain-link fence came with the house. It's been fine for my garden, and my flowers never tried to escape."

Jake chuckled, then backed up a few steps. "Let me know if you need my help."

"Sure. See you around."

Jake gave a salute and turned, taking off at a brisk pace.

"Let's go, boy." A raindrop splatted on my face. "Rita hired me to create flower arrangements for the bank and the Moore house. It's time to get busy."

We had one local florist, Yarrow Martin. She was recovering from hip replacement surgery, and her daughter, Violet, was caring for the woman. They'd asked me to pick up the slack until she returned to work, and I'd agreed. In our little town, the florist didn't do a huge business, but it was important to help her survive. Neither of us could've predicted a funeral for a prominent citizen during her recovery period.

I led Cowboy through the yard to the back door and let him into the kitchen before gathering the flowers I'd already cut for Willow's arrangements.

My bungalow had been built in 1925, and I'd worked hard updating it over the years while retaining its original charm. Three bedrooms and two baths had been perfect for Abby and me. The third bedroom served as my office. An extra refrigerator in the garage worked to keep my flowers cool, and the kitchen was where I created flower arrangements. For the bank, I worked on a spray with yellow and white daisies, white mums, and red carnations. Creating something for the Moore house was a bigger challenge, knowing the couple was about to divorce. I chose to go with hydrangeas, white cosmos, and green filler in an antique vase I'd bought at a flea market.

Cowboy stood beside me, wide-eyed and tail-wagging.

"Do you need a treat?" I opened the large box of bone-shaped biscuits, and he sat. "Hmm, is that how you do it? Sit obediently when hoping for a treat? Here you go." I tossed it his way, and he caught the biscuit before it hit the floor. "Good boy. I've got to take a shower."

He followed me to my bedroom and lay at the foot of the bed while I cleaned up. I dressed in black slacks and a black blouse, thinking my outfit was respectful and appropriate to work in. I slipped on my red flats in honor of Willow. The rain transformed from a pitter-patter to a downpour, so I decided to drive instead of walking to the bank.

Within fifteen minutes, I entered the bank with the wire easel and floral spray. I set the display near the front door and noticed the lace was unraveling. The deluge continued, and it didn't make sense to get drenched, walking to my truck for supplies to fix the damage.

Instead, I carried the arrangement to the employee break room in hopes of finding supplies to repair the damage. In the past, I'd provided flowers for celebrations in the employee area, and I knew where they kept scissors and tape. I slipped into the room unnoticed, gathered some materials I thought would work, then busied myself fixing the imperfection.

Elevator music floated throughout the main floor, and a talk show played on the small TV in the break room. Gina Zimmerman and Heidi Bauer sat at a table drinking coffee, deep in conversation.

Heidi fanned herself. "Rita's ex is super hunky, and he's out of prison. I keep expecting him to walk through the front doors any day and claim his woman."

Gina said, "But she's got a crush on Mr. Moore."

"Honey child, when she lays eyes on Dave, all thoughts of Vince Moore will disappear. There's really no comparison."

I cleared my throat. "Sorry, I don't mean to interrupt, but I don't want to eavesdrop either."

Gina's eyes grew wide. She was older than my daughter but still in her twenties. "Hi, Ms. Justice."

"Please, call me Emma."

Heidi was closer to my age, and she didn't bat an eye. "I was telling Gina here that Dave Smith is out of prison. Mark my words, we'll see him in town soon. He and Rita were engaged before he got himself arrested."

"What does he look like?"

Heidi's eyes sparkled. "He's one fine Black man. Trim and not quite six feet tall. No tattoos and short black hair. Sometimes he has facial hair, but not always. He's full of charisma. If you ever meet Dave, you'll see what I mean."

Chills raced up my spine. One of the men Rita had spoken to earlier was a slender African American. The other guy was Kevin. "I may have seen him on the square this morning."

"You don't say." Heidi took her mug to the sink, and Gina followed her lead. They walked to where I stood, repairing the loose lace and taping it back together. "Where exactly did you see him?"

"In front of the bank." My voice squeaked, and I cleared my throat again. "I drove by in time to see two men on the sidewalk, and Rita came out of the bank and talked to them."

Heidi snapped and pointed at Gina. "See? He's come back to claim the love of his life."

Gina gasped. "Did they kiss?"

I shook my head. "No. They were only talking when I saw them, but it doesn't take too long to drive around the square." No need to tell them I'd been spying on the three people, and there was definitely no reason to mention the tender touch.

Gina's shoulders slumped. "Oh, coconuts. I really wanted to see him. Rita always seems so uptight, and it'd be nice to see her happy."

Heidi leaned a hip against the counter. "Our lives are much easier when Rita's happy, if you know what I mean."

I didn't want to say something ugly, and these women had provided a good clue, so I knew it was time to set up the flower display. "I better get this out there. Y'all have a great afternoon."

Rita appeared while I worked on the arrangement in the lobby. "It's lovely, Emma. Add the expense to my bank tab."

"Sure. Are you certain it looks okay?"

"Willow would've been pleased." She clasped her hands together. "Have you been by the house yet?"

"It's my next stop. Hey, congratulations. I heard your ex-fiancé is back in town."

She narrowed her eyes. "If he is, it means nothing to me. History won't repeat itself between us."

Not quite a denial. Man, she was good at keeping her secret hidden.

Chapter Twelve

Monday meant it was book club night at my house. Light food, books, and good friendship always filled our evenings. I'd prepared a veggie tray, pretzels, and a meat and cheese board. The cold foods chilled in the refrigerator that had become much too empty since Abby left for college.

Cowboy watched my movements with interest. I rolled slices of Lyoner with olives and peppers and speared each one with a colorful toothpick. His ears perked up when he smelled the Black Forest ham, and I gave him a slice. As skinny as he was, I leaned toward allowing him to eat real food. "We need to fatten you up, but don't tell Dr. Erb I gave you anything besides his fancy dog food."

Cowboy devoured the ham and barked.

"One more slice, and that's all." I cut up the slice and placed it in his bowl. "There you go, boy."

He gobbled it up in less than twenty seconds.

After I cleaned the kitchen, Cowboy followed me to my home office. The rain had quit, but the weather was dreary. It both felt and smelled like it could rain again any moment. I sat at the desk, and Cowboy lay at my feet while I added notes to my tablet on what I'd learned about Willow.

I'd discovered more about Rita and her ex-fiancé and created a new entry on them. They probably had nothing to do with Willow's death, but Dave was a newcomer and an ex-con. Had he been out of prison long enough to have crossed paths with Willow? I didn't see how he could've had a motive to off her.

The doorbell rang, and Cowboy raced to the front door, barking until I joined him. "No barking."

Cowboy quieted, but his tail continued to wag.

I looked out the upper window panes before opening the door to Paige. "Hi, you're early."

She nodded as she entered, then stopped in front of Cowboy and pet him as I shut and locked the door. "When'd you get a dog?"

"I found him this weekend and adopted him after Dr. Erb told me that his owner died. Evidently, if I didn't adopt him, he could die next."

"That doesn't sound right to me. I bet they only said that to guilt you into adopting him."

"I looked it up. It's okay to euthanize shelter dogs, as in it's legal." I shivered.

"Still, it doesn't sound like something Dr. Erb would do. He's in the business of healing pets, not killing them." She removed her rain jacket, and I hung it on a coat rack made from a birch tree limb. Paige wore a light blue T-shirt featuring Jane Austen.

"That makes me feel better about Dr. Erb. Let's discuss something besides death." I headed to the kitchen. "Would you like a drink?"

Paige and Cowboy followed me from the living area, through the breakfast room, and into the kitchen. Paige plopped onto a barstool, and Cowboy headed to his water bowl.

"I'd love a drink, but nothing with caffeine. I'm wired enough." Paige ran a hand through her hair, messing up her already messy bun.

"I've got the perfect thing." I filled a glass with ice. "The Agatha Christie book was good."

"Hers usually are. It's why they've stood the test of time." She stared into space and replied with a flat tone.

I pulled out a pitcher of lemonade from the refrigerator and filled her glass, then dropped a mint sprig on top before passing it to her. "What's going on? Has there been a new development?"

"Chief Young questioned me again. I almost puked when he walked into the store this afternoon. I had to close for about three hours while he grilled me." She drank the entire glass of lemonade at once and passed it back to me.

"What kind of questions did he ask?" I refilled her glass.

"What was my relationship like with Willow? Where was I when the murder occurred? Do I have a witness? We went over the timeline of Friday morning again. Oh, Emma, I know they are going to arrest me." Her knuckles whitened as she held the glass. "They're trying to catch me in a lie or something."

"Surely not."

"I'm going to be sick again." She dashed out of the kitchen and toward the bathroom.

Cowboy whined.

"Do you need to go out?" I opened the back door and followed him as far as the patio. "Don't think about trying to escape. I'm watching you tonight."

A metallic sound yanked my attention off Cowboy. "Who's there?" Shadows filled my yard, but it wasn't dark yet. Although, Willow had been murdered in the light of day.

My dog poked his head up from the flowers and raced to the side of my house. His bark sounded happy instead of threatening.

The fence surrounded my flower gardens and the sideyard. I inched my way toward the side area, unsure what to expect. At least Paige was in the house and could call for help if this went sideways. Taking a deep breath, I peeked around the corner.

Jake had a wrench in one hand and was moving the gate door back and forth.

I gasped. "What are you doing?"

His eyes grew wide. "I wanted to come by and see if we could discuss the murder, and it seemed like a good time to take a look at your gate."

"I planned to get to it." Wait, that didn't sound thankful. Willow's murder must be getting to me. "I appreciate your help, but don't you have better things to do?"

He shrugged. "It beats sitting around the bed-and-breakfast."

"What about Brett?"

Jake shut the gate behind him and knelt beside Cowboy. "Celia wanted some time alone with Brett before she has to head back to Waco. What can I say? My little sister has me wrapped."

Cowboy licked Jake's face.

"Thanks for helping, but Paige is inside." I rubbed my hands together. "I can't desert her."

"No problem. I'll finish this up. Cowboy can stay with me."

"I hate to take advantage."

"You're not. I'm offering. We'll be fine." He patted Cowboy, then stood. "Go hang out with your friend."

"If you're sure."

He motioned for me to leave. "Go on."

I only glanced back once at Jake working on my gate with Cowboy sitting beside him watching. The puppy was well-behaved. Was he special, or had he been trained? The things I knew about dogs could fill a spoon.

In the kitchen, Paige sat at the counter. Her face was pale, but she must've run a brush through her hair. It looked much neater. "Sorry about that."

"Don't worry. Do you feel any better?"

She blotted her forehead with a damp paper towel. "I'm not sure I can lead our discussion tonight."

"Let me text our group and postpone until next week." I picked my phone off the counter and began a group message.

"That will only work if I'm not in jail next Monday." She squeezed her eyes shut.

"Aw, Paige, don't think like that. You're innocent."

"There are lots of innocent people in prison."

I hit send, then sat beside my friend. "We know you didn't kill Willow, so who else had a motive? The spouse is always a suspect, but Vince is obvious. If we rule out you and Vince, who does that leave us?"

"I don't know." She reached for her lemonade and took a drink. "I heard Rusty was questioned."

"It's hard to believe he'd murder Willow. Maybe if she'd been run over by a drunk or stoned driver, Rusty could be considered." I flattened my hands on the cool granite countertop. "Although, he doesn't have a car, so that doesn't make sense."

"His parents moved to Austin last year. The dad made a fortune working the oil rigs or investing wisely or something." Paige wadded up the paper towel. "None of this is helping prove my innocence."

"We eliminated Rusty." My phone pinged twice.

"Right, but it doesn't help me. We're eliminating more people than finding suspects." My friend gasped. "You've got to help me catch the killer. You usually solve the mystery first in book club. Don't just say you're going to help. Dig in and catch the killer. I'm not imagining Chief Young's desire to arrest me. It's going to happen."

I'd never seen Paige come unglued. She was normally confident and optimistic. "Hey, you're innocent, and the truth will prevail." I pulled out the meat and cheese board as well as the veggies and placed them on the counter. Maybe Paige's blood sugar had dropped. Her mood was for sure bleak. My phone pinged again, and I glanced at it.

Paige took a big breath. "I guess that's our group replying."

I checked. "Yes. You know we're all on your side."

"Yeah." She eyed the food. "I haven't eaten all day."

I pulled out a stack of Thun Bohemia Rambler pink flower plates I'd inherited from my Grandmother Fair. "Eat something. I'm sure you'll feel better with food in your stomach."

There was a tap on the back door followed by a bark.

"That's Jake. Do you mind if he comes in? He's had police training, and he's been helping me solve the mystery." I walked to the door but kept my focus on Paige.

"What can it hurt?" She reached for the crackers.

I opened the door for Jake and Cowboy.

Jake stood in the doorway. "The gate should stay closed for you now. If not, let me know. I'll try something else."

"Thanks, but you don't need to worry about it."

"It's best to stay busy. Keeps me out of trouble." He winked.

"Okay, I don't want to be blamed for you getting into trouble. Why don't you come inside? We're going to eat a little and discuss the murder."

Jake wiped his feet on the doormat, then pointed to the sink. "Do you mind if I wash my hands?"

"Sure. Would you like lemonade?"

"Sounds good." He was taller than my brother who had been about the only man in my kitchen. Jake's presence filled the space.

I poured drinks for us.

Paige pointed to the veggie dip. "This is delicious. Did you make it?"

"No, I bought it from Sophie. I'm going to grab my tablet to take notes on what we discuss." I left her picking two little slices of rye bread off the board.

When I returned, Jake was loading up his plate.

"Let's sit at the table." I pointed to the long French harvest table I'd gotten for a steal at a flea market after I bought my bungalow. It was long and narrow and fit the space perfectly.

The three of us moved the food, and I sat at the end of the table with Paige on one side and Jake on the other. "Jake, Paige is concerned Matt will arrest her for Willow's murder. Do you think it'd be a good idea to dive deeper into Willow's life?"

He swallowed and wiped his mouth. "Yeah. That'll give us a better idea of who might have a motive to kill Willow. What do you two know about her?"

"She's rich." Paige rolled a carrot between her fingers. "Always has been wealthy."

"Then it sounds like money is a legit motive." Jake nodded.

"I wonder who will inherit her fortune?" I added the question to my notes.

Paige said, "Probably her children, but there's no way they murdered Willow."

"I agree." From a distance, I'd watched the kids grow up. They loved their mom, and I'd never seen an altercation between either child.

"I don't know the kids, but it wouldn't be the first time a teen murdered their parents. How old are the children?" Jake frowned.

Paige played with her ring. On and off it went. "Seventeen and fourteen, but they seem like good kids. They've helped me at the store for special events. Both are polite and appeared to get along with Willow."

Jake nodded. "I'll trust your assessment for now."

I added money to my list of motives. How many people had been killed because of greed? The more immediate question was, who had the most to gain financially from Willow's death?

"Blake plays baseball for the high school, and you know that parents of athletes can get hostile." Paige sighed.

"It's early in the season. Do you think he took somebody else's spot on the team?" I knew most of the high school parents because of my daughter Abby.

"Benching a player is bad if they're hoping to earn a college scholarship." Paige left her ring alone and took a cracker. "I'll ask around and try to find out if baseball could be a possible connection. I know it seems like a long shot, but I'm that desperate."

"Unless Willow was on the coaching staff, it doesn't seem a likely motive." Jake tapped the table. "Emma, I think you're onto something about Willow's past. I wonder if she was being blackmailed for some reason."

"Blackmail? That's an interesting angle. Willow appeared to be a pillar of the community, but what if she did something bad?" I wasn't sure what it could be, but I'd dig into her background, starting with social media.

Chapter Thirteen

Paige stared at her plate. "Don't forget Nick Jones was at the store when I left."

I glanced at Jake. "He's the exterminator."

"Got it. You mentioned him before."

I found Nick's name in my notes. "It'd be interesting to know if Nick and Willow had issues. But Nick has been infatuated with Paige for a while."

Jake looked at Paige. "I take it you're not interested in dating Nick?"

Cowboy walked over to his water bowl and lapped it dry.

Paige said, "No, and I've asked him repeatedly to back off. He keeps asking me out and making inappropriate comments."

"Jake, you should know Nick's first wife died mysteriously." I popped a grape into my mouth.

"If he's as dangerous as you two are insinuating, why do you have him handle your pest control?"

Paige shrugged. "I'm afraid to change."

Jake frowned. "That's not good. Do you think he's stalking you?"

"I don't think so, but isn't that part of being a stalker? Your victim doesn't know you're watching?"

"Some stalkers want you to be aware. It gives them a powerful feeling to scare their prey."

Beside Nick's name on my tablet, I struck the question mark key. "Nick could've accidentally killed Willow, thinking he was going after Paige. If he's guilty, we don't know of any other motive."

"Correct." Paige reached for a slice of Lyoner with olives and peppers and two little slices of rye bread. "I think it's more likely to be Vince who killed Willow. With her death, he probably remains in charge of the bank even though her family started it."

I documented her words on my app. "I wonder why we haven't seen Willow's family?"

Jake said, "I met her mother and brother at the coffee shop. They were heading to meet Willow's kids, Christine and Blake. Right?"

Paige nodded. "That's right. I met Willow's family many years ago, but it's doubtful they remember me."

I stopped taking notes. "I saw the kids the other night, but Vince's parents were at the house with them. With the divorce coming up, I'm sure it's a sticky situation between Willow's family and Vince. Jake, how did you know those people were related to Willow?"

"They each ordered coffee, then got into a big discussion about what the kids would like to drink. I suggested the fruit smoothie that's popular with the youth around here, so they ordered two." He bit into his sandwich.

"Anything else?"

"I offered my condolences and mentioned how we were the ones who found Willow's body." He pointed his finger between himself and me.

"Wow, I doubt I'd have had the nerve to confess that to the family." I took a drink.

"Why? We didn't do anything wrong."

"Yeah, but still." Guilt niggled my conscience. If I'd gotten there a few minutes earlier, would Willow still be alive? Like background music in a coffee shop, the accusation was constantly on my mind.

Paige dropped her carrot. "Did they mention me?"

Jake ran a hand across his mouth. "Kinda. They know Willow was working for you, but they didn't accuse you of killing her. The mother was weepy, and the brother was stoic. I think his name is Cal."

"Cal Hoffman." I met Jake's gaze. "Who do they think killed Willow?"

"Vince. They asked my opinion, and I confessed how new I am to the area." He fixed another little sandwich with the cocktail-sized rye bread. "These are good."

My stomach growled, and I reached for a chunk of cheese. "Thanks. Eat as much as you like. We canceled our book club meeting tonight."

Paige finished her sandwich and reached for a slice of ham and crackers. I'd never seen her eat so much at once. The stress must be getting to her.

We ate in silence for the next few minutes, and Cowboy lay on the floor between Jake and me.

I finished and moved my plate to the side. "Jake, did you learn anything else from Willow's family that might be useful?"

"No, I'm afraid not." Jake scooted his chair back and stretched out his long legs, crossing them at the ankles with his top foot bouncing. "I gave them my phone number in case they wanted to talk or had questions."

"Okay. I'd like to hear more about why they think Vince is guilty. His parents were so pleasant. Zig Meier told me that Vince runs with movers and shakers, or something like that. I've never seen Vince get angry or rude. In fact, he's always been nice when I've been around."

Paige leaned forward. "As long as you're not married to him, he's fine. Willow and I weren't besties, but we were friends even though the police are looking at me for committing the crime. Vince's philandering ways hurt her."

I returned to taking notes. "Um, did she think he did a good job running the bank?"

Paige sighed. "I guess so. He provided his family with a nice home and lots of extras. Vacations, country club membership, good clothes, and things like that. He was also able to afford an apartment to live in plus keep up house payments when he moved out."

My ears tingled. "He has an apartment?"

"I mean, probably. Where else would he live?" Paige shredded her napkin into thin strips.

Jake said, "There's an extended-stay hotel between here and Waco, or he could be living with his latest girlfriend, assuming he really has a woman on the side."

Paige tossed the demolished napkin to the side and broke her cracker in half. "The rumor is she's not from around here."

"Again, we're all assuming Vince is having an affair. What if it's only a rumor?" Jake's tenor voice questioned us without sounding accusatory.

"He's done it before." Paige ate the cracker.

The urge to doodle struck me, and I pulled a notepad out of a drawer. When I couldn't pull weeds or work in the garden, drawing was a great way to relieve tension, and solving the murder was stressful. "I wonder why she stayed with him all these years? And if she put up with him this long, why not wait until the kids left home?"

"Like I said, we used to be close before I asked for her help getting a loan." Paige reached for another napkin and tore a strip. "Willow wanted to stay together for the sake of the kids, but it got to be too much of an emotional strain."

Jake unfolded his legs and leaned forward. "Story as old as time."

I sketched Paige's ring. "Was there a pre-nuptial agreement? How did he know he'd lose his job when they divorced?"

"It was part of the contract for his executive position with the bank. All executives must live respectable lives. No affairs. No drugs. No gambling. That kind of thing."

I nodded. "Faith said the same thing."

Jake asked, "Why didn't she help you get the loan?"

"Willow used to run the bank. Her dad was the youngest of the brothers, and the last living sibling. When Willow's dad died, she bought the cousins out and took control. Although family is still involved, like maybe on the board or something."

"Sounds like she was smart." Jake rubbed his chin. "What about her brother? Did he want to be more involved?"

Paige quit shredding the napkin. "He's a doctor and not interested in running the bank full time. Willow has a good head for business. She gave me some solid tips about my bookstore. I shouldn't have gotten upset with her."

I patted Paige's hand. "It's understandable. Your business is in trouble, and you've poured your heart and soul into it."

"Still, friendships should be more important than the store." Paige hopped up so fast her chair fell over. "I didn't handle the rejection well."

"What do you mean?" I dreaded her answer.

"There may be some horrible text messages on Willow's phone from me. I was terrified of losing everything I own. The only way I could see to save it all was for the bank to give me a loan. I wasn't myself. If she didn't erase the messages, and the police see them, I'm doomed."

Jake said, "It's possible to retrieve deleted texts."

"I was afraid of that. I've gotta go." She hurried away.

I followed her to the door and handed her the rain jacket. "I'm so sorry you're going through this darkness. The truth will come out."

"I hope you're right, Emma. It's hard to believe right now." She walked to the driveway and took off in her sedan.

I returned to the kitchen, where Jake was clearing the table. "Oh, thanks, but you didn't have to do that."

"No problem. I thought you and Paige might need a moment alone." He glanced around the kitchen. "Do you have plastic containers for the leftovers?"

"Yeah." I pulled them out of my hidden pantry.

"Hey, that's pretty slick. I thought you had regular cabinets there." Jake walked over and looked into the pantry. "Perfect hiding place."

I laughed. "It's the perfect place to hide my junk so the kitchen looks neat."

"It'd also be a good place to hide if somebody breaks into your home."

Chills covered my body, and I stepped into the brightly lit kitchen. "Let's hope it never comes to that."

"True. How many people know about this?" He stepped into the space and turned around.

"Abby, of course. Sophie and my sister both know. My brother doesn't have a clue, but we're not that close. There are no windows, so it's my shelter during tornado warnings. I like how it flows with the kitchen design and disguises the fact it's a small room. Anyway, you're now one of the privileged few who know my secret." Sophie was my best friend, and she and my sister had always stood by me. There wasn't much they didn't know about me, and I wasn't sure how I would've survived without the two of them.

Cowboy barked.

"I probably should take him for a walk. Do you want to join us?"

"Sure thing." He re-entered the kitchen and shut the pantry door, admiring the craftsmanship. "This is very impressive."

"You're right. I guess you can add the construction guy who remodeled this place to the list of people who know about the pantry."

"Let's walk your dog and discuss something more pleasant than murder. Are you a baseball fan?"

"I can watch it with other people and understand the game, but I'd never turn on a game if I'm home alone. Reading a good book or watching a mystery on TV is more my speed." I leashed Cowboy, and we took him out the front door, making sure to lock it behind us. Even though I had a secret pantry, there was no way I wanted to use it for a hiding place. "That was quite the bombshell Paige dropped on us."

"About the text messages? Yeah, and I'm sure Matt will discover them. It's one thing to argue about something, but to have evidence of the debate on your phone is bad."

"I've got to help her find the real killer. What are your thoughts on Nick Jones?"

"I plan to see if Brett uses him at the coffee shop. If so, I'll arrange to have a conversation with the man."

"Do you believe he's the killer?"

"Maybe. Maybe not. Either way, I'd like to speak to him. Scaring women isn't acceptable where I come from."

I paused for Cowboy to sniff around a street sign. "You really are a man of integrity, aren't you?"

"I've been called a lot of things in my life, but most can't be repeated in front of a lady."

I shook my head. "You need to learn to take a compliment."

Jake ran a hand over his mouth, then laughed. "Thank you, Emma."

"You're welcome." In two days, my opinion of Jake Hunter had transformed. How many times would I change my mind about who the killer was?

Chapter Fourteen

Clouds filled the sky on Tuesday morning, and I needed to weed, deadhead, and fertilize. I stirred the compost bin and slipped on my gardening gloves. Brett always saved coffee grounds and tea leaves for me, and it helped. My acid-loving plants thrived with the dregs, worms loved them, and they repelled slugs, ants, and snails.

Cowboy snoozed on the back patio, and I enjoyed having his company even if he was asleep.

I worked the soil in the area designated for herbs, then planted chives, rosemary, oregano, and lemongrass. Thoughts of Willow's murder plagued me. The motive would probably lead me to the killer.

Cowboy barked and darted to the back door.

"What's the matter, boy?" I removed my gloves and headed to the patio for a drink of water from my insulated glass.

The doorbell rang, and I heard it from my spot near the door. I toed off my garden shoes and walked through the kitchen and breakfast room to the gathering room, and opened the front door. Cowboy stayed by my side every step of the way.

Rusty Ramirez stood looking down at his faded, holey Converse tennis shoes.

"Hi, Rusty. I'm glad to see the police let you go."

Cowboy barked a friendly greeting.

"Yes, ma'am. I didn't kill Mrs. Moore." Rusty rubbed Cowboy's head.

"I didn't think you did. Do you want to come inside?" I stepped back so he could enter.

"Yeah, it's best if nobody else hears what I'm about to tell you."

If Rusty didn't have my attention already, his declaration intrigued me. "Come on back, and what do you mean?"

The young man followed, then leaned a hip against the kitchen counter. "Were you serious about offering me a job if I get myself clean and sober?"

"Absolutely." I met his bloodshot gaze. "Do you have a plan?"

He looked back down at his tattered shoes. "I talked to my parents this morning. They're on the way here from Austin. I'm going to some fancy clinic, and this time I want to get cleaned up."

"What do you mean this time?"

"They've taken me there before, but I was just playing the game until I could get out and score my next fix." He shrugged. "Dad's got plenty of money these days, and he was patient with my mom and her addiction. He believes I can turn my life around too."

"Why will it be different this time." God bless his parents for not giving up on Rusty. I'd heard those places were pricey.

"It's time to grow up. If I keep going from one high to the next, it's gonna kill me." He returned to staring at his shoes. "Either directly or indirectly."

"I'll hire you when you get back to Lutz, but I feel like there's more to this sudden interest in getting sober." I watched his expression. "Do you know who killed Willow?"

"Maybe. Possibly."

"Is that what you told the police?"

His head jerked up. "No way. I'm trying to live through this, not get myself killed too."

Cowboy nosed Rusty's leg.

"I'm glad you adopted him. He kept me company a few cold nights. It's a terrible thing to abandon a dog."

"I agree." I pointed to the bar chair. "Have a seat. Would you like a Dr. Pepper or a Coke?"

"Dr. Pepper sounds good." He sat on the chair and propped his arms on the countertop.

I retrieved two cans of soda from the refrigerator and filled glasses with ice. "Are you hungry?"

"No, ma'am. This is good." His hands shook, but he appeared to be sober, probably from the time he spent at the police station.

"What aren't you telling me?"

No answer.

"Your therapy might go better if you're not carrying a secret. Is it possibly a deadly secret you're keeping to yourself?"

He stared at his drink. "I didn't kill Mrs. Moore, but I was paid to do it."

I gasped. "What happened?"

"I needed a fix and would've agreed to anything once I saw a wad of cash." He rubbed his hands on his jean-covered thighs. "I never planned to kill her, but I took the money anyway."

"Who paid you?" I held my breath, expecting to hear the name Vince Moore.

"The fella wore a new Texas Rangers baseball cap and sunglasses."

"What else do you remember?"

"The sunglasses were black and wire-rimmed. He would've been smarter to hire Gambler. That dude has a rep for killing anyone in order to make his gambling debts disappear." He made a motion with his hands like a magician. "Poof."

Maybe the gambling guy did the job when Rusty didn't. "Who is Gambler?"

"He's a local legend. There are a lot of stories about him. I figure he's your age or older. No way he could've murdered as many people as they say if he's my age. The dude likes to hide the bodies. What I can't figure out is, if he killed Ms. Moore, why didn't he hide her body?"

"Good point. Willow was found behind the bookstore. Can you give me a better description of the man who paid you?"

Rusty's eyes grew wide. "I've said too much. I need to disappear, but you say it's okay to contact you when I'm clean?"

"Yeah. Where are you going until your parents get here?"

He slid off the stool, and with hunched shoulders, he walked to the front door. "Don't worry about me. I probably know the shadows of this town better than anybody. See you around, Ms. Emma."

"No need to be formal. Call me Emma."

He saluted and jogged away.

I closed the door and patted Cowboy. "I've got a possible idea who paid Rusty, but I'm clueless about Gambler. Lots of people wear Rangers ball caps and wear dark sunglasses. Can I narrow down the suspects by looking at hats?" Dave had recently been released from prison. It stood to reason he'd have a new hat, but I needed more than a gut feeling to include him on my list of suspects. What would be his grounds for committing the murder? If he was still in love with Rita, it'd make more sense to kill Vince. Eliminate the competition.

The morning had flown by. The Moores decided to cater a meal instead of letting the church ladies help out after the funeral. If I was going to assist Sophie in serving food at the Moore house, I needed to shift into high gear.

Chapter Fifteen

Once again, I wore my nice black slacks, a black blouse with the sleeves rolled up, and I slipped on my red flats in honor of Willow. My traditional outfit included black shoes when I helped Sophie cater an event. Trays of food were prepared and laid out on the dining room buffet. Katie Paxson, Abby's friend and one of Sophie's employees for big events, would be focused on serving drinks, non-alcoholic, because of all the teens who'd show up to support Willow's children. My job was to circulate with appetizers.

Rita hurried into the kitchen. "They're here. Everybody ready?"

Sophie wiped her hands on a towel. "Relax. We're prepared."

"Good. We may have a few more guests than I predicted."

What had happened to a small family affair? I watched Sophie's professionalism rise to the surface. "It shouldn't be a problem. I always prepare a little extra."

"Good." Rita disappeared with a click-clack of her black stilettos.

I sidled up next to my friend. "She's not wasting any time taking over Willow's territory."

"I normally admire a woman who knows what she wants and goes after it, but Rita's actions are morbid." Sophie took a deep breath. "That was unkind. Vince is lucky to have such an efficient assistant."

I laughed. "Girl, you're too much." Sophie's tender heart endeared her to everyone she knew.

The back door opened, and Vince entered with his parents and children. His eyes widened. "Oh, I forgot you'd be here. I don't know where my mind

94

is."

I spoke up, "Can I get you anything before you face your guests?"

"Thanks, but I know where the liquor cabinet is, Emma. Take care of my family." Vince left us standing in the kitchen.

Mr. Moore looked like he'd aged since I'd last seen him. His shoulders slumped more, and his complexion looked like a shade of gray. Mrs. Moore was harder to read. Christine's splotchy face revealed her pain, but Blake scowled. The boy's fists were clenched as if ready to punch somebody.

Having raised a daughter, I was accustomed to dealing with girls. Blake's anger was beyond me, but most guys liked food. "Blake, can I get you something to eat? You can stay in here with us if you don't want to face your visitors."

The boy glared at me without uttering a word.

Sophie picked up a plate. "How about y'all take a seat? I can fix a plate for each of you. My guess is once you leave the kitchen, you won't have time to eat. Everybody will want to talk to you."

Mrs. Moore tugged on her pearl necklace. It was longer than the one she'd worn the first time I met her. "Yes, I think that's a good idea. Sophie, isn't it?"

"Yes, ma'am." Sophie pulled an upholstered chair out for the lady to sit on at the farmhouse table.

Blake sat by his grandmother but remained tight-lipped.

I poured sweet tea for everybody, then fixed each person a plate of food and served the four of them. "Can I get you anything else?"

Mr. Moore gave me a tight smile. "No, dear. This is good."

I backed away instead of hovering over them. No doubt they'd been under a microscope at the funeral and cemetery.

Sophie patted my shoulder. "Why don't you take a tray of Kentucky Hot Brown sliders to the visitors? Katie is circulating with drinks."

I picked up a silver platter and entered the dining room. Rita and bank employees stood around in small groups, chatting in low tones. Approaching a circle of people always made me feel awkward. I paused a little distance away, waiting for a lull in conversation.

Heidi Bauer, one of the tellers who'd told me about Rita's ex, stood close to one of the executives. Too close. The man said, "We'll need to give Vince at least a week off."

Heidi looked up at the white-haired gentleman. "Will he be able to keep his job now that Willow has passed?"

The man's mouth turned down. "As long as he didn't kill her, I don't see why not."

"I should hope he didn't." Heidi laughed, and the man stepped away from the circle and bumped into me.

"I'm so sorry." My face warmed. "Would you like a slider?"

His expression cleared. "Don't mind if I do. Have you seen Vince?"

I handed him a napkin and held the tray higher. "I expect he'll be out soon. He's been through a lot and probably needs a moment to compose himself."

"I understand." The gentleman picked up the slider closest to him and took a bite. "Um, delicious. I bet Sophie Becker is catering."

"Yes, sir. If you give me your name, I'll let Vince know you're looking for him."

"I'm Todd Russell, and on the bank board." He finished eating his slider and reached for another one.

"Are you related to Willow?"

He shook his head. "No. The board is made up of more than family members."

I leaned closer. "So, do you have the power to fire Vince?"

"I can suggest it, but we'd take a vote. Why? Is there a reason to terminate Vince?" His eyes narrowed.

"No, I'm not suggesting that at all. I was curious how a board of directors works." I smiled and ignored my shaky knees. "I'm so sorry. This was a terrible time to voice my questions. Please forgive me."

"We'll forget this conversation ever took place." His white hair didn't move when he nodded.

"Thank you, Mr. Russell." I kept the smile pasted on my face. "I better get back to work."

"Take care." He bit into the Kentucky Hot Brown appetizer, and I circulated.

Vince appeared, and I headed to him. "Hey, there's a Mr. Todd Russell looking to speak to you."

"I'll find him." The smell of alcohol drifted out with his words.

"Vince, no offense, but would you like a breath mint?" I pulled one from the stash in my black apron pocket.

He shook his head, but took the peppermint. "I didn't know it was obvious. Even though I didn't have the best marriage, I loved Willow." He popped the mint into his mouth. "Thanks."

"Death is never easy."

"Ain't that the truth." He left me standing with my almost-empty tray, so I headed to the kitchen.

Sophie looked up from preparing another serving dish. "How's it going out there?"

"It's a somber group which makes sense, and I decided to replenish my tray." I placed it on the kitchen counter. "Where'd Vince's family go?"

"Mrs. Moore and Christine went upstairs to freshen their makeup. I thought Mr. Moore and Blake joined the others." She passed me a serving dish full of Texas eggrolls.

I popped a peppermint into my dry mouth and snatched up a fresh stack of napkins before carrying the appetizers back to the gathering.

New faces appeared, and I worked the room. Mr. Moore and Blake sat in a corner by themselves, looking at a photo album. Vince joined them and sat on a leather ottoman.

My earlier conversation with Vince confused me. He surely knew he was a suspect in his wife's murder, and if Willow had survived, they'd be in divorce court this week. Yet, he claimed to care for Willow. Love could be so fickle. How did one find the courage to fall in love and make a lifetime commitment?

"Emma, hi." A feminine voice distracted me from staring at the Moore men.

I turned. "Hi, Celia. What are you doing here?"

"Because we found the body, I thought I should pay my respects to the family. I came with Brett and Jake." She pointed to my tray. "Whatcha got there?"

"Texas eggrolls. Try one."

Brett and Jake walked up, each carrying a glass of tea.

"Hi, guys. Who's watching Anytime Coffee?"

Brett shrugged. "I closed before the funeral and left a sign saying we'd reopen tomorrow morning."

"That was really nice. I need to circulate, but maybe we can talk later." I gave them time to grab some eggrolls before moving through the room.

Vince stood at the front door, shaking hands with the group of men who'd stood with Rita earlier. The men and Heidi left, but Rita remained. She touched Vince's arm and spoke. He leaned down to hear her words, and they looked like a couple.

Acid churned in my stomach, but I couldn't quit watching. Was it possible there was no affair? Did the relationship between the two of them only exist in Rita's mind? I never wanted a marriage to fail.

Katie appeared. "Are you okay? I'm sure this is a challenge since you found Willow's body and all."

I blinked and shifted my focus to the girl. "Oh, thanks for asking. I'm not sure I've been right since Friday morning. It breaks my heart."

"Let's go back to the kitchen and give you a chance to take a deep breath." The young woman nudged me and pointed to the kitchen.

"If you're not majoring in psychology, you need to reconsider." I smiled. "But seriously, thanks."

Sophie was washing dishes when we entered the room. I left my platter on the counter and sat down with my insulated water bottle.

Katie shook her head and handed me a glass of tea along with a cookie. "Take a minute for yourself. I'll replenish the buffet."

Sophie dried her hands and joined me. "What's going on?"

"I'm struggling to keep my mind off the murder and wondering who killed Willow. You know it could be somebody in this house." I bit into a chocolate chip cookie.

"True, but it could also be a complete stranger. One of those at the wrong place at the wrong time events." She squeezed my hand. "Do you want to leave?"

"No. I refuse to let you down, and I'll stay until the end."

"Okay, but feel free to change your mind. I'd completely understand."

"Thanks." I finished my cookies and tea then freshened my lipstick and headed out with another tray. Mini quiches with jalapeños this time.

Willow's mother and brother appeared. They looked around the room, then walked to the loveseat where Christine and Blake sat. Mr. and Mrs. Moore spoke to Willow's family, then walked away.

My respect for Vince's parents grew. If I had half the class his mother possessed, I'd be proud of myself.

I turned my attention to the garden club ladies. The women huddled together in the far corner, whispering.

Jake appeared. He leaned down and spoke in hushed tones, "How are you holding up, Emma?"

"It's a lot, you know?"

"Yeah, I do. Brett took Celia back to his place. They're going to walk Rufus."

"Why'd you stay?"

His eyebrows rose. "I wanted to make sure you were okay."

"Oh, that's so nice." Yes, I was one of those blubbery women. Good or sad. It didn't take much to make me weep. I inhaled deeply, fighting the urge to break down. "I appreciate it."

One of the garden ladies tapped my shoulder. "I need a fresh drink. Is there anything stronger than tea?"

"I'm sorry, but we're not serving alcohol today out of respect for the children. I'll get you more tea."

She plucked two quiches off my tray before I headed to the kitchen.

Jake followed me. "I'll hang out until this thing is over."

"No, you should go. We'll need to clean the kitchen and load the van and all the things a caterer does."

"I can help. Let me know when you need me." He turned on his toe to rejoin the other visitors, and I entered the kitchen.

Katie was about to exit with a tray of drinks.

"Would you go to the garden ladies first? They are thirsty, and I told them tea is the strongest thing we're serving."

Katie scrunched her nose. "Message received. Don't let them trick me."

"You got it." I laughed and reached for a fresh tray of sliders even though the crowd had thinned.

Both sets of extended family sat with Willow's children. They all appeared to be on their best behavior. If my daughter had been murdered, and her husband was a suspect, would I be as calm? If it protected my grandchildren, maybe.

I swapped my full tray for an empty dish on the buffet.

Movement near the stairwell going to the basement caught my attention.

Rita walked down the stairs. Vince looked over his shoulder before following his assistant.

I hesitated, then grabbed a small plate of cream cheese pickles and followed them at what I hoped was a discrete distance.

This was like no basement I'd ever seen. Pool table, large screen TV with comfortable seating around it, a bar, a ping pong table, and a wine room. Boy howdy. This place was nice.

Rita and Vince stood at the bar with their backs to me. Vince's arms were propped on the gleaming wood surface, and one black shoe was hooked on a metal foot rail.

I slipped into the dimly lit wine room, but kept the door open enough to watch and listen. I placed the plate of pickles on a mini-fridge and hid in the shadows.

"What do you need to discuss, Rita?" His voice sounded weary.

"Vince, it's finally time for us to be together." Rita purred and placed her hand on his arm.

His head jerked back like he'd been slapped. "I don't know what you're talking about, Rita. My wife just died."

"I know, but you never loved her. And Willow never loved you the way I do." Her voice rose. "There's nothing standing in our way. I love you so much, darling. Don't you see? It's finally our time."

Vince jolted away from Rita. "I don't know what to say."

"Say you love me." Rita closed in on him and latched onto both of his arms.

"I can't. It's not appropriate."

"Darling, I understand. We'll keep our relationship a secret until a proper amount of time passes."

"It's not that." He disentangled himself from her clutches once more. "What I'm trying to say is I don't love you, Rita."

"No!" She slapped Vince across the face. "After all I've done, how can you say you don't love me?"

"I'm sorry. You're a trusted employee and friend, but I don't feel the same."

"You're going to regret this, Vince Moore." She stomped away from him and up the stairs.

I dropped to the floor right before Vince strode across the room with his long-legged stride.

"Rita, hold up. Let's talk." His words faded away with each step he took.

I stood and wiped my hands on my slacks before grabbing the plate I'd brought downstairs. If Vince had killed his wife, it wasn't so he could be with Rita Flores.

Chapter Sixteen

After we helped Sophie unload her delivery van at the bakery, Jake and I walked around the town square. My home was down Main Street and across the train tracks, and it was a nice evening for a stroll.

I carried a bag of leftovers and couldn't wait to dive in. "Now that we're alone, you won't believe what I overheard."

"I watched you follow Rita and Vince downstairs."

"Oops, I thought I was discrete. Did you notice I carried food with me on the pretense of working the crowd?" I was proud of myself for that move.

He chuckled. "Smooth. So, spill it. What'd you learn?"

"Rita told Vince she is ready to take their relationship to the next level or something like that, but he doesn't feel the same way." We stopped at the street crossing and waited for our signal to walk.

A sleek black Audi sports car screamed up Maple and ran the red light.

Sirens blared, and a police car followed.

We stood in place and watched the commotion. The cop blocked the Audi into a corner of the square near the yoga studio.

Jake grabbed my hand and led me to the doorway of the closed coffee shop. "In case this goes sideways, let's stand back here." He unlocked the door and turned off the alarm. "Get inside."

We stood near the window and watched the officer approach the fancy sports car.

I squinted and leaned forward. "Do you know who that is?"

Jake nodded. "Yep. It's Rita's ex-fiancé."

"You're right. Dave Smith. I wonder how he can afford such a fancy car when he just got released from prison. We need to make sure he doesn't get away with only a speeding ticket. I'm sure Chief Young wants to question him."

"On it. I've got his personal number." Jake pulled out his phone and called the police chief while I continued to watch the scene play out.

Doubts plagued me. Maybe Dave was only guilty of driving too fast. It'd be wrong to suspect Dave because he was connected to Rita. Yes, Rita loved Vince, but it didn't mean Dave was a suspect in Willow's death. Rusty was the one who'd led me to consider Dave.

Jake ended his call and slipped the phone into the pocket of his slacks. "Matt's on the way."

"Should we stay here or go on home?" Heat crept up my neck. "Uh, I mean, you walk me home. Then you'll go to the bed-and-breakfast."

He winked. "I know what you mean. Have you told the chief what you learned yesterday at the bank about Rita's relationship to Dave?"

"No." For once, Jake's wink didn't annoy me. Was it possible the man was growing on me? "I also haven't had time to tell him Dave may have been the one who paid Rusty to kill Willow."

"Say what?" Jake faced me.

"Oh, yeah. Rusty told me this morning. A man paid Rusty to kill Willow. Of course, Rusty took the money and used it to buy drugs."

"Lady, your cheese must've slid right off the cracker. Why in the world would you wait to report this? Where's Rusty now?"

I backed away and faced Jake. His rudeness had returned. "I don't need to explain myself to you."

"If we're working together, you need to share explosive information."

"The only explosive thing around here is your attitude." I pulled open the door and left him standing in Anytime Coffee House. I walked across the street and toward home. Street lights shone, but the red and blue flashing beams from the police car cast an eerie glow over town square.

The coffee shop's alarm beeped, and the key clicked in the door. Jake had locked the store and secured it. Fast footsteps followed me, then his fingers circled my arm. "We're close to the police station, and I think we should head there first."

"What about my dog? He probably needs to go out." I didn't have a clue how long Cowboy could last between potty breaks, but I wouldn't willy-nilly go along with Jake's plan.

"Fine." Jake ran a hand down his face. "I'm sorry about losing my temper."

"It's okay." I watched the cop who was still writing the ticket for Dave. "I guess Matt will be here soon. Oops, Chief Young. I'm not supposed to call him Matt in front of his men."

"I understand you know him as a friend and as a professional, but he is an authority figure, and I get his logic. Shall we go check on Cowboy?"

I nodded. "Yeah, then I can drive us to the police station."

Over an hour later, we sat in Chief Young's office, answering his questions after I updated him on my findings.

His nostrils flared, and multiple times he ran his hands through his hair, but he let me tell my story without interrupting.

At last, I leaned back into the chair and sighed. "That's it."

He glanced at his notes. "Let me sum it up. Yesterday you learned Rita Flores used to be engaged to Dave Smith. Today, Rusty Ramirez told you someone possibly resembling Dave paid him to kill Willow Moore. Instead of killing Willow, Rusty used the money to buy drugs, and now he's holed up in a hoity-toity rehab facility. It's possible Dave hired another person—"

"It could be Gambler."

"Got it, but this is all hearsay. The first problem is your source is a drug addict. Even if we decide to question Gambler, we don't know who he is. Once we determine the man's real identity, we need concrete evidence to arrest him." He tapped his pencil on the desk. "I don't guess you have any evidence up your sleeve?"

I lifted my hands. "Afraid not."

"Most murders linked to the mysterious gambling man don't fit this MO."

Jake said, "What do you mean?"

"Gambler usually kidnaps his victim. Then he executes them and leaves their bodies hidden in the woods or behind abandoned factories."

Jake rubbed his hands together. "Gotcha. Willow was shot, and her body was found behind the bookstore."

"You two go home, and I'll contact you tomorrow." Matt ran his hands through his hair once more. "Try to stay out of trouble."

Jake paused at the doorway. "I'm beginning to think trouble follows Emma."

Chief Young massaged his temples. "You could be right."

Chapter Seventeen

I overslept Wednesday morning. Nightmares about Willow's murder had kept me tossing and turning. If it hadn't been for Cowboy's nudging, my cold feet would still be buried under the covers along with the rest of my body.

We headed out for his morning walk before my first cup of tea. I couldn't take my dog inside Anytime Coffee House, but I texted Jake and asked him to fix me a cup of green tea with honey.

Brett had a small seating area set up on the sidewalk in front of the shop, and I waited there with Cowboy. The dog barked a friendly greeting, and his tail swished each time a person walked by. Most people pet his head and spoke to both of us.

Jake walked out with an environmentally friendly cup. "Good morning, Sunshine."

"Um, Sunshine?"

"Yeah, for your sunny disposition, and you're a flower farmer."

"Morning." I caught my reflection in the shop's window. Strands of red hair had escaped the ponytail, and my always-pale complexion appeared pasty. I passed him the money. "Thanks for doing this."

"No problem. We're fully staffed this morning, so it was easy." He pocketed the money, knelt beside my dog, and rubbed his head. "Cowboy looks good."

"Thanks. I keep reading books on the best way to care for him. Puppies need to burn up their energy, and they need love and attention."

"How are you doing? Er, not taking care of the dog, but you personally."

"I'm exhausted. Between work, helping cater, and answering Matt's questions last night, I didn't want to roll out of bed this morning. Cowboy had other ideas, though." I sipped my tea.

"Say, do you know of any affordable apartments for rent?"

"Affordable? Not sure." I took another sip. "I guess it needs to be in a reputable complex."

"It can even be a house. I can't afford to keep staying with Faith and Zig. Once Celia leaves town, I need to get my own place."

"Do you have any interest in buying a house?" A loud truck rumbled by, and I tightened my grip on the leash, but Cowboy behaved.

Jake jumped, but tried to act nonchalant. "Not yet. If I get on with the police department, then I might buy my own place. For now, I only need a rental."

"Let me ask around. I'll get back to you."

"Thanks." He stood and moved toward the shop. "I'll see you around, Emma."

"Bye." With the cup in one hand and gripping the leash with my other hand, I led Cowboy to the park a few blocks away. I let him loose in the dog park area where he could run free, and I wouldn't worry about him trampling my flowers.

Leaning against the fence, sipping my tea, I watched Cowboy run the perimeter. Another pet owner played toss with her beagle. Dog toys. Why hadn't I thought of that? Later I'd stop by the dollar store and buy some toys for Cowboy so we could have fun.

I snapped a picture of the dog and sent it to Abby. **I finally got the puppy you always begged for.**

My thoughts turned to Willow's murder. Nick Jones had been left alone with Willow when Paige took off on her morning run. Nick had been upstairs spraying the apartment over the bookstore. Paige had said she wanted to rent the space out as an apartment, so it made sense she'd want the place to be free of insects and rodents.

Cowboy ran to me, panting.

"Hey, boy. I probably should've brought you a bowl for water. I promise to get better at being your owner. Water, water bowl, and toys. It makes sense you're thirsty."

The beagle's owner pointed to a water spiggot. She said, "Maybe you can get your dog to drink from that. The only trick is to make sure he doesn't choke."

"Thanks." I went to it and turned the knob. Cupping my hands together, I caught the water. "Cowboy, come here."

The golden retriever gave me a curious look.

I spilled water and started all over. "Drink."

He sniffed my hands, then lapped up the water.

"Good boy." I repeated the process with him until he appeared satisfied, then I attached the leash to his harness, and we left the park.

The sight of an approaching car slowed my steps, and we edged toward the grass. It was the black Audi from the previous night. My heart beat hard against my ribs.

I stopped, and Cowboy whined.

The car slowed to a crawl, and the window lowered. The driver pointed his front finger toward me and thumb up. Like a gun. "If you know what's good for you and that mutt, you'll mind your own business." Dave Smith stepped on the gas and disappeared.

My racing heart and shaky limbs made it impossible to walk.

Cowboy rubbed against my leg and barked.

Deep breaths. I couldn't fall apart on Second Street in Lutz, Texas. Cowboy depended on me to get him home. Breathe in. Breathe out. One foot forward, then the other. I could do it.

The long walk home was a blur. Dave Smith had threatened me. If I believed Rusty, Dave may have been the same man who'd paid him to kill Willow. Why wasn't he in jail? Probably something like lack of evidence.

Somehow, Cowboy and I made it to the house. Once inside, I locked and bolted the door before collapsing on the couch.

Willow was dead. Dave Smith was free as could be. Rusty was in rehab. Dave was Rita's ex-fiancé. What did he have to gain by Willow's death? It opened the door for Rita to be with Vince, making it harder for Dave to rekindle the flames of love. Although, Vince had turned Rita's proposition down flat. Rumor was Vince had a mistress. Had Vince asked Rita for the best way to get rid of his wife before the divorce? Had she agreed, thinking Vince wanted to be with her? If sorting through the clues was as easy as weeding my garden, I'd be much closer to an answer.

It was simple for me to distinguish between a flower and an unwanted plant. Pull a weed, and throw it out. The trouble with Willow's murder was I didn't know the difference between clues, red herrings, and lies. So far, Dave's threat scared me more than anything else.

If I continued trying to prove Paige's innocence, it'd be best not to let Dave find out.

Chapter Eighteen

I'd pulled myself together enough to meet Paige for lunch at Anytime Coffee House. We sat in a booth at the front window. I'd ordered coffee because a jolt seemed in order after my sinking experience with Dave. A chicken salad sandwich with a side of apple slices filled me up.

Paige finished her salad and cut her cookie, passing half of it to me. "I'm supposed to meet Chief Young again this afternoon at the police station. Thankfully, he gave me time to line up someone to run the store."

"Thanks." I took the cookie. "Your meeting with the chief could be positive."

"How do you figure?"

"They're not arresting you yet." I broke off a chunk of the cookie and popped it in my mouth.

"Yet is the key word." She tore a strip off her paper napkin. "It's simply a matter of time."

A fist landed on our table so hard, the dishes clattered.

My heart nearly leapt out of my chest.

Nick Jones leaned toward Paige. "I can't believe you ratted me out."

Paige's face paled. "What are you talking about?"

"You told the cops I was the last person to see Willow alive." He glared at her.

"That's not what I said." She wadded up the napkin and edged away from the man until her back touched the glass window.

"Then why are they questioning me?" He growled.

I said, "Nick, did you see anybody else at the store before you left? Or what about near the store as you were leaving? You could've seen the killer."

His eyes narrowed. "I treated the apartment, gave Willow the bill, and left. I didn't touch the woman, and I didn't see nobody."

Jake appeared. "Hit the road, mister."

Nick spun and pulled his arm back. He swung at Jake's face.

Jake dodged the punch, then pulled Nick's arm behind his back. He dragged him through the coffee shop and pushed him out the door. "I better never see you in here again."

Nick cursed a blue stream. The door closed and muted the man's tirade.

Jake reopened the door. "Move along, or I'll call the cops. Got half a mind to do it anyway."

Nobody uttered a word until Nick walked away, then the room buzzed.

Jake returned to the table. "Are y'all okay?"

Two threats in one morning. It was way more than I was equipped to handle. Holding back tears was easier to accomplish than stilling my shaky hands.

Paige said, "He's mad and trying to scare me. He's nothing but a big ole bully who thinks he's a ladies' man, which is a terrifying combination if he's coming after you. That guy's one of the most horrible men I know."

Jake motioned for me to slide over. After I complied, he sat beside me. "Who was that?"

"Nick Jones, the pest control guy." My voice croaked.

Paige broke into giggles. "He's the biggest pest around. Isn't it ironic that he makes a living getting rid of other pests?" Her laughter continued.

Jake looked from me to Paige.

I reached for her hand. "Paige, honey, pull yourself together." Easier said than done, but she needed to calm down.

Her laughter died. "I'm losing my mind."

"No, you're not. We all react differently to stress. You laugh, and I usually cry."

Jake said, "Can one of you tell me what happened? Should I call the cops?"

"No, please don't. It'll only make things worse." Paige recapped our encounter with Nick.

I listened but kept wondering how long it'd taken Nick to spray the space over her store. When she finished, I asked the question weighing on me. "Do you have much to do to convert the space over the store to an apartment?"

Paige ran her hands over the edge of the table. "It's ready to go. I'm either going to rent it out or sell my house and move there. It'll help my finances, and I refuse to lose my store without a fight."

I elbowed Jake.

He wrote his phone number on a napkin and slid it across the table. "It just so happens that I'm looking for a place to rent. Can I see it?"

Her eyes grew wide. "Yes. I've got an appointment with Chief Young, but I can call you when it's over."

"Sounds good."

Paige gathered her belongings and stood. "Thanks, Jake. Let's hope I only need money for my store to survive. I don't know what will happen if I have to come up with the funds to pay an attorney to prove I'm innocent of Willow's murder. Whatever happened to innocent until proven guilty?"

I said, "You can only take one step at a time. Go to your appointment with the chief, then give me a call."

"See you two later." She left with a wave but no smile.

Jake began to slide out of the booth, but I latched onto his plaid cotton shirt. He met my gaze. "What's wrong?"

Wow, was I that bad at keeping a secret? "I ran into Dave Smith this morning."

His jaw clenched. "I can't believe that dude's not in jail."

"Yeah, I was shocked." My eye twitched, and I rubbed it.

"How'd you know where to find him?"

"I didn't find him. He found me near the park. After we stopped here, I took Cowboy to the dog park. Dave pulled up in his expensive sports car and threatened me."

Jake's hand covered his mouth, and he stared at the empty seat across from us. "Dave warned you, and Nick bullied Paige. Two potential suspects. Two different motives. You need to be extra cautious, Emma, especially since they both threatened you today."

"Are you blaming me for what happened this morning?" I drew as far away from Jake as possible in the bench seat.

"No, I'm only saying be careful. Maybe we should back away from helping Paige. I don't want you to be in danger."

"She's my friend and asked me to help." I kept my voice low. "I can't walk away."

"I get it, but do you understand what I'm telling you?" He didn't sound angry. More insistent.

"I guess."

"Do I need to explain why this situation is so alarming? Willow was killed, and if you're stirring the pot, you could be next. Do you understand?"

Did he think I was an idiot? Yeah, I got the point. "Hey, don't get all military on me. I appreciate your service to our country, but I don't need a lecture. Not from you and not from anybody else." I pushed him to move because I was trapped between him and the storefront window.

Jake stood, and I escaped from the booth.

He reached for my arm. His touch was gentle. "Sweetheart, I'm scared for you."

His words moved me, but I couldn't back down from helping Paige. "I've been taking care of myself for thirty-eight years, Jake. I appreciate your concern, but don't waste your time worrying about me." I fled the coffee shop before he could reply.

Chapter Nineteen

I spent the afternoon pulling up weeds and cutting pretty daffodils, larkspur, and snapdragons and placing them in clean buckets of fresh water. The weeds were tossed into an old cracked pail. Why couldn't I weed through the lies and deception surrounding Willow's murder?

What if I plotted out my murder notes like I'd strategized my gardens? With pencil and paper, I'd drawn a plan for where everything should go in my garden. Could I reverse the process and solve the mystery by organizing my notes by hand?

Who knew Willow the best? The snobby ladies I'd seen at the farmers' market and at the Moore house? Willow had money, but she'd never treated me bad like her friends did. Willow had always been kind to me, even if we didn't travel in the same social circles.

Still, Willow's friends had gossiped about her. Had she been aware they couldn't be trusted? Or had she confided in them?

What about Faith? I tugged off my garden gloves and texted Faith. **Can I bring over some fresh-cut flowers and ask you a few questions?**

I didn't have to wait long for a reply. **Sure.**

After cleaning up, I walked to Heart of Texas Bed-and-Breakfast with a spring bouquet of African Daisies.

Faith took me to the TV room, and I placed the flowers in an empty vase on the oak coffee table. The table was a shade darker than the white-oak cabinetry filling one wall. The cabinetry held the television and hid all the cords. Open shelves displayed books and games. Perpendicular to the wall were sliding glass doors, revealing the yard and an outdoor swimming pool.

Two couches formed a L-shape. "I bet your guests spend a lot of free time in here. What a great place to relax."

"Thank you." She pointed to the matching taupe couches. "Have a seat, Emma. What's on your mind?"

I sat on the soft microfiber material. Very nice. "The other day, you told me you felt like Vince was behind Willow's murder. Do you still feel that way?"

Faith settled onto the other couch and crossed her legs. "Yes, and my head still believes it."

"But?"

"Vince seemed so torn up at the funeral, and it made me doubt. Did he love Willow, or is he a good actor?" She threw up her hands.

"He told me he loved his wife. I did a little eavesdropping and discovered he's not having a fling with Rita." No need to reveal how I'd followed them to the basement.

"Yeah, the assistant seems too obvious, especially with her big crush on him. Although, sometimes, the obvious answer is the correct answer." Faith reached for a pillow and ran her hand over the fabric. "I still believe he was unfaithful to Willow."

"You mentioned she had proof of at least one affair."

"Right." She sighed. "The forensic accountant Willow hired found proof Vince was spending money out of town on hotels and expensive dinners. What else could it be?"

"Did Willow mention offshore accounts or anything like that?" I pulled my phone out. "Do you mind if I take notes?"

"Why do you want to take notes?"

I pressed my lips together until coming up with an acceptable answer. "Paige is in serious trouble. The cops are looking at her, and she asked me to help."

"I know she was one of the last people to see Willow, but what do they think her motive is?"

"Willow wouldn't help her get a bank loan."

Faith laughed. "The logic behind that is flawed. I'm pretty sure Willow would've given her the loan after Vince got the boot. She liked Paige and appreciated having a job at the bookstore. Willow was always loyal to her true friends."

True friends. Exactly what I'd wondered about. "I heard some women gossiping about Willow at the house last night."

"Yeah, well, they weren't her friends. So many people pretended to be close to Willow because of the bank. She told me it had become hard to know who to trust." She tossed the pillow to the side. "In the past year, there weren't many people Willow trusted. I was one of the few, and I know she appreciated having a job. Willow had been under enormous stress, with the divorce looming on the horizon. She never would've asked Vince for a favor, but in my heart, I believe she would've given Paige a loan once she regained control of the bank."

Interesting. I added the word trust in all capital letters. "You didn't answer my question about offshore accounts."

Faith stood and paced in front of the glass doors. Her blond ponytail swished each time she turned. "Willow was suspicious, because money was missing. The accountant was working on finding proof of more secret accounts."

I told her what Jake had heard at the farmers' market. "It didn't seem to be a secret."

"That makes me so mad. The accountant is married to one of those women, and believe me, I know who you're talking about. One day they'll get their comeuppance." Faith fisted her hands. "I wish Willow would've hired an accountant from Austin or Dallas, anywhere but here. She always believed in supporting local businesses, even if it didn't work in her favor."

"It sounds like the offshore bank accounts could be real, then." I added the information to my notes.

"All I can say for sure is that Willow believed it." Faith leaned over and sniffed the flowers, then moved them to the bookshelf. "Vince has done some terrible things to his family, but if he's responsible for Willow's death, the kids will be devastated."

"I know. At least they have grandparents who love them." The flowers crowded the shelf. "How about the table between the couches?"

Faith moved them and shook her head. "Maybe the sofa table."

"Stay there." I stood and moved the arrangement to the solid wood table behind the couch.

"Looks perfect. I can see them from here, and if a guest props their feet on the coffee table, they won't get knocked over."

"What's going on in here?" Zig entered the room and went straight to his wife. He kissed her cheek, then smiled at me. "Good afternoon, Emma."

"Hi, Zig. I can leave if you and Faith need to do something. I was just picking her brain about Willow's murder."

His eyes grew wide. "Mind if I join the conversation?"

"I'd love to hear your thoughts on Vince and their marriage. Shoot, I'm happy to hear anything you want to share."

The three of us sat on the couches, and I raised my phone. "I'm taking notes, if you don't mind."

"Don't mind at all." His deep voice gave me the feeling everything would turn out okay.

"Do you think Vince was involved in Willow's death?"

The tall African American leaned forward with his forearms resting on his thighs, and he clasped his hands. "Vince and I weren't close. I don't know if it's because I'm faithful to my wife, and I don't flirt with other women. We have friends in common, so we've spent time around each other. But we're not tight. Never have been, and I don't predict we ever will be."

"Did you two ever get into an argument or have a confrontation?"

"Naw, nothing like that. Maybe it's my race, or maybe it's because I don't party hard. It's probably a two-way street. I'd rather spend time with my wife or respectable men. I'm sharing this with you to show I may not be the best person to question. But I don't believe he killed Willow. Leastways, he didn't do it himself. He's not the kind to get his hands dirty. Paying somebody to carry out his evil desire, now that could be a different story. He's definitely the type of person to throw money at a problem."

I typed Zig's thoughts. He'd left acting after two hit TV comedies and a few appearances on the big screen. Faith hadn't known how to deal with his fame and the media, so they'd settled in little Lutz, Texas, to run the bed-and-breakfast. "I agree about Vince not doing it himself, but I wonder who he would've hired."

"Shouldn't you focus on your pretty flowers? Why are you getting involved?" He rubbed his large hands together.

"Paige is my friend, and she asked me to help. The police are looking hard at her." I gave him a brief update on the situation. "If you or Faith asked me to help, I'd be there for you."

"Ah, ha. Cause we're friends." His big smile revealed sparkling white teeth.

"Exactly. That's what friends do."

He leaned back and slipped his arm around his lovely wife. "Good to know."

Faith said, "If I die, there'll be no need to look at Zig. We became best friends before we fell in love. If there's one person I trust on this earth, it's Zig Meier."

My heart melted at her words. Would there ever be a man in my life I trusted and loved so deeply? I made my farewells and headed home to digest all we'd discussed.

If Vince was behind his wife's death, he'd probably paid somebody else to do the deed. Dave Smith had recently been released from prison. He'd been engaged to Rita at some point, so had he lived in Lutz? Why had he gone to prison? Had Willow been involved? Was he getting back at her for his incarceration? Or had he been paid to kill her and was outsourcing the job?

When I got home, I would start digging for clues into Dave. He'd threatened me, leaving no doubts that he was involved in something nefarious. Willow's murder? It was possible, and I didn't believe in coincidences. Had he done it as an act to win back Rita in some twisted way? If so, did that mean Rita was the mastermind behind asking Rusty to murder Willow?

Chapter Twenty

A **puppy? I'll call after my study group. I need details.** Abby attached a smiley face emoji at the end of her text message.

Cowboy barked, then the doorbell rang.

Chills broke out all over my body. I snatched my phone and walked from my home office at the back of the bungalow to the front door.

Cowboy beat me there, and I peeked out the upper windows.

Jake stood on the porch holding a box about the size of a sheet of notebook paper.

I opened the door, and Cowboy jumped on Jake's legs.

"Sit, Cowboy. Sit." I reached for the golden retriever's collar and pulled him away from Jake. "Sit, boy."

My dog sat, and his tail swished along the floor.

Jake laughed and rubbed Cowboy's head. "Good boy."

I stepped back and stuffed the phone into the pocket of my jeans. "Hi."

"Howdy. I tried to call, and when you didn't answer, I decided to take a chance and drop by."

I looked at my phone and saw he'd tried to call when I'd been with Faith. "Oh, sorry. Come on in." I led him to the office and placed my phone on the charging station. "What's up?"

"First, I got this for you. I'm sorry about our disagreement earlier." He handed the beautiful gold box to me.

"Godiva?" My mouth watered.

"Seemed appropriate. I won't read you the riot act again. You scared me, and I acted poorly."

I ran my hands over the box. "Apology accepted. What's your other reason for coming over?"

His posture relaxed. "You know Paige invited me over to look at the apartment, and I was hoping you might go with me."

"Really? Why?"

"Not all women are comfortable around strangers, and Celia's too busy to come along. Would you please accompany me? Last thing Paige needs is to feel awkward about being alone with me." He batted his eyes in a silly manner.

"Sure. Let me put Cowboy up, and I'll be ready."

I got my dog settled, but Jake hadn't followed me. My little bungalow made it easy to find him still in my office. "Whatcha doing?"

He pointed to my poster board where I'd written notes about the murder. "You're getting ahead of me on finding clues."

"It's because I know people. Maybe we can work together on looking into Dave Smith's background. Unfortunately, his name is pretty common, and I'm not having a lot of luck."

Jake nodded. "Sounds about right. I'll be happy to work on it right after we check the apartment."

It only took me three tries to find my keys, then we walked to the bookstore to see the upstairs rental space.

Paige smiled. "Hi, guys. The apartment door is in the alley. I hope that won't deter you from renting it. The place is clean, with one bedroom, a small kitchen, one bathroom, and a large living space. There are wood floors that need to be refinished, but I'll make sure it gets done. The original owner lived here and worked downstairs, but we'll lock the connecting door that leads into the store's back room. I believe it'll be a good place to live." Her words came out so fast, they ran together.

"I'm sure it'll be fine." Jake winked at me as if he understood how nervous Paige was.

She opened the door and led us up wood stairs, and we entered the kitchen. "I'll let you look around and meet you in the store." She opened the other door that led to Paige's Turn Bookshop. "Like I said, we'll keep this locked if you decide to rent the place."

"Sounds good." Jake's voice echoed in the empty space.

Her footsteps padded down the stairs, then silence.

"Wow, she must really be worried about your decision. You'd be a good renter, and it'll ease her money woes."

Jake walked to the far end of the room and looked down on the street from the huge window. A vehicle backfired in the distance, and the man flinched.

I pretended not to notice and busied myself checking out the little kitchen. Jake always seemed so confident and brave. The thought of him suffering from PTSD saddened me. I opened the refrigerator. A lonely box of baking soda was the only item in it. Was Jake lonely, or did he have a lot of friends outside of Lutz? I sniffed the refrigerator. "It smells clean in here."

Jake disappeared into the bedroom on the alley side of the apartment, then reappeared. "I can do the floor work if it'll get me in here sooner."

"What's the hurry?" I inspected the cabinets.

"Celia leaves this weekend, and it's time for me to get my own place. Sometimes a man needs space to think. Faith and Zig are great, but I don't always want to have a conversation when I get home at night."

"You're not the biggest talker I've ever met, so I get it. Pitching in at the coffee shop probably requires being extroverted." I leaned against the kitchen counter. "There were plenty of days I didn't want to be social after spending ten hours in the pharmacy. Now that I work with flowers, I have a better balance of quiet times and periods when I need to be more social. How do you imagine you'll decorate this place?"

"The main things I need are a bed, TV, couch, and maybe a place to eat. Although, eating on the couch is an option."

My heart sank. "You'll need more than that. Maybe on Sunday, we can go to one of the flea markets or vintage sales."

He raised his hands. "Let me stop you before you get too carried away. I'm not a shopping kind of guy."

"Oh, but you can find so many interesting things when you go to antique sales."

"Not gonna happen." He left me and examined the bathroom located close to the bedroom. "I need to add a shower curtain to my list."

"It sounds like you're going to rent this place."

"The price Paige quoted me on the phone fits my budget, so yeah." He stuffed his hands in the front pockets of his jeans. "What do you think?"

"It's functional, but will the traffic bother you? Big ole trucks and motorcycles can be loud." The desire to protect him surprised me. My pulse throbbed in my temple. Jake was a grown man, a Marine no less. He didn't need me watching out for him. Still, I'd seen him flinch and hated for him to suffer needlessly.

"Hmph." Jake crossed his arms, then walked to the window and looked out again. "During the day, I'm sure this will let in lots of natural light. With the bedroom in back, I don't believe the noise will bother me. It'll be okay."

Dag gumit. You couldn't protect people who didn't want your help. "Fine. Let's tell Paige."

Jake touched my arm. "Are you upset with me?"

"No." My eyes watered. Stupid desire to shield him from trauma. I avoided meeting his gaze and turned my back on him. "I'm exhausted, and Willow's murder has me on edge."

"Aw, now. It's gonna work itself out. First, let's tell Paige I'm taking the apartment."

"And second?"

"I want you to share with me what you've discovered today."

A black Audi was parked across the street. "Jake, turn off the lights."

He obeyed without questions, then joined me at the corner of the window. "What?" His breath tickled the back of my ear.

I pointed. "That could be Dave Smith's Audi."

Jake fiddled with his cellphone, then looked at it. "It is Dave. Look through my binoculars app."

I took the phone from him, and our fingers brushed. He let go and stepped away.

I used the phone, and sure enough, Dave sat in the car. "Wonder what he's doing?"

"I'd say he's either spying on Paige or us."

"If he'd been there when we arrived, wouldn't we have noticed?"

"There's quite a bit of traffic this time of day, and we were focused on meeting Paige. Be right back."

I turned my focus back to the Audi. "What are you up to, Dave Smith?" With a beautiful box of Godiva chocolate waiting for me at home, it wouldn't be hard to spend a few more hours researching the man in the fancy sports car.

Chapter Twenty-One

The evening had gotten away from me. Earlier, Jake had called the police about Dave, but he disappeared before an officer arrived. Lutz was a little town with a small police force. There'd been a domestic dispute in one of the nicer neighborhoods, and the cops had been focused on saving the family. I understood setting priorities. All survived the family drama, but it was too bad they didn't question Dave.

By the time Jake signed the papers to lease the apartment, I was beyond hungry. Jake walked me home. "Sorry the night got out of hand. Do you want to get dinner, then work on the investigation?"

I opened the door. "How about a bowl of cereal? It's quick, easy, and filling."

Jake laughed. "I had my heart set on something heartier, but cereal it is."

We fed the dog and ate our crunchy oat cereal and blueberries before spreading out at the breakfast table. Country music played on the local radio station. Jake had my tablet, and I worked on the laptop. I said, "Can you find out why Dave was in prison? Was Willow Moore involved in any way with his incarceration?"

"Like did she turn him in or testify?"

"That's right. While you do that, I'll try to find old yearbooks online or reunion pictures on social media; anything I can do to link Willow and Dave."

"Sounds like a plan."

I checked yearbook websites. Willow had been close to fifteen years older than me, and we'd only become friends while raising our children. I typed in names of schools, but nothing worked. "I may need to go to the library."

"The local high school probably has all the yearbooks. It might be a good place to look." Jake's gaze remained fixed on the tablet.

"Good idea. They know me there because of Abby."

Jake whistled and lifted his hand. "Wait until you hear what the cat dragged in."

My ears tingled in anticipation. At last, I couldn't stand it any longer. "What?"

"Dave's been arrested more than once. The first time he pled guilty to first offense with intent to distribute cocaine."

I added this information to the murder document I'd created from my phone notes. The document was much easier to read on my laptop. "Is that why he was in prison?

"No, there's some kind of act for young adults. It allowed the judge to send him to therapy and get counseling or an intervention. He took classes and earned his GED."

"It sounds like Dave was given a wonderful opportunity to redeem himself."

"You'd think so, but hold on." He winked at me before turning his attention back to the tablet.

"How about some decaf tea?"

Jake nodded.

I prepared herbal mint tea and poured it into two antique English mugs with hand-painted roses. I added honey and stirred. With cautious steps, I brought the mugs to the table and set them on sunflower stone coasters. While waiting for Jake to share, I doodled on a clean sheet in my sketchbook. Drawing often stimulated good ideas for me. Most of my sketches involved flowers and plants, and I got lost in the activity. My brain took a moment to relax from the stress of life.

Jake clapped, and I jolted. "I found out why he was in prison."

I placed a hand over my heart and sat straighter. "The suspense is killing me. Whoops, it's not killing me, literally, but you know what I mean."

"Yeah, I do." He chuckled. "It appears Dave kept himself clean for a few years, or at least he didn't get caught until the drive-thru drug operation at a neighborhood home in Dallas."

"Drive-thru?"

"Kinda. Neighbors started reporting an unusual amount of traffic in their normally quiet neighborhood. Investigators believed the informants and watched the home in question. Motorists arrived and parked in the drive, in the grass, and anywhere they could find a spot. A person would walk up to a window and make a transaction. After a week of watching, an undercover agent approached the window and made a purchase. Cocaine, but they could've bought heroin, meth, or pot. Different agents followed the subjects who made purchases. The customers only received tickets. No jail time."

"Sounds like a full-service drug dealer. Is this what landed him in prison?"

"Once the officers got a warrant, they found thousands of dollars' worth of drugs packaged in plastic bags for distribution. Cash, loaded guns, ammunition, and drug paraphernalia were also confiscated. Dave's charge was possession with intent to distribute the drugs. The jury found him guilty, and he served his time."

"Then it sounds like selling drugs is the lane he stays in. If he's involved in Willow's death, what's his motive?"

Jake reached for his mug and leaned back in the dining chair, sipping his tea. "How does a person transition from dealing drugs to getting involved in a cold-blooded murder? It'd be more understandable if Dave shot one of his customers."

"Like a drug deal gone bad." I tapped my pen on the paper. "It makes sense."

"Exactly. It's too bad we didn't find a connection between Dave and Willow. She lived in Lutz for years, and his drive-thru venture was in Dallas. To be clear, I don't believe Willow was a drug abuser."

"Yeah, me either. I feel like we're on the cusp of something big, but what?" My heart picked up its tempo. "Why did Dave come to our little down after getting released?"

"To see his ex-fiancée?" Jake ran his thumb along the rim of the mug.

"That's our theory. Otherwise, why wouldn't he return to Dallas, where he could get lost in the crowds? Houston would've been a good option too.

Leaving Texas might have been his smartest move."

"True, unless the terms of his parole restricted where he could live."

"That never occurred to me. I'd love to know how long Rita has been working for Vince Moore. I'm also curious how she and Dave got together." I reached for my drawing pad and wrote the questions before drawing rough caricatures of Rita, Dave, and Vince.

"What bank do you use?"

"Lone Star Cattleman Bank of Texas. How's that for a mouthful?"

"Vince's bank." He smiled. "When's the first time you remember seeing Rita there?"

I paused my pen's strokes. "I mostly used direct deposit when working at the drug store. It wasn't until I began my business this past year that I started noticing Rita. It's like she's been around, but I didn't really know her. She's been good to order flowers from me though, while Yarrow closed her business. Rita claims she likes to support local businesses, and boy howdy I appreciate that."

"Sounds noble. Who would know her length of employment?" He returned his mug to the coaster, and I gave him mental points for good manners.

"Sophie and Paige have been in business longer than me. Let's see if they know." I shot a text to both of them.

Jake stood and stretched his arms. A joint popped.

"Did that hurt?"

"Naw, I'm used to it."

My phone beeped, and I read the message from Sophie. **Rita has been at the bank about five years. Why?**

I relayed the answer to Jake, then replied to Sophie. **Still trying to catch the killer.**

Jake put his mug in the dishwasher. "I better go. Brett's expecting me to open the coffee shop tomorrow morning."

My phone rang, and Sophie's picture flashed on the screen.

"Good timing because I'm probably going to get a lecture from my best friend." I followed him to the door.

"Lock up."

"Don't worry about that. See you later."

Jake stood on the porch. "Good night."

"Night." After I turned the lock and deadbolt with a soft thunk, Jake walked away whistling a popular country tune. I returned Sophie's call. "Hey, sorry I didn't pick up."

"Have you lost your mind? After Dave Smith's warning, you should be curled up on the couch reading a good book or watching TV."

"Jake's been here helping me." I let Cowboy out the back door and updated Sophie on everything that'd been happening. Downplaying my suspicions about Rita seemed to be the smartest option to keep my friend safe. No need to put Sophie in danger.

We chatted until Cowboy came inside. Our conversation ended with me promising to be careful, however, I didn't promise to drop my investigation.

Chapter Twenty-Two

After a morning of gardening and playing fetch with Cowboy, I fixed a small tulip arrangement and took it to the local high school. Once the school secretary recognized me through the glass doors, she buzzed me right in.

"Paula, how's it going?" I handed her the vase of tulips.

"These are beautiful. Thanks." Paula placed them on her organized desk, then turned back to me. "Nobody has brought me flowers since Abby left for college. You've always been so kind to brighten my day. How's your daughter?"

I leaned on the tall counter where parents signed students in and out. "Great."

"How are you holding up?" Her long brown hair was in a bun, and it emphasized the fact one of her eyes opened more than the other.

"I miss her like crazy, but I adopted an abandoned puppy, and being a flower farmer keeps me busy." I sighed. "We talked on the phone last night, but life's not the same with her gone."

Paula nodded. "Empty nest syndrome is very real and painful."

"Do you have children?" Why didn't I already know the answer? "I must seem so selfish not to know more about you."

"Don't feel bad. I'm here to help the students and their families. When you walk in here, the focus should be on you and your child or children."

"You didn't answer my question."

"Very few people know my real story."

"I'd love to hear it if you want to share." I lowered my voice. "You can trust me to be discrete."

She looked over her shoulder before meeting my gaze. Her voice lowered to almost a whisper. "I have a daughter, but she lives with my parents for safety reasons."

My heart dropped. "How old is she? And what do you mean safety reasons?"

"Sixteen." Paula positioned herself closer to me. "I can't believe you didn't hear the gossip. I used to be married to Nick Jones. I was his second wife."

"The exterminator?"

She pressed her lips together and nodded. "Yes. After we got married, I started hearing rumors about his first wife dying under suspicious circumstances. One night we went out to eat, and Tess Carranza, the town librarian, came up to us and accused Nick of murdering his wife. Tess said she'd prove it one day. Nick was furious. I'd never seen him mad before. We left the restaurant, and when we got home, he began to throw dishes. He even punched a hole in the wall. I was terrified. I'd planned to tell him I was pregnant after dinner."

"Oh, no."

"During his explosion, he hit me. That wasn't the life I signed up for, and my baby would not be subject to a monster."

"What'd you do?"

Again, she looked both ways, but not a soul was in sight. "I heard you didn't have the best marriage before your husband died. Maybe you can understand my actions. Again, not many people know."

I kept my voice low. "You can trust me. What'd you do?"

"I lied and told Nick my mother had a heart attack and needed me to help for a few days. At first, Nick called me every day and sounded so sweet and concerned about my mother. If it hadn't been for the swelling in my face and bruises on my neck and arms, I might have reconsidered. Then his calls turned dark. He wanted me to come home and cook for him and do his laundry. He cussed me out on a daily basis. My dad had taken pictures of my face when I arrived. He begged me to divorce Nick, and I listened to him. I ended up staying with my parents until my precious daughter was born. We'd all decided the safest thing would be for them to raise her."

I gasped.

"Hear me out. If we'd divorced, Nick would get some kind of custodial rights. Even if it was only every other weekend, the risk was too great. I made a choice for the safety of the baby."

What a sacrifice she'd made for her child. "You were so brave."

"Not really. I did what was best for my child. Kylie. My parents moved to Louisville, Kentucky, and changed their names. They legally adopted my daughter. We did everything possible to protect Kylie. It was close to a year later when I returned to Lutz. There were personal items I needed at the house, and I wondered if I should give Nick another chance. It was possible he'd become a better man. No such luck, though. Nick beat me when I got home, and I called the police. From the hospital, I filed for a restraining order and hired a divorce attorney. The cops were wonderful through my nightmare with Nick."

"Did you consider moving away?"

She shook her head. "I've always been terrified he'd follow me and find Kylie. The threat was too great. One day we'll tell my daughter the truth, but she's had a happy and safe life."

I prayed her daughter would understand when she discovered the truth. "Paula, do you think Nick could've killed Willow Moore? He was the last person to see her."

The woman closed her eyes and rubbed her face. Mascara smeared, as well as her lipstick. "If she made him mad enough, I truly believe he's capable of murder. I heard the police questioned him, and it's the reason I decided to share my story with you today. Nick can't be trusted. If you're trying to prove he's guilty, you need to be extremely cautious. He's dangerous."

I slumped against the counter. "Would you tell Chief Young?"

"No, ma'am. I don't intend to cross Nick Jones ever again." She reached for a tissue and blotted a stray tear. "I'm sorry for Willow, but the police will have to solve her murder without any help from me."

"I understand. I've seen his ugly side. Once, but it was enough." I jammed my cool hands into my pockets.

"Why'd you come by today, Emma?"

"I was hoping to go through the yearbooks. I'm trying to find a connection between Willow and another person on my suspect list."

"You'll need to go to the public library. In the flood of 2016, water ruined almost every book on campus."

"That's a shame. Paula, I'm part of a book club, and we meet at my house every Monday night. Why don't you join us?" I wrote my cell number on a sticky note by her phone. "Call me."

"Thanks, Emma. I might surprise you and call."

The principal walked out of his office with two students.

I waved to Paula and headed to the public library. Even if they didn't have the local high school yearbooks, I could always question Tess Carranza about the murder of Nick's first wife.

Chapter Twenty-Three

"Welcome to the society of women who suspect Nick Jones of killing his first wife." Tess Carranza led me to the private meeting room in the library. "Be right back."

"Okay." I walked around the table and chose a seat where I could see anyone enter the room.

Tess joined me a hot minute later, carrying a stack of yearbooks. She locked the door and sat catty-corner to me. She stared at me like a momma lion with her cubs. "Paula called and told me you were heading this way."

Wow. I don't know what I'd expected, but her bluntness surprised me. "I appreciate you are prepared."

She placed the books on the table. "I understand you're looking for connections to Willow Moore."

"Yes. Were you and Willow friends?"

Tess shook her head, but her brown hair with blond streaks didn't budge. Her full lips parted into a smile, revealing teeth so white I almost squinted. Tess was the flashiest librarian in the great state of Texas. "I knew Willow from the years she brought her children in for storytime. She was always polite, and I hate that she was murdered. Do you believe Nick is guilty of murdering her?"

"He's on my suspect list." I described the scene from the coffee shop when Jake forced Nick to leave. "Paige is really scared of him, and of course, Paula is too."

"Those are two smart women, if you ask me. I could talk all day about Nick, but let me briefly list the facts about his first wife's death. Rhonda

Bogle Jones and I grew up together. Her last name was Bogle, and with mine being Carranza, we often sat close together in class. Rhonda was the sweetest person. We both loved to read, and we were both terrible at sports. At recess, we were always the last to get picked for teams. We remained best friends through high school and college. When we came back to Lutz, she met Nick. He said all the right things, if you know what I mean." Tess rolled her eyes.

"Did you ever like Nick?"

"I saw through him from the beginning, but she hadn't dated much and fell for his lines. They ran off to Vegas and got married by an Elvis impersonator. Cliché and tacky, yes. Rhonda didn't care because she was Nick's wife, until death did they part."

"Why do you think he killed her?" I pulled the sketchbook from my oversized bag and began taking notes. Writing on paper would save the battery in my phone.

"Rhonda had inherited her grandmother's house, and she had a little savings built up. There was also her life insurance policy. Nick killed her for financial reasons."

"I don't understand why he wasn't content living in the house with Rhonda."

"He's a selfish—excuse me." She inhaled, then released it slowly. "He's selfish. We'll leave it at that. A couple of months after they were back from their honeymoon, Rhonda started having stomach pains. She began journaling about her health issues. Thank the good Lord she gave me the journal before Nick could destroy it."

"Aren't you as smart as a dolphin?"

"Not smart enough to save my friend's life. My notes cover her relationship with Nick and my suspicions." Tess patted a bright pink leather journal. "I can make you a copy if you like."

"Yes, please."

Tess nodded. "Rhonda's symptoms grew worse, and I dragged her to the doctor. He didn't have any good answers, so we went to a specialist. They put her in the hospital, and she began to feel better. When she went home, she got worse again."

"What kind of job did she have? Could the health issues have been related to asbestos or mold?"

"Doubtful. She was in charge of marketing for the farmers' market. This was in the early days. Not quite twenty years ago." Tess glanced at her hi-tech watch. "My time's running out. Let me copy the notes for you."

"I'll pay whatever it costs to copy them."

"It's on me. In fact, I'll copy the journal and my notes while you look at the yearbooks. I'm so happy someone is taking me seriously." She reached for the book with her well-manicured hands. "Be back soon."

I waited until she left me alone in the plain room. Tess had movie-star beauty, and it amazed me she'd never gotten married. I reached for the oldest book and found Willow's picture as a freshman. Uncertain what to look for, I leafed through the pages and searched for images of Willow. There were pictures of her with different groups of teens, and even a shot of her with the mean ladies, but there wasn't a single photo of her with an obvious boyfriend.

Tess returned with a folder stuffed full of papers. "Here, I'm sorry, but duty calls. Let me know if you have any questions."

"You've been wonderful. Thanks so much, Tess."

"Even if Nick didn't kill Willow, I feel good showing somebody the evidence I have on Rhonda's murder. I contact Chief Young about once a month, but he's grown tired of listening to me. It's definitely a cold case."

"Maybe when he hires a new cop, the case will get reopened."

"God willing, and the creek don't rise. I'd be the happiest person in town for Rhonda's case to be investigated." She slipped away, and I spent the next two hours studying Tess's notes and looking through the yearbooks.

At last, my growling stomach insisted I leave. After returning the yearbooks to the librarian, I walked home with a bag full of research papers and a heart full of urgency. Willow's killer needed to be caught. Sooner rather than later to prevent another death.

Chapter Twenty-Four

Nick Jones was sitting in his work truck, and it was parked in my driveway. My house was located on Main Street, but there wasn't much traffic at the moment. My grip on the bag of murder notes tightened. Potential evidence against Nick filled my bag.

What to do, what to do. I dug for my phone and dialed Jake. Sophie was my best friend, but when it came to facing a deadly bully, my chances would be better with a strong man at my side.

"Hey Emma, what's going on?" Jake answered right away.

"I'm walking home, and Nick's in my driveway." Not true. I'd stopped cold in my tracks.

"Turn around. Come to the coffee shop. I'm on my way." The urgent tone told me I wasn't overreacting.

Why hadn't I thought of that? No doubt he figured if my brains were ink, I couldn't dot an *i*.

Nick turned his head my way.

Our gazes locked.

The man frowned.

"Oh no, Jake, he saw me." My cold hands grew damp.

Nick jumped out of his exterminator truck, painted to resemble a roach. "Hey, stop right there."

I turned and sprinted in the opposite direction, clutching my bag tight against my side. "Jake, I'm running to you, but Nick's coming after me." My cutesy tennis shoes weren't made for serious running, but I'd never been more serious.

The hefty man's feet pounded on the blacktop. "Stop."

I sprinted over the train tracks and continued toward downtown where there'd be people and safety.

Nick yelled obscenities.

A car drove by without stopping.

Jake appeared on the sidewalk running in his jeans and red-and-black plaid shirt. "Emma, go to the coffee shop. Brett's in there. You'll be safe."

Nick's steps slowed. The stocky man huffed. "Shoulda known you'd call for help."

With Jake at my side, I faced the exterminator. "Nick, I don't have anything to say to you."

His eyes narrowed, and he stopped about six feet away. "Don't believe all them rumors going around town. I didn't kill Willow. Got no reason to."

I kept a firm grip on my bag of evidence against him regarding the death of his first wife. "That's for the cops to settle."

"Right, and if they're competent, you'll find out how innocent I am." His voice had turned deadly calm, scaring me more than the lunatic screaming curse words. "Mind your own business, Emma. Don't dig into my life. Past or present."

How'd he know what I'd been doing? "Have you been following me?"

"I'm not a stalker, if that's what you mean."

"You were sitting in my driveway like you knew I'd be home soon." I didn't mention the library in case he hadn't followed me throughout the day.

Jake pulled out his phone. "Why don't we call Chief Young?"

Nick spat. "No need to call the cops. I'm leaving."

Jake lifted his chin. "Stay away from Emma."

"Or what?"

"You'll have more than the cops to worry about."

Nick muttered something and stomped away.

We didn't move until he disappeared from sight. "Why didn't you leave when I told you? I could've handled him for you."

I reached for Jake's hand. "You probably won't understand, but I'm not used to having others handle my problems. Still, it was nice to know I could call you. I appreciate you standing *with* me. Thanks for coming." There were few men in my life, and becoming friends with Jake amazed me. He'd dropped whatever he'd been doing at the coffee shop and came to my aid.

He nodded. "Thanks for calling. I don't trust that guy."

"Wait until you hear what I learned today. You'll trust him even less." I shivered.

"Let's go to the coffee shop so you can get warmed up." He slid his arm around my shoulders, and we walked up the hill. "You need to try my new blend of coffee. I call it the Jakester."

"The Jakester?" Relief filled my body with Jake at my side. I wasn't ready to go into an empty house yet. Although I would have if necessary, and at some point, I'd need to go take care of Cowboy. "Cute, but you know I'm more of a tea person."

"Yes, ma'am, which is exactly why I want you to try this." We reached Anytime Coffee, and Jake opened the door for me. "Humor me. If you don't like it, I'll prepare your usual green tea and honey."

"Deal." I met his earnest gaze and smiled. "Do you have time to look over the notes with me?"

He smiled. "You bet, but is it safe to discuss here?"

One man sat at a window seat journaling, and a couple sat in the back, holding hands and talking softly.

I nodded. "I believe so. We'll keep our eyes open for trouble."

Jake nodded. "Sounds like a plan. Why don't you take the back corner booth, and I'll be right with you?"

After I settled, Brett appeared. "Emma, it's good to see you. Jake said you were in trouble right before he took off at warp speed. Are you okay?"

"Yeah, and it's probably due to Jake's appearance. Nick Jones was waiting in my driveway when I got home, and he chased me."

"You know, I'm your friend too. Call me anytime." His dark brown eyes shone.

"Thanks, Brett. Will you tell me what's going on with you?"

He sat across from me. "Can you keep a secret?"

"Yes. You can trust me." I dreaded the words about to spill from his lips. I braced myself to hear the word cancer.

"I had hemorrhoid surgery."

Relief flooded through me, and I rounded the table and hugged his neck. "Oh, Brett. I'm so relieved."

He patted my back. "Thanks, I think."

I returned to my seat. "Jake never hinted at what you were going through, and of course, I feared the worst. I mean, I realize it's surgery and all, but still. Why don't you want people to know?"

He turned his hands, palms up. "It's embarrassing."

"Trust me, you're not the only person in town to have that surgery. Remember, I used to work at the pharmacy. How are you healing?"

"I'm fine. End of conversation." He shook his head. "You going to try the Jakester?"

"Yeah, I don't have much choice. Jake seems so proud of it."

"Here he comes now. Be sure to mention you notice a hint of hazelnut."

"Got it."

Brett walked away and spoke to the lovey-dovey couple.

Jake placed two mugs of coffee on the table and claimed the seat Brett had vacated.

"So, this is the Jakester?" I lifted the mug and sniffed. "Mocha?"

"Yes, but there's more to it." His smile made my heart pitter-patter.

I blew on it and took my first sip.

Jake studied me as if he cared about my opinion.

"Yum." I took another sip. "I detect a hint of hazelnut and something fruity."

"Right." He sipped from his blue mug. "What else?"

I didn't want to ruin the moment and hurt Jake's feelings. Another sip. I let it flow over my tongue and swallowed slowly. "It's delicious, whatever you chose."

"Dates."

I snapped my fingers. "Excellent choice. This is my all-time favorite cup of coffee. You can make it for me anytime."

He laughed. "Perfect since we're Anytime Coffee House. Can I take your picture and quote you for social media?"

Yikes. "I must look a fright. Let me freshen my lipstick first."

He gave me a lopsided grin. "You look beautiful."

My heart went from a gentle pitter-patter to an all-out gallop. I hadn't been in the market for romance, but Jake seemed to find ways to worm himself into my heart, probably without even trying. Earthworms were beneficial for my gardens. Maybe Jake would be a positive addition to my life even after we caught Willow's murderer.

Chapter Twenty-Five

Later that day, Jake joined me when I took Cowboy for a long walk in the park, insisting after my run-ins with Dave and Nick, it'd be better to have company.

"Cowboy has a lot of energy." If I kept up with him, I was bound to shed a few unwanted pounds.

"It's not surprising for puppies to be full of get-up-and-go."

We approached a bench where the Nelle sisters sat.

Jake slowed. "Evening, ladies. It's a fine night to be outdoors."

All three agreed with nods and yesses.

Ruby, the youngest of the sisters at eighty-one, said, "Looks like y'all are exercising your bodies and not your mouths like some folks." She pointed toward the entry gate of the dog park area.

Rita and Dave wore workout gear, but Ms. Ruby Nelle was correct. The couple argued instead of working out. "Do you know what they're discussing?"

Gaby, the middle sister, tapped her ear. "My hearing aids don't work so well these days."

"Even though I don't work at the drug store now, I'll help you replace them anytime," I replied.

She removed the hearing aid and dug out a small card with batteries attached. Handing both to me, Gaby said, "You always are such a dear."

She heard well enough to understand my offer. I passed the leash to Jake. "This won't take long."

"Cowboy and I'll meet you near the fountain."

"Sounds good." I turned my focus to the task at hand.

Ms. Ruby said, "We miss you at the pharmacy, but we're about to move to a retirement community. They have a program to help with our medicine." She adjusted the vivid red scarf at her neck.

"Nice." I popped out the dead battery and slid it into the pocket of my jogging pants so Ms. Gaby wouldn't accidentally put it back in the hearing aid. In no time, I'd loaded a fresh battery into the device and returned it. "There you go. I like your earrings."

She fingered the dangling large beads. "Thanks." Her eyes sparkled.

Cowboy barked, and I turned to see what the commotion was about. Jake and my dog passed close to Rita and Dave. Cowboy wasn't happy about something.

"Uh oh. I better go help. See you ladies later."

Gaby waved. "Thanks, Emma. Be careful around those two."

"Yes, ma'am." I smiled, then hurried to Jake and Cowboy. No, he'd told me to meet him at the big fountain where children played in the hot weather. He probably thought I was too strong-willed for my own good, because I hadn't gone along with his directions very often. This time I'd surprise him.

When I reached the splash pad, I stretched while keeping a discrete eye on Rita and Dave. Even though Dave had threatened me, the Nelle sisters were watching. I'd be safe. Nothing got past those three.

Rita was pointing at Dave and frowning. He held out his hands, palms facing her. Before I knew it, he touched her shoulders.

What was happening? Rita had declared her love for Vince in his home after the funeral. Vince had claimed he wasn't interested. Dave had a history of nonviolent crimes, but it appeared that he'd gotten pulled into somebody's wicked scheme. Had Vince hired him in order to avoid a divorce? Had Rita hired him so she could be with Vince? Dave clearly cared about Rita, so why risk going back to prison by taking part in the murder? Maybe he'd threatened me to protect Rita. Suppose he was innocent. Who else could've been part of the plot?

How did Nick fit into the grand scheme of Willow's murder? Could Nick be Gambler? What had Rusty said about Gambler other than the man would kill a person to pay off his debts? I needed to review my notes.

Cowboy barked and ran to me, jumping on my legs.

"Hiya, boy. Did you go for a run?" I rubbed his head.

Jake wiped sweat from his forehead. "I'm not sure who dragged who. Dave's back was to us, but Rita saw me. My only hope is that she was too steamed to pay us any attention. Let's get outta here."

"Look at them now." Rita's posture had softened, and she leaned toward Dave.

"Well, I'll be."

"Do you think it's safe to leave the Nelle sisters alone?"

His shoulders drooped. "We'd never forgive ourselves if anything happened to them."

"A week ago, I wouldn't have been concerned, but these days it's hard to know who to trust."

We returned to the bench where the elderly sisters sat and chatted with them before escorting them to their car. Once they drove away, I elbowed Jake in the ribs. "I think Ms. Ruby might have a little crush on you."

His face reddened, but his only reply was to take Cowboy's leash and walk away. "Keep up, Sunshine. We've got a mission to accomplish."

"Yeah, like find out how you can get in touch with a certain lady." I laughed and teased him all the way home. Once inside, I headed to retrieve my phone from the office charger. "Oh, I missed a message from Faith." I swiped the phone.

The police arrested Paige for Willow's death.

"Oh, no." I dropped into a chair.

Jake met my gaze. "What's wrong?"

"We need to work faster. Paige was arrested."

"I'll speak to Chief Young and see what I can learn."

"Good, you don't seem to irritate him as much as I do. I'll make some calls and do more online research."

He passed the leash to me. "Don't question anybody without me. Your investigation is more dangerous than swimming alone. You need a buddy."

My throat constricted. "Okay."

"I'll call you when I learn more about Paige."

"Thanks." I locked the door. Paige's worst fear came true. She'd been arrested for the murder of Willow Moore.

Cowboy and I settled down in my bedroom with the notes I'd taken with me from Tess. My eyes closed before I'd barely begun, and I fell asleep next to Tess's treasured research on Nick Jones and the death of his first wife.

Chapter Twenty-Six

While my tea steeped on Friday morning, I reviewed my notes on Gambler. Rusty hadn't revealed much, but I couldn't get past the fact Willow's body been found in the alleyway. By me. I removed the tea infuser, set it to the side, and added honey to my green tea.

Rusty had been paid to do the job but backed out. Rather he never intended to kill Willow, but he definitely took the money. Had Rusty's involvement led to a delay that prohibited Gambler from his usual method of murder? No matter who the killer was, I needed to determine who had bankrolled the hit.

Did Willow need to be gone before the divorce proceeding? That could be another explanation for the rush. If preventing the divorce was the motive, Vince would have the most to gain from Willow's death. Even if he didn't inherit anything in the will, he'd keep his job and standing in the community.

Cowboy nosed my leg. After studying up on golden retrievers, I'd discovered he was underweight. Dr. Erb had encouraged me to only feed Cowboy the expensive dog food at the vet clinic. One online authority claimed feeding him real food was best, but only as long as it was healthy. The puppy nosed my leg again.

"What's the matter? Do you need to go outside? It's not even eight o'clock, so you can't bark and wake the neighbors."

His ears perked up, and he tilted his head.

"You are so adorable, and you're right. There's probably not anybody close enough to bother." I rubbed him before opening the back door. Cowboy leaped out to the patio, then growled. Chills raced up my spine, but I followed him outside. "What's wrong?" *Please be a cat, please be a cat.*

My retriever looked right and left. The growl came from a deep place in his chest.

I pulled my phone out of the pocket in my shorts. These days I always carried my phone. I dialed Jake's number from heart. He was no doubt regretting his suggestion for us to work together on Willow's murder.

"Emma? What's wrong?"

"I'm not sure, but Cowboy's spooked by something in the backyard. It could be nothing, though."

"Are you in the house or outside?"

"I'm on the patio with Cowboy. Can you hear him growling?"

"Yep. Get inside. I'm on the way." A sense of déjà vu filled me. Hadn't we had the same conversation the day before?

"Come here, boy." He approached ever so slow, watching the yard with every step. I wrapped my cold fingers around his collar and led him inside. "It's going to be okay."

Cowboy paced at the back door while I raced across the house to verify the front door was secure. Paranoia was an ugly feeling.

I'd bought my bungalow when Abby was a toddler. It'd been a fixer-upper before the term was popular. One of the contractors who'd helped me referred to it as an airplane bungalow because of the second story. My home had always been my comfort zone, at least until Willow's murder. Now I was jumping at shadows.

I prayed we'd be safe from whatever scared Cowboy. The dog hadn't been with me long, but I'd already learned he wasn't afraid of cats. If he saw one, he ran after it. Same with squirrels. So what had disturbed him?

My phone vibrated before it rang. "Jake?"

"Yeah, I'm in the driveway. I don't see anybody in the front yard or on this side of the house. I'm going to check the back. I'll let you know when it's safe."

"Thanks." I returned to the kitchen to watch out the window. Seconds turned into minutes. "Cowboy, what's he doing? Why can't we see him?

Should I call the police?"

The dog stood alert at the door. His deep growl sent shivers up my back.

I craned my neck to get a better view of the sideyard. For the love of daffodils! Jake could be injured, needing assistance while I stood in my safe kitchen like some damsel in distress. "We're going out, Cowboy."

My brother Wyatt had given me a baseball bat for a housewarming gift when I moved into my home because it was on the outskirts of downtown. I snatched it out of the pantry and walked onto the concrete patio with Cowboy beside me. "Jake?"

He appeared from the sideyard, hands on his hips. "You were supposed to wait for me. Inside."

"Let's review our relationship. We're friends, but I don't take orders from you." Shame hit me right away. "I'm sorry, but I was worried you'd gotten hurt."

Cowboy barked a friendly greeting to Jake before running the perimeter of the yard.

"A ball bat is your weapon of choice?"

"Well, yeah." I glanced down at the Louisville Slugger gripped in my hands. It seemed dangerous to me.

"You're aware it won't stop a flying bullet, right?" His nostrils flared, but his voice softened.

"Sure, but what if I'd snuck up behind somebody holding a gun on you? I could've whacked him on the shoulder or head, you'd grab his gun, and we'd be safe." I gave Jake what I hoped was a dazzling smile.

"Oh, Emma." Jake shook his head. "Sometimes I don't know whether to shake you or hug you."

He wasn't muscular like Henry Cavill or Arnold Schwarzenegger in his younger days, but Jake's muscles were well-defined by his gray T-shirt. "I vote for hug."

He wrapped me in his arms, and I dropped the bat. "I'd really appreciate it if you'd be more cautious."

I inhaled and took in his scent. It was a mix of coffee and spices. In a very short time, I'd grown to admire Jake. "Yes, sir. Did you find anything?"

He pulled away. "I think somebody was in your yard, which is what spooked Cowboy. See for yourself."

Cowboy circled us, then trotted to the sideyard.

Near the gate, my dog sniffed a fast-food brown paper bag.

Jake said, "Stop, Cowboy."

The dog paused.

I hurried to where Cowboy stood and wrapped my arms around the pup. "Jake, that's not mine. What do you think it means?"

"It's time to call Chief Young. Somebody could've planned to tempt Cowboy away with the food, or it could be poisoned, or who knows what?"

"This has gone too far. I can't believe the killer would go after an innocent puppy to warn me to back off."

"Emma, the plan could've been to hurt Cowboy in order to get to you." He punched numbers into his phone. "Or some creep could've spent the evening here watching you."

I rubbed my tight jaw. "If that's the case, I must be close to solving the case. Although none of my clues are solid." I led my dog away from the bag.

He dug his feet in.

"Let's go inside where it's safe for you to eat. I'll get you a treat."

Cowboy tilted his head.

"You can trust me. Let's get a treat." I put emphasis on the last word, and my dog followed me inside.

Jake remained on the patio. "Hey, Matt. It's Jake Hunter."

Once inside, I found a bacon dog treat and gave it to my golden retriever.

The dog may have saved my life, and Jake may have saved both of us. I longed to work with my flowers and forget about Willow's murder. If Paige hadn't been arrested, maybe I could walk away.

I'd faced many challenges in my life, and this creep wouldn't force me to back away from attempting to solve the mystery. My friend needed me, and I wouldn't let her down.

Chapter Twenty-Seven

Chief Young drove out to question us personally. He'd also called in a team to handle the evidence and process the area around the gate and food.

Jake took off after giving his version of the event but promised to check on me later.

When the police chief started to leave, I followed him to his official Charger. "Matt, have you figured out who Gambler is?"

He opened the car door but placed his hand on the roof and stared at me. "Emma, focus on your flowers. Willow's murder doesn't fit Gambler's MO." He pushed on his sunglasses.

My heart raced as I stared at the police chief. "Paige is innocent."

He glared at me. "I'm handling the murder, not you."

I didn't argue and gave a halfhearted wave as he drove away. Back in my house, I added the police station to my list of flower deliveries. Two reasons. One was to be nice, and the other was to show Matt I was focusing on my flowers. Yellow tulips with a bit of purple verbena made a beautiful arrangement without being too frilly. It seemed the perfect arrangement for Matt and his officers, both men and women.

Yarrow Martin, the local florist, had emailed me and announced she planned to open the store on a limited basis. Her recovery from the hip surgery was progressing. I replied, then busied myself cleaning up.

After a hot shower, I hid my sketchbook and the files Tess had given me in the pantry behind Cowboy's big ole bag of dog food. Was it too obvious? I separated the files and placed them in a stack of tablecloths. I sealed my sketchbook in a plastic bag and buried it in the dog food. That should do it.

Paranoid or smartly cautious? Who knew? But if someone broke in, and if they discovered my secret pantry, hopefully, they wouldn't find everything related to Willow's death.

I loved on Cowboy, then left him alone to nap. After the excitement, he deserved some peace and quiet. My first stop was the library, where I replaced flowers and checked on Tess. She took me to the side. "I guess you heard Paige was arrested."

"Yeah, I'm afraid so. Have you heard why?" It'd be easier to prove she was innocent if I knew what the evidence was.

"No." Her grip on my arm tightened. "Have you had time to read Rhonda's journal yet?"

"No, but I plan to this afternoon. Nick was waiting in my driveway when I got home. It's possible he's been following me. We need to be extra careful because he acted like he knew I'd been here. Call the police if you're scared."

Her eyes widened. "Forget about me. What about the journal? Is it in a safe place?"

"Yes, and I didn't put my dog in his crate today as an extra security measure."

"Okay, good." She wrung her hands. "I'm glad Nick didn't hurt you."

"Me, too."

"Call me after you read Rhonda's journal. I want to hear what you think."

A library patron approached the counter and motioned she needed help from Tess.

"I'll let you get back to work, and I'll be in touch after reading the diary." I left and stopped by Sophie's Bakery. Customers stood in line examining the cases full of pastries with intriguing names like lebkuchen, fruit and cheese plunder, franzbrotchen, raisin schnecke, hazelnut bars, pretzels, donuts, Danish, and kuchens. The wonderful aromas stirred my hunger.

Sophie met my gaze but continued helping the people in line.

I washed up, then filled the blue and white pottery with my cuttings. Forsythia went into the bigger pieces and cosmos in the smaller vintage pottery. Sophie was predictable in where she liked the arrangements, so I spread them around the shop in their usual places.

Once the crowd thinned, Sophie left her assistant to handle business and met me in the kitchen. "How's it going?" She reached for a cherry Danish and handed it to me.

"Girl, you know my weakness." I bit into it. "This has been the best thing to happen to me today." Not really. Cowboy was safe, and Jake was becoming a good friend. Nothing more.

"Come on back to my office. Tara will holler if she needs help." Sophie led me to the cramped room and sat behind her large desk. "Spill."

I dropped into the only other chair and faced her. "I'd much rather enjoy my treat."

Sophie giggled. "I should have known better than to offer you food first."

"You got that right." I finished eating while Sophie sorted through a stack of mail. "It seems like forever since we were together. You've got a nice mid-morning crowd."

"Ja." Sometimes Sophie slipped into her native language, but she was fluent in English. "Tell me about you."

I updated her on recent events.

"Lieb haben. You have feelings for Jake." Her practical assessment surprised me.

I licked the sticky off my fingers. "Why do you think that?"

"We have been friends for over ten years, and there has never been such a sparkle in your eyes." She folded her hands and placed them on the desk. "There is also a spring in your step."

Heat infused me, and I reached for a catalog and fanned myself. Wasn't I too young for hot flashes? Like way too young? "Um, I don't know how to answer."

"When was the last time you dated? Scratch that. You haven't been in a true relationship since Bo died."

"Bo burned me, and you know I've been too busy to get into a romantic relationship."

"True, but Abby's in college now. Jake is here, and you two have the ingredients for a special recipe. A romantic recipe, if you know what I mean."

"I survived Bo, but it's like the smoke clings to me from the flames of our marriage." A shiver ripped up my spine. "I don't think I can endure another relationship like that."

Sophie tapped the table. "You are older and wiser, and most important, Jake is not Bo Justice."

"I hear you." If I wasn't careful, I could easily fall for Jake. I'd even allowed him to hug me, but I needed to wise up. "Who has time to date?"

She shook her finger at me. "Excuses, excuses, excuses. You are not getting any younger, but you are also not too old for romance."

I fanned the magazine faster. "I've got more flowers to deliver."

"I understand, but keep your heart open to love."

I stopped fanning and made eye contact with my best friend. "What about you? You're not dating anybody either."

"It is difficult to spend time with a man when you work a baker's schedule."

"Look who's making excuses now." I stood. "It sounds like we need to find a man who works second or third shift for you to meet. Then I can meddle in your love life."

Sophie shooed me out of her office. "Enough crazy talk. Have a good day, my friend."

After our discussion, I changed my delivery route. Anytime Coffee House was my closest stop to the bakery, but I wasn't ready to face Jake, especially after my conversation with Sophie.

Instead of Jake, I headed to the police station.

While I didn't want to fill my mind with crazy romantic notions, I couldn't deny my attraction to Jake. Yet, I was a sensible businesswoman who didn't require a man in my life to be complete.

Chapter Twenty-Eight

Heart of Texas Bed-and-Breakfast wasn't far from the police station, so I dropped by to chat with Faith about her needs for the weekend. The woman was always prepared. She'd written a list on a piece of pale blue stationary.

"I'll have these back to you before your guests check-in today."

Faith stood across the kitchen island from me. "How would you feel about providing flowers for a small wedding. It's an older couple, and it'll be a simple affair. The wife is a practical sort, but her future husband wants her to have a bouquet."

My thoughts raced. "Frugal but beautiful?"

"Exactly. Can you handle it?"

"No problem." I pulled a few business cards from my bag. "Have the groom get in touch with me. I like to check on allergies and preferences."

"Ah-ha. Can't have the bride sneezing through her wedding." Faith laid my cards on the counter. "I guess we'll see each other later when you deliver flowers."

"Yes. Don't get up. I can see myself out." I walked to the front door, but it swung open before I could touch the knob.

Jake met my gaze and paused. "Howdy. Whatcha doing?"

"Flower deliveries and taking orders." My neck grew warm, but I willed myself to stay cool. Jake had no inkling about my conversation with Sophie. There was no reason for me to be embarrassed. "How's your day going?"

"Great, actually. I move into Paige's apartment later today. She doesn't have enough staff to keep the store open, and I'm not sure she'll be able to raise bail. My moving in will give her a little income." He stepped into the entry area and closed the door.

"The store is closed?"

"Not right now. I helped her find someone to work the next few days until she has a better feel for the situation. Did Matt stay long after I left?"

"Not really." I lowered my voice. "He basically told me to butt out."

"Nothing new there. Are you going to quit your amateur investigation?"

"Not a chance."

"Just what I expected. Okay, you know the locals. Who else can we add to your suspect list?"

I looked around the front hall to make sure nobody was snooping. "The timing still makes me think Willow's death is linked to the divorce."

"If divorce was the motive, you've got Vince, his kids, and his parents."

I laughed. "Vince is the only suspect there."

"You've got to open your mind to other family possibilities. Just watch the news or listen to podcasts. Unfortunately, kids have been known to murder their parents."

"I'll try to keep an open mind, but you don't know Christine and Blake. For now, let's consider other possibilities. It'd be nice to find out if Nick Jones likes to gamble. Maybe he lost and couldn't pay his debt. Maybe Dave approached him with enough money to get him out of trouble. If that's the case, then he intended to kill Willow. It wasn't mistaken identity."

"Whoa, that's a whole lot of speculation."

I lifted my chin. "Yeah, but how else do you find a killer? Speculate and rule out or look harder."

"How would Dave know to approach Nick?"

"Don't criminals hang out together?"

"Oh, honey." Jake crossed his arms. "I'll ask Brett if he knows about local poker games or whatever."

"It's doubtful he'll be much help. Brett's all into nature and working out when he's not at Anytime Coffee."

"True, but he might hear things at the gym or the shop. It can't hurt to ask."

"You're right. I plan to read Rhonda's journal when I get home."

He tilted his head. "Rhonda?"

"Remember? She was Nick's first wife."

"Oh, yeah. There are enough in-and-outs in this little town to make a man's head spin. Be careful, Emma."

"Always. See ya' later." I made tracks to Anytime Coffee while Jake was occupied at the bed-and-breakfast.

The next hour of deliveries took me to the bank, the yarn shop, and the yoga studio on the way to Paige's Turn Bookshop. The Nelle sisters were sitting on a bench under the American flag. A quick glance in my bag assured me I had enough flowers, so I detoured to where they sat. "Good afternoon, ladies."

Ms. Gaby wore leather earrings today. "Where's your young fellow?"

"You too, Ms. Gaby? He's only a friend, and we're close to forty." I cleared my throat and pulled three bright yellow tulips from my bag, and handed one to each lady.

"Thanks, hon, but closing in on forty is all the more reason to hook up with that man. Even with a cataract, I can tell he's handsome." Her eyes sparkled.

The ever-practical Ms. Rosalita said, "Don't forget kind. Lots of people pass right by us saying nary a thing. Your young man's not like that, though. He always has a pleasant word for us."

My face grew warm.

"Emma, thank you for the flowers. If you don't want to be sitting on a bench with only your sisters or friends forty years from now, take a chance on Jake Hunter." Ms. Ruby twirled the tulip in between her fingers.

I stepped back and, one by one, made eye contact with each of the three sisters. "Nothing gets by y'all, does it?"

Ms. Rosalita shook her head. "Not much, dear."

As much as I'd like to know their ideas on Gambler, I didn't want to endanger them. That was a line I didn't want to cross. "I hope you have a nice afternoon. I've got to keep working." I turned on my toe, and the dahlia print wrap dress swirled around my legs. I loved wearing clothes with a floral theme. Shoes were a different story. Periwinkle flats matched the blue tones in my dress, and they provided good support for my feet and back as I walked to the bookstore.

A silver Toyota SUV pulled into a parking space in front of Paige's place, and Jake hopped out.

I couldn't seem to catch a break when it came to ignoring Jake. With a smile plastered on my face, I waved to the man who'd consumed my thoughts since our morning hug.

"Well, if it isn't the town's flower lady. Are you following me?" With sure moves, he zigged around me and opened the door.

"Flower farmer, and no. I'm not following you." I tossed my hair over my shoulder.

"What happened to your sunny disposition, Sunshine?" He winked.

My heart skipped a beat. "Calling me Sunshine seems rather insulting if you really mean I'm grumpy."

"Didn't mean no disrespect, Emma." Smile lines framed his mouth.

I entered the store and looked around.

Celia stood at a display table arranging best sellers. "Just what I needed, a friendly face and fresh flowers. Thanks, Emma."

I drew to a stop. "What are you doing here? I thought you were going back to Waco."

"I've accumulated so many vacation days, it's not funny. When Jake mentioned Paige's troubles, I decided to lend a hand." She rearranged local pottery on the next table.

"First, you pitched in to help Brett and now Paige. You may be the most generous person I know."

She lifted a shoulder in a half-shrug. "It could be selfish. I enjoyed my first week of vacation so much, my brother didn't have to twist my arm to return to Lutz."

Jake slid an arm around his sister's shoulders. "As long as you stay away from Emma and the danger swirling around her, you'll be fine."

Celia's eyes widened. "Danger?"

"Yeah, we gotta watch this one. Both Dave Smith and Nick Jones threatened her." Jake gave me a smug grin.

So much for thinking I could intimidate Jake. "Celia, we all need to be extra cautious until the killer is caught."

A young mother entered the store carrying a baby and holding hands with a little girl. The toddler had a red ponytail and stopped when she saw me.

"Momma, she's got red hair too."

The woman gasped. "I'm so sorry. She has no filter yet."

"It's nothing to worry about." I reached for my basket of flowers and knelt by the child. "Us redheads need to stick together because there aren't many of us. Would you like a flower?"

Her mouth rounded into a perfect circle. "Yes, please."

I tugged out a Prairie-Fire stem and passed it to her. "This almost matches your hair."

"Oh, Thank you so much!" She looked at her mother. "Look, Mommy, she gave me a flower."

"I see. It's nearly as beautiful as you." She touched her child's head in a loving gesture. "Let's find you a book."

"Yay. This is the most special day ever."

I stood. Oh, to be young and innocent.

The mother made eye contact. "Thank you. The new baby has been an adjustment for her, and I appreciate you taking time to make her feel special."

"She brightened my day too." I'd never imagined how much I'd miss Abby when she left for college. "Time passes much too quickly. Enjoy your children while you can."

"You better believe it. These two are the reason I left a good marketing job in Dallas." She followed her daughter to the children's area.

"Celia, I'll leave you some flowers. We can talk later, but you'll be safe in Lutz." With her big brother and Brett keeping an eye on Celia, no harm should come to her.

"I'll look forward to chatting with you." She left me standing with Jake, and I discarded the dying flowers and created a new arrangement featuring the Prairie-Fire.

I glanced at Jake. "Speaking of time flying, it's been right at a week since we found Willow's body. The police have arrested the wrong person."

"They can't arrest a person without sufficient evidence. There must be a good reason for Matt to arrest Paige."

"But she's innocent. What could they possibly have as so-called proof? Vince said he believed Paige killed Willow, but surely that's not enough to get her thrown in jail."

"Try to stay calm." Jake rubbed his earlobe.

"It almost seems like more than one person needed to get rid of Willow, and they teamed up to kill her. Can you imagine the logistics? Two people want Willow dead. They discover each other, then they work together to commit the murder."

"Stranger things have happened." Jake shook his head.

"True, but in Lutz?" My little town had always been so friendly. How was it a murder had occurred, and now I was studying multiple suspects?

Chapter Twenty-Nine

L ate Friday afternoon, Cowboy and I headed out for another walk. The sixty-something temperature caused me to shiver, and I wrapped my warm scarf around my neck and fastened the buttons on my quilted jacket. "Cowboy, I'd never survive in Montana or Colorado."

He tugged on the leash, and I hurried my steps. We soon reached the square and ran smack into Jake, Celia, and Brett. It'd be easier to put socks on a rooster than put some space between Jake and me. "Hey, y'all."

Celia approached and pet my dog. "How's Cowboy?"

"We're getting used to being a family."

"He already looks healthier. You must be treating him good."

I laughed. "Honestly, it's hard to tell. I've never been responsible for a dog, and he's being super patient with me during the learning process. I've already made a few mistakes. One was a wonky gate, but Jake helped me fix it. What are y'all up to tonight?"

She hugged me and whispered in my ear, "Can you take Jake off my hands? I'd like to spend a little alone time with Brett."

No, no, no. Her request meant I'd have alone time with Jake, and that's the last thing I needed in order to conquer my crush on the man. "I don't think so."

"Please? I'll owe you one." Her hopeful expression reminded me of Abby, even though Celia was close to ten years older than my daughter. Aw, shoot. Who was I to ruin her chance at love?

"All right." I turned my attention to Jake. "Do you have time to discuss you-know-what after Cowboy's walk?"

Deer in headlights look was the only way to describe Jake's expression. "Uh, we're about to go bowling."

Celia nudged Brett.

Brett coughed, looked at Celia, then grinned. "You know, I'm not sure about lifting those bowling balls yet. Backgammon might be more my speed."

"Oh, man. That's too bad." Celia would never win an award for acting. "Backgammon is for two players only. Jake why don't you go with Emma, and I'll hang out with Brett?"

Jake's hands went to his hips, and he studied the three of us. "Feels like I'm being set up."

I touched his shoulder. "Be a good sport and play along."

Celia gave me another hug. "Thanks so much."

"You're welcome."

Brett winked at me, then the two of them disappeared in the direction of Brett's house.

Jake's forehead furrowed. "Let me guess. Celia dumped me so she could have time with Brett, right? No chaperones and no interruptions."

I tightened my hold on Cowboy's leash and walked to the corner. "If you know what she's up to, it doesn't seem like she duped you."

Jake laughed so loud the dog and I both stopped and watched. "Emma, sometimes you crack me up."

I fought the feeling of pleasure his words gave me. "How about a cookie or something from Sophie's Bakery? She stays open later on Friday and Saturday evenings."

"If I ever turn down something from Sophie, check me into the hospital."

"Deal. Same goes for me." I smiled.

We walked the short distance and entered the bakery.

Sophie was alone in the store. "Emma, I love you, but Cowboy can't be in here."

"Sorry, I wasn't thinking." I backed out and handed Jake a five. "Anything with chocolate or cherry."

"If you don't like what I pick, we'll trade." He returned to the counter, and I sat outside on a bench with my puppy.

Trucks and cars followed the traffic pattern around the square. I angled myself to see the Lonestar Cattleman Bank of Texas. Lights blazed inside, but I didn't see a guard. A cleaning cart was in plain sight, though. I got lost in my thoughts and jumped when Jake appeared.

"Jumpy? Sorry about that." He sat beside me. "German chocolate pie for you. It's a new recipe that Sophie assured me you'd like. I ordered cheesecake with rhubarb for myself and a dog treat for Cowboy." He pulled our deserts and forks out of a canvas bag and dropped the treat to the dog. "Sophie also wants the bag and utensils back. Something about saving the environment and knowing you wouldn't mind helping."

"Yeah, she and I are funny that way. Did Brett mention that he saves the coffee grounds for me?" The pie was topped with whipped cream, chocolate shavings, and toasted coconut. I slid my fork into the concoction and took the first small bite. My taste buds sang for joy at the deliciousness.

"Why?"

I processed Jake's question. Why what? Oh, yeah. "It makes good compost, and if I use them instead of Brett throwing the grounds away, the environment benefits."

"All right, we'll keep saving them for you. I'm all for protecting the earth." He cut into his cheesecake.

"Interesting tidbit, if you ever need to get rid of expired medications, you can add them to still-warm coffee grounds. The drugs disintegrate, and nobody can abuse them."

The fork stopped midway to Jake's mouth. "Do you use drugs in your compost?"

I gasped so hard, I choked. More like I hacked up a lung.

Jake thumped my back, and Cowboy quit chewing his treat and watched with his eyes wide and his head tilted.

Tears streamed down my face before the coughing spell ended.

"Are you okay?"

I nodded. "Yeah, I'm fine. By the way, I'd never use coffee dregs laced with drugs for compost. They go to the landfill."

"Good to know, or else customers might start eating your flowers instead of smelling them." He took his first bite of the cheesecake. "Um, this is amazing."

"Here, try a bite of my pie." I forked him up a bite, and he gave me a bite of his.

I allowed the creamy dessert to settle on my tongue before chewing. "I didn't expect to like it so much, but you're right. Sophie's the best."

"She has a sign on the counter advertising only traditional Texas desserts for the next two days."

"You know March second is Texas Independence Day, and she's preparing Texas recipes every weekend this month."

"Good for her. It's important to explore all Texas has to offer. The history of Germans immigrating here in the 1840s is part of our heritage."

"Sophie is actually German." We finished our desserts in silence. "I've been watching the bank. There's a cleaning crew, but I don't see a security guard."

"Interesting." He dropped his arm along the back of the bench while watching the bank. "You're right. I see the cart. Maybe the guard is on a break."

"I wonder what cleaning company the bank uses, or do they have their own maintenance staff?"

"Whoever does it must have to pass a background check, but it concerns me that the guard isn't visible."

Cowboy lay at my feet and breathed heavily.

"I never knew dogs snored before this week."

"Every dog I ever had did the same thing."

"Why don't you have a dog now?" I kept my attention focused on the bank.

"I've been busy the last year or so, and it wrecks you when they pass."

I did a double-take. Big ole Marine Jake Hunter had a soft side. "Let me guess. Celia and dogs are your weakness."

"Shh, let's keep that our little secret."

I returned to watching the bank. Maybe Jake would open up if I didn't look straight at him. I reached for my cell phone and took pictures of the bank. "Tell me about your dog."

"Chase was a mutt I rescued from the animal shelter. He was part border collie, and who knows what else? We ran together in the mornings. He'd chase anything I threw his way and always returned with it. Sticks, discs, balls. You name it, and he'd chase it."

"Is that the reason for his name?"

Jake chuckled. "Yep. That first day when I learned he'd play fetch as long as I'd throw things, I named him Chase."

"That makes sense. Maybe I should've named Cowboy something like Scout since we found him in the alley, probably searching for food." I glanced down at my golden retriever.

Jake grunted. "It's a good name, but I think Cowboy fits him."

"Yeah, I agree." I zoomed my phone's camera app in and took more pictures of the bank.

"My Nikon would work much better. Too bad it's in storage until I get settled."

"I could always move closer to the bank."

"Not a smart idea. What are your most recent notions for motive?"

"The motive for Willow's death could be the divorce, the bank, the mysterious mistress, or something totally different."

"Rumored mistress. Let's return to the other options you've mentioned. What if Willow wasn't the intended victim? The killer might have meant to kill Paige. Does she have any enemies?" He crossed his ankle over his knee.

"Nick Jones is the obvious answer because Paige refuses to date him. I don't see how Nick would mistake the two women. They look nothing alike." Speaking my thoughts out loud to Jake confirmed my instinct Nick was innocent of Willow's death. I wouldn't go so far as to say he hadn't killed his first wife, though.

"Paige left the store, and Nick and Willow were the only two there. Would Nick have another motive to kill Willow?"

Jake had my full attention. "Is it possible he asked Willow for a loan too? His business could be slow."

So much for ruling out Nick. "Or he might want to expand. Hiring more employees and buying more equipment can be costly. How many people work for Nick?"

"He probably has an officer manager, but I've always seen him driving the work vehicle." I'd be sure to follow up on Jake's question. "I don't think there's anyone else."

A person wearing a security uniform opened the bank door, and two women exited the building. They walked close to each other and disappeared around the corner. The guard locked the door and vanished into the bank's shadows.

"Did you notice the so-called guard is short and stocky with a beard?"

I shifted my attention back to the man in question. "Um, is that a ponytail out the back of his cap?"

"Looks like it. If I was a gambler, I'd bet that was Rita's friend, Kevin." Jake pointed at the man.

"Why do you suppose he stayed? The bank only has a security guard when it's open. At night, they set the security system. Before you ask, Willow told me once."

"So many questions come to mind. First, how active was Willow in the bank?"

"Her family started the business, but when she had her first baby, Vince took up the reins. Now that the kids are older, Willow dropped into the bank unexpectedly and frequently. No doubt her attorney could shed more light on her motives. My guess is she planned to take charge once the divorce was final."

"How did you find out about the bank's security?"

"Last year, Vince turned fifty-five. I hadn't started my business yet, but Willow knew about my plans. She asked me to help set up flowers and balloons in the bank for Vince's birthday. Yellow roses and red, white, and blue balloons. After we decorated his office and the lobby, Willow set the alarm and explained about the security system." I rubbed my hands together. "She also had me take pictures for a portfolio. Even though I'm more focused on growing flowers, I decided it couldn't hurt."

"Let's see."

I scanned my phone and found the photos, then passed it to Jake.

CHAPTER TWENTY-NINE

He whistled. "That must be the biggest desk in central Texas."

"I think Vince's life motto could be something like, go big or go home. His parents seem so down-to-earth, and Willow must've seen something special in Vince since she married him. I wonder if he changed, or maybe she liked his flashiness?"

"Some women go for that." He hunched over the phone, enlarging and studying the pictures. "It doesn't appear Vince had a photo of Willow in his office, but it's possible I can't see well enough. Do you remember?"

We'd been all over his office, and I'd taken pictures from different corners of the room. "Now that you ask, I can't remember a picture of her or them as a couple."

"Did she talk like she still loved her husband?"

"Willow was excited to surprise Vince. Sophie was going to provide pastries for the employees the next morning and cookies individually wrapped for bank customers. Willow didn't hold back."

"Okay. Either she loved him then, or she wanted to get into the bank to spy without any prying eyes. Was she in your line of vision the entire time you were together?"

"Jake, you're amazing. We had a ton of stuff. Willow turned off the alarm, and I carried the vases, balloons, ribbons, and all the party supplies inside. She parked in the alley just in case Vince drove by. She didn't want him to see us and spoil the surprise. Even more interesting, she wasn't always standing at the door to let me in right away. I had to pound on the glass door with my fist."

"Sounds like she was snooping to me. If she was questioned, the party was the perfect excuse to be in the bank after hours."

"Do you believe Vince stole money from the back in addition to hiding personal money in the Cayman Islands?" My heart sped up. "If they got divorced, the bank would have fired him. Willow would've taken control. I bet a bank auditor would've combed the books, accounts, or whatever and discovered Vince's crimes."

"Hold on. We're leaping to a lot of assumptions, and we're all over the board on suspects. Vince, Nick, unknown person, and maybe Rita?"

Movement at the bank ended our conversation.

The security guard exited and locked the door.

A black car approached, and the guard got into the passenger seat. The car took off before the boxer-shaped man shut the door.

Cowboy barked.

I dropped a dog bone to him. "Shh, boy."

His attention turned to chewing on the bone.

Jake swooped toward my body and embraced me right as the vehicle's headlights swept over us.

My heart kicked it up another notch as Jake's breath tickled my face.

Brakes screeched. The sports car stopped. A car door slammed.

Was one of the goons heading for us?

Dread left me gasping for air. Had the fake security guard and his driver seen us watching them? If I died tonight, Abby would be an orphan.

Chapter Thirty

"Wrap your arms around me," Jake whispered.

I snuggled closer to him and circled my arms around his neck but kept my gaze on the action.

"Dude, the bakery's still open." The pretend bank guard signaled the driver with his hands.

The car engine shut off, and another car door slammed. Footsteps pounded and disappeared.

"Jake, we've got to protect Sophie." I glanced over his shoulder. "Oh, no. Dave is the driver, and he followed Kevin into the bakery."

"Is there a back entrance?"

"Yes. All the stores on the square have a back entrance from different alleys. Dave won't be happy to see me. What if you go in the front where the men are? I'll text Sophie to unlock the back door. Cowboy and I can hide in her office and call the cops if we need them."

"Sounds like a plan." Jake jogged the short distance to the bakery.

I texted my friend, then scurried with Cowboy to the back entrance. We avoided walking past the bakery windows. I touched the back door handle, but it didn't budge. I knelt and hugged Cowboy. "I'm sure she's busy serving Kevin and Dave. She'll be safe with Jake. They've got five minutes before I call the cops." Talking to your dog was acceptable. Right? Even if he didn't understand.

Like a watched pot doesn't boil, observing a clock doesn't make time go faster, and staring at a door handle doesn't unlock it. At last, the door opened, but nobody was there. With one hand on the leash and my phone in the other hand, I entered the bakery's back room.

Low voices murmured from the front. Normal tones reached my ears. Nothing threatening.

"I hope you enjoy your sandwiches and the pie. Have a nice evening." Sophie's voice rang out clear and strong.

I leaned against the wall. Seconds ticked by.

Jake appeared. "Crisis averted. Rather, I don't believe there was any foul play intended. Even criminals need to eat."

Sophie appeared. "I'm locking up, then you two can walk me to my van and explain what just happened."

I eyed Jake. "She may give us a talkin' to."

He laughed. "It's possible we deserve whatever speech she's about to dish out."

It took less than thirty minutes to ride home with Sophie, receive her well-thought-out tongue-lashing, and walk to my house. Cowboy headed to his crate and fell asleep without any persuasion. Jake and I sat in my little office in order not to disturb the sleeping pup.

I sat at my desk and faced Jake. "It feels later than it is."

"Living on the edge will wear a person out." He stretched his long legs. "Are you working at the farmers' market tomorrow?"

I yawned. "Yes. The exposure will help my business more than traditional advertising. What about you?"

"You'll see me there in the green VW van again."

Turquoise and white van, but who was I to correct him? "I understand if you want to call it a night. It'll only take me a few minutes to search for Kevin."

"Knowing his last name might make your work easier." His eyes sparkled.

"You've been holding out on me." I wadded up a piece of scrap paper and threw it at him.

"Hey, now. I learned it at the bakery. The nametag on Kevin's shirt said Anderson."

I searched for Kevin Anderson. "Rita must've played a role in hiring Kevin."

"No doubt."

I added Texas to my search criteria, but there were still a lot of Kevin Andersons to go through. "This is ridiculous. How can so many people have the same name?"

Jake shrugged. "Beats me. What do you think about Matt Young?"

"He's been here for going on fifteen years. I've never had any problem with him. He used to come into the pharmacy and ask law enforcement questions about suspects. Matt's divorced. Our girls took dance classes together years ago. That's when I first got to know him and his wife. I like both of them. It seems like she wanted the divorce saying he was married to his career as a cop. At least that was the word around town." I glanced up from my laptop. "Have you heard from Matt? Has he offered you a job?"

"Not yet."

"I'm sure it'll be soon. Are you worried?"

"The thing is, it appears to me all the men on the force are locals. They're very protective of the chief. There are no women cops, which is bothersome. How does he get away with only hiring men? My gut instinct has been wrong on occasion, and I'm probably misreading the situation."

"Maybe it's part of living in a little town. It's possible women don't apply for law enforcement jobs in Lutz."

"Could be." He avoided eye contact.

"Jake, are you cut out for small-town life? For better or worse, everyone will know your business."

"I've been a rambling man for way too long. It's time to put down roots and make friends. Lutz will be close enough to Celia, and my best friend in the world lives here. I can handle the busybodies."

I laughed. "Oh, Jake. The Nelle sisters will try to set you up with someone. Once the single ladies of Lutz realize you're here to stay, they'll be bringing you casseroles galore. Your desire to remain single won't stand up to the women of Lutz."

"I don't mind dating the women, but don't expect me to get in any kind of serious relationship."

There was my answer. Jake had decided not to get involved. Another reason for spending less time with him once we'd solved the murder. "Time will tell."

"Brett's still single."

"Is he? Really? Do you think maybe he resisted because his heart was already set on your sister? If you would give those two your blessing, they'd be the two happiest people this side of the Rio Grande."

Jake sat straighter. "They don't need my permission."

"No, but they both love and respect you. They'd prefer your blessing before they date."

"Honey, I'm not sure about your theory." He rose and walked out of the room. "But I'll give it some thought."

"Trust me. It'll make a difference." I walked him to the front door in silence. Jake didn't seem like the type who would appreciate me going on and on, so I kept my mouth shut. Once he left, I returned to my internet search. Ten more minutes, then I'd go to bed.

Chapter Thirty-One

Cowboy's barking woke me the next morning. I jumped up from my desk and checked the time. I'd overslept, and the crick in my neck demanded ice and ibuprofen. Hustling to the kitchen, I opened the back door to let my dog out. My dog. Yeah, I liked that.

"Good morning, Cowboy. Go potty while I prepare your breakfast." Fresh water in one bowl and kibble in the other.

There was no time to fix coffee or hot tea. Instead of easing into the morning, I organized the flowers I planned to take to the farmers' market.

Cowboy barked once, and I let him back in. He ate while I freshened up and changed clothes. Five minutes was a new record for me getting ready. Of course, it probably didn't appear I'd made any effort.

In very little time, I organized fresh flowers in coolers, then loaded them all into Ms. Daisy. Dried lavender was something I wanted to try selling today. The purple color was beautiful, and there were so many benefits to the plant, it seemed worth a shot. After locking Cowboy in the house, I hightailed it to the farmers' market.

It was easy to spot the turquoise and white VW van. There was already a line with nearly a dozen people at the window where Jake sold customers their desired morning brew. Too bad there wasn't enough time for me to swing by.

This week I felt more confident organizing my booth, and it didn't take as long. Farmers were early risers, and many were already selling produce to shoppers. I'd get an early start next week.

A twenty-something woman appeared, holding hands with a small girl.

"Good morning." I reached for a daisy and passed it to the child. "How are you two today?"

The little girl took the flower and softly said, "Thank you."

The three of us chatted about our favorite flowers, and before I knew it, my day started.

Mid-morning, I reached a lull and sat on a red folding chair.

"Morning, Sunshine." Jake's voice greeted me.

"Good morning." I'd rarely had a nickname. Emma Fair Justice. Plain and simple, yet I kinda liked Sunshine.

Jake handed me an insulated travel mug. "Green tea with local honey. Celia dropped by and is handling the coffee van, so I decided to check out the market."

"It's hopping today, that's for sure." I sipped my tea. "Delicious. Thanks."

"No problem." He covered a yawn with his large hand.

Rita walked by with Dave. Was it possible Dave had seen Jake and me together? I hopped up and reached for a bundle of dried lavender. "I guarantee this will help with sleep issues. Keep it on your bedside table, and you can even put a stem in your pillowcase." I sneezed.

Jake's eyes grew wide. "Bless you."

Rita glanced my way. When she recognized me, she waved.

"Hi, Rita."

She and Dave joined us. "Did I hear you mention a sleep aid?"

"Yes. I was explaining to Jake that lavender has been shown to help people sleep." I reached for another bundle. "Have you met Jake? He's helping Brett at the coffee shop."

Jake nodded. "Good to see you again."

We stumbled through the introductions.

"Rita, are you also having difficulty sleeping?"

"It's a new development. I think Willow's death hit me harder than I expected."

I passed a few sprigs of lavender to her. "Some people claim this helps stress as well as being a sleep aid. Your boss could probably use some too. How's Vince doing?"

"He's fine." Rita's clipped tone intrigued me, and possibly Dave too.

With raised eyebrows, Dave studied the petite woman. "You're the fine one."

Rita was stunning with gently layered jet-black hair, dark eyes, and a trim figure. It would've been easy to imagine Vince falling for her. If I hadn't overheard him reject Rita, I'd still believe they were having a fling.

Jake cleared his throat. "You've convinced me to give it a try."

"I will too." Rita smiled at her ex-fiancé, and he paid me before they wandered off.

"Hope I didn't break up the party before you grilled them."

"We learned Rita isn't sleeping and is possibly stressed. It could be chalked up to a broken heart or a guilty conscious."

"It sure enough could be either reason. I need to shove off. How much do I owe you?"

"Nothing. When I saw them, selling the lavender to you was the first thing that came to mind. Keep it in case they watch you walk away."

Jake tilted his head. "You're not getting paranoid, are you?"

"It's not paranoid to believe someone is watching you if they really are watching. Know what I mean?" How many times had I said 'Know what I mean, jelly bean' to Abby? It was lucky I stopped myself.

"I hear ya. Be careful, Emma."

"You too, Jake."

He trudged away, and I sipped my tea between customers. I might not be making a lot of money at the market, but people were learning about my business. If I kept my eyes open, I might even find another clue to the mystery of Willow's death.

The last hour of the farmers' market wasn't busy, and I allowed my thoughts to wander. I couldn't think of a solid reason for Nick to be the killer. Mistaken identity seemed far-fetched, and there was no proof he and Willow had business dealings.

Paige didn't fit the profile of a killer, and how could she have done it while Nick was around and spraying for bugs?

Rusty had admitted to taking money to kill Willow, but he'd said he never intended to do anything other than get high. I believed him.

If Vince killed Willow, it wasn't to be with Rita. I figured his motives were to keep his job as bank president and prevent himself from being humiliated in court. There was also the rumor about him having a girlfriend and offshore accounts. Were the accounts related to the supposed other woman? Or was Vince embezzling to be greedy? If that was his motive, how would I prove it?

The Nelle sisters walked by at their normal slow pace.

I approached them. "Good afternoon."

Ruby, the youngest, reached me first. Today she wore a straw hat with a red ribbon. It matched her red blouse and shoes. "Morning, Emma. We're having Vince Moore and his parents over for dinner tonight, and I'd like a pretty flower arrangement."

My heart leapt at the budding opportunity to find a clue, but how without placing the sisters in danger? I reached for a vase. "Will it be the six of you?"

"Yes. The children have a youth group event at the church tonight and won't join us." She pressed her red-tinged lips together.

"Perfect. We don't want the arrangement so high you can't see each other around it." I began filling a vase with bluebonnets and white snapdragons. "You know, I'm not busy tonight. If you prepare the food, I can be your server. That way, you won't get pulled out of the conversation by making sure everyone has enough iced tea or pulling hot rolls out of the oven. Sophie uses me for catering jobs on occasion, so I know what to do."

"Dear, that's nice of you to offer." She lowered her voice. "Too bad I don't have a budget for that kind of thing. The flowers are my big splurge."

"Hey, I won't charge you for tonight."

"Why would you do that? I'm sure a young woman like you has better ways to spend her Saturday evening." Her eyes sparkled, and she smiled. "One lovely option would be for you to spend time with Jake."

"Er, I'd rather hang out with y'all. It's what friends do for each other." I finished arranging the wildflowers. "What time should I be there?"

She smiled. "Dinner is at six."

"I'll arrive at your place no later than five. When you get home, put water in the vase. Is there anything else?"

Her fingers fluttered on her chest. "No, dear, you're being more than generous."

Ms. Rosalita Nelle approached, blotting her hairline with a linen handkerchief. "Emma, how are you holding up, dear?"

I took a deep breath. "I'm doing okay." I didn't mention the nightmares I'd experienced from the sight of Willow's dead body. There was nothing she could do to help, so why bother?

We concluded our business, and Jake appeared carrying three clear plastic glasses of iced tea.

"Ladies, I'm closing up shop and thought you could use some refreshment. How about I walk you to your car?"

The Nelle sisters giggled like teenagers and accepted his offer. Jake carried the floral arrangement, and they sipped on their drinks. It didn't surprise me one little bit to notice Ruby slipping her free hand into the crook of Jake's elbow. People often called the sisters the Nosy Nellies, but I thought of the youngest as Romantic Ruby.

I packed up my belongings and headed for the truck. In less than three hours, I was due at the Nelle home, where I hoped to find a clue of some sort.

Chapter Thirty-Two

Wearing a black skirt and a black short sleeve blouse, because it was way too hot for slacks, I walked around Ruby's rectangular dining room table, removing empty salad bowls.

The table was covered with a vintage damask tablecloth. The sisters had fine china, silver flatware, and Waterford crystal glasses. The conversation flowed with talk of the weather, music, and good books.

The sisters wore their Sunday best clothes. Mr. Moore wore black slacks and a black turtleneck. I didn't know if he chose the color because of Willow's death or if he preferred black. Mrs. Moore wore a dark green dress and another set of pearls with matching earrings and bracelet.

In the kitchen, I dished up chicken casserole, lemon-sesame green beans, and honey-glazed carrots. Vince's parents were served first, then Vince, then the Nelle sisters. Last thing I did was pull yeast rolls from the oven and took eight of them to the table in a serving bowl. I returned the rest of the rolls to the oven and lowered the heat. The conversation around the table had transitioned to financial issues.

Hot dog! Maybe I'd get more out of this evening than being nice to Ruby, although I would always be happy to lend a hand to the sisters. I reached for the tea pitcher and refilled glasses.

Vince said, "I'd be glad to review your finances and find ways to better invest your savings."

The hair on the back of my neck stood up.

Ruby ran her fingers along the single-strand pearl necklace she wore. "I don't want to do anything risky. At my age, there would be no way to recover."

Vince pointed at each of the sisters with his fork. "Y'all might be surprised."

Gaby shook her head. "I'm fine leaving things the way they are."

Rosalita elbowed Gaby. "Amen, Sister."

"It's a sure thing, trust me." Vince's eyes shone, and his smile reminded me of the bad wolf in the fairy tale.

My stomach churned. What kind of game was Vince playing? And right in front of his parents.

Ruby's fingers tightened on her necklace. "Daddy told us that there's no such thing as a sure thing."

Mrs. Moore touched her son's arm. "Darling, let's not discuss business at the dinner table. These ladies have prepared such a nice meal. Don't spoil it."

Vince glanced at his mother. "Yes, ma'am."

Mr. Moore dabbed his mouth with a napkin. "We're considering moving to Lutz to help Vince with the children. This seems like a right nice neighborhood. Tell us about it."

I returned the pitcher to the marble-top table in the corner and reached for the empty bowl of rolls. Once again in the kitchen, I removed more rolls from the warm oven and refilled the bowl. The doorbell rang. I placed the bowl on the corner of the table, then hurried to answer the door.

Rita stood on the stoop.

"Hi, Rita. Can I help you?"

"Where's Vince? Don't try to deny he's here. That's his black Escalade in the driveway."

"He's right in the middle of dinner."

Rita narrowed her eyes. "I thought you lived downtown."

"Yeah, I live on Main Street. This is Leisure Lane."

"Then what are you and Vince doing here? Is this a vacation rental?" With both hands, Rita pushed me back. I stumbled as she stormed to the dining room. "Vince!"

All talking ceased in the dining room.

I steadied myself, then hurried to catch up. "Rita, you need to leave."

"Ah, ha. The Nosy Nellies. What's going on, Vince?"

He stood. "Rita, have you lost your mind? These kind ladies invited us to dinner."

Fists on hips, the bank employee's gaze darted from one person to the next.

I plastered on my best smile and hoped to diffuse the uncomfortable scene. "I bet you're hungry. Why don't you come in the kitchen with me? I'll fix you a plate of this scrumptious food."

"No. Thank you, though." Her lips trembled, but it appeared her sanity may have returned. "Vince, please. We need to talk."

Ruby stood, but placed a hand on the back of her chair as if to steady herself. "Feel free to step out on the back patio. It should be lovely this time of the evening."

"Actually, if you don't mind, I'll walk Rita to her car." Vince's eye twitched so hard, he had to press his fingers against the visible throbbing. "Please, excuse me. This won't take long."

The two of them disappeared without another word.

I turned to assess the food situation. Empty plates littered the table. "Would anyone like seconds?"

Silence.

Ruby said, "How about dessert? I'll help Emma clear the table."

There was my cue. I gathered the dinner plates two at a time so as not to ding them. It took more trips to the kitchen, but there was no damage from rushing.

"I've started the coffee. Decaf, of course." Ruby leaned against the counter and crossed her arms. "I'd so hoped for a nice evening for the Moore family after all the sadness tied to Willow's passing."

"We're not going to allow Rita to ruin the evening. Let's serve dessert with a big ole smile like there wasn't an incident. What are we serving?"

"German blueberry cake. Sophie made it."

"Go back to your guests. I've got this."

Ruby shuffled toward the dining room and at the last second, lifted her chin. "Thanks, Emma."

Vince returned as I passed around dessert plates with slices of cake, and the evening finished with chatter and laughter. I washed and dried the porcelain plates. The tiny pink flowers and green leaves made the plate feel like a garden. If I ever collected china, this would be my pattern.

My mind drifted to Rita. She'd seemed to wonder if I was alone with Vince. Her distress told me she hadn't given up on a relationship with her boss despite the fact I'd seen her earlier with Dave. If Rita was still hung up on Vince, was it a powerful enough motive to murder Willow?

The red slingback shoe found inside the store made me believe the confrontation began in the back room. Had Willow seen her attacker approach? Or had the killer snuck up from behind? Did the lone shoe indicate she'd run right out of her pretty red slingback? The red shoe had haunted my dreams.

A headache formed over my eyes, but I continued cleaning.

"Emma dear, our guests have gone. Why don't you head home?"

It'd been a long day, but the thought of not finishing my task wasn't an option. "I'm almost through."

The refrigerator door opened. "The least I can do is send you home with leftovers."

"Thanks, Ruby."

She hummed an old jazz song until we completed our tasks.

"Here you go, my dear. Now be careful driving home."

"Yes, ma'am. I'll see you later." I took the paper plate of food and walked to Ms. Daisy on achy feet. The evening had turned out to be more of a good deed than picking up any clues.

My only real concern was Vince's offer to help the sisters invest their money. What had motivated him to make the proposal? Kindness? Or was there something sinister behind his proposition? Were the rumors about overseas bank accounts connected to him supposedly helping people invest in a sure thing? Was a Ponzi scheme involved? Or maybe he was only hiding his personal money from Willow.

If Vince had stolen money from customers, the bank Willow's family had started would be ruined. Had Willow discovered hidden money and accounts? If so, it'd make more sense for Willow to kill him than vice versa.

Chapter Thirty-Three

Cowboy's barking could be heard from the driveway. I shook off the chill running up my spine and entered the house, locking the door before checking on him. Nobody would sneak in the front door while I was distracted. "Cowboy, what's wrong?"

Rrowff. Rrowff.

I opened the door to his crate. "It's okay, boy. I'm here. Do you need to go potty? I wasn't gone that long." Four hours. Tops.

Cowboy zipped past me and nosed the back door.

"Hold on. You can go out." I turned on the floodlights but hurried to the pantry and grabbed the baseball bat Wyatt had gifted me. With more confidence, I stepped outside with my puppy.

Disaster greeted me. I gasped. The fenced-in area of my little flower farm had been destroyed. Dirt and flowers from raised beds had been tossed here, there, and yonder. Someone had pulled them up by the roots. Other plants appeared to have been stomped on and broken in half. A few had even been ground into the dirt like a smoker crushing a cigarette.

Cowboy ran the perimeter of the yard, barking.

"No, boy. Come back." With one hand gripping the bat and the other clasping my phone, I called the police.

Some might call it my comeuppance for trying to catch a killer. They could be right. I'd never had my home or land harmed before Willow's murder.

Why had I thought I could become a flower farmer and run my own business? An even bigger question was why had I thought I could help prove

181

Paige was innocent? Reading mysteries didn't mean I was qualified to solve a real-life murder.

"Ow!" A masculine voice yelled. There was movement in the shadows at the back corner, then a deep growl.

The man cussed.

Cowboy yelped.

A dark hooded figure appeared. The only thing preventing his escape was me.

"Stop." I swung the bat. Missed. The man shoved me to the ground and darted away. I landed on my backside but didn't drop my weapon. I stood and gathered my wits.

The gate clinked.

That settled it. I was smart enough not to chase the culprit into the darkness.

I stuffed the phone into the pocket of my black skirt and ignored the emergency operator. Gripping the bat with both hands, I walked across my yard in search of my puppy. "Cowboy, where are you?"

He appeared from the shadows, limping.

"Oh, Cowboy. You poor baby. Let's get you inside." I picked up my golden retriever puppy and trudged to the house. "This would be a good time for you to be a chihuahua. On the other hand, a little dog may not have frightened the intruder. You're such a brave boy. Lots of treats for you. I'm so sorry you got hurt."

Sirens sounded as I entered the kitchen with Cowboy. I opened the cookie jar of dog treats and gave him the biggest one. "Alright, let's see what's bothering you."

Chapter Thirty-Four

The police didn't provide much hope of catching the yard wrecker. The extent of damages wouldn't be completely evident until daylight.

Cowboy and I stood at the front door talking to the chief of police.

Matt stuffed a little spiral notebook in his shirt pocket. "While we try to solve a murder, your case won't get much attention. Contact your insurance agent about the damage, and see a doctor if you're hurt. I'll look into your case later."

"Matt, don't you think the two incidents could be connected?"

He laughed. "Not for one minute. See you 'round." He sauntered toward his car.

A tall figure appeared, running on the sidewalk. My heart stuttered. Nobody would try to hurt me with a police car in front of my house.

The runner was dressed in shorts, a T-shirt, and a ball cap. Not a hoodie, but that'd be easy enough to toss.

Matt looked toward the other man and spoke.

The runner waved to me while talking to the police chief.

Jake.

Woof. Woof. Cowboy barked a friendly greeting.

The two men parted, and Jake walked to me and loved on my dog. "Hey, there. I heard you got into a scuffle."

"Yeah. Matt says he's worked with lots of dogs and thinks Cowboy is okay." I ran my hand over Cowboy's head. "If he's limping tomorrow, I'll call Dr. Erb's office."

Jake stood. "I meant you. Are you okay?"

I glanced down at my dirty black blouse and skirt. "Yeah, but the baseball bat wasn't much help. I swung and missed. The thug pushed me down and got away."

Jake swiped at the perspiration beading his forehead. "I see you're safe, but are you okay? Physically and emotionally?"

I pressed my lips together. Leave it to Jake to ask how I was handling the invasion, or attack, or whatever you called it. My legs shook. "Do you want to come in? I can get you a glass of water."

"Sure." He followed me to the kitchen, grabbed a paper towel, and swiped his damp face. "You still haven't answered my question."

I poured two glasses of water and passed one to him. "I'm physically okay. Might need to go to the batting cage and work on my swing, though."

He chugged his water. "Emotionally? Don't try to convince me this didn't affect you. It's bound to have rocked your equilibrium."

I leaned against the counter, and Cowboy lay at my feet. "Honestly, I'm devastated. I've dreamed of being a flower farmer for years. Step by step, I bought this property with enough land to grow flowers. It took years of hard work, but I transformed my yard into raised beds to grow flowers. My goal was to grow more flowers every year. The countless hours and money poured into the land, and my business were demolished in a short time." The attack on my gardens felt like a knife to my heart.

"Sounds bad, but all situations look darkest before the morning."

I threw my shoulders back. "You know what? Standing around and feeling sorry for myself won't fix this problem." I stormed out of the kitchen and toward the bedroom.

"What are you going to do?"

"Change into something else, then see what I can salvage. Thanks for stopping by, Jake. If you don't mind, lock the door on your way out." In no time, I ditched my dirty catering outfit and pulled on my garden clothes. The sound of a door shutting comforted me. Jake wouldn't try to dissuade me from working on my yard in the dark. I didn't have time to argue.

After turning on all the upstairs lights, I ran downstairs and turned on every possible light. For protection. To discourage the previous intruder. "Cowboy, you need to rest your leg. Let's get you in the crate."

He obeyed without a whimper, and I rewarded him with a treat. "Good boy. I'd rather have your company outside, but you're injured. This is best for you."

My phone vibrated, and a message appeared from Jake. **I'm in your backyard.**

I walked out. "Jake, what are you doing? I thought you left."

He appeared with one handful of snapdragons and a clay flowerpot. "I thought I'd help, but it turns out I don't know exactly what to save. If it has roots, I'm picking the things up."

Tension eased from my shoulders. "Seems like you know what to do. I've got extra gloves in the shed. The hardware store was having a clearance sale, and I bought a bundle of all sizes." I walked to the small woodshed, where a bag of garden gloves sat in a box on a shelf.

"Go ahead and grab two extra-large pairs and a smaller one. Brett and Celia are on the way over with coffee and a hankering to help."

Sophie would've been the first person I'd have called if she didn't have a big Sunday order. "That's so nice." It was hard for me to ask for help, but my business was on the line. Pride wouldn't stop me from saving my flowers.

When the others arrived, we devised a system for sorting and replanting what I thought might survive the attack. Fighting doubts and worry was easier with a group surrounding me. Alone, I probably would've been a big ole blubbery mess.

After a few hours, Brett said, "Emma, we've tackled as much as I think we can in the dark. I can close the shop tomorrow, er, I guess today, and be back in a few hours to continue."

I stepped closer and touched his arm. "You'll do no such thing. Go home and get some sleep. You're still recovering from surgery, and yet you showed up and helped. I can't thank you enough for all you've done."

"It ain't no thing."

Celia joined us. "I'm heading home later today. My assistant started having contractions, and the doctor told her to stay in bed for a few days. Is there anything else I can do now?"

I hugged her. "No. Go get some sleep and enjoy what time you have left with Brett and of course, your brother. We've been through a lot in a short time."

She held me tight. "You can say that again. Take care, Emma."

Jake tugged off his gloves. "Why don't you crash at my apartment? That way, you won't wake any guests up at the b-and-b."

"Oh, I hadn't thought of that." Celia nodded. "Thanks for the offer, Jake."

"Let's roll. Emma, we'll see you later."

"Thanks again, y'all."

I locked myself inside and headed upstairs. After showering, I collapsed in my comfy bed. Every bone in my body ached, but after our hard work, there was a chance the attack on my gardens would only be a setback. Not an end to my business. I thanked God for good friends and promptly fell asleep.

Chapter Thirty-Five

After early service at the community church, Sophie followed me home to assess the damage in daylight. She sat on a chair in my bedroom, and I pulled out work clothes for each of us.

"I wish you'd called me. Sundays are my easy day. I only bake for special orders, and they're all picked up before ten."

"I knew you had a big order, and I didn't call the others. Jake saw the police lights when he was out for a run. He rallied the others to pitch in." I met her gaze. "Before you ask, I told Abby everything."

"Good, and I think it's a good thing Jake moved to Lutz."

"Yeah. Me, too." I tossed her a pair of socks. "Do you feel like I should have stuck with my job at the pharmacy?"

Sophie's brown eyes widened, and she fingered her long hair back into a ponytail as if getting ready to tackle something. "No. As long as I've known you, you've put others first. You raised your daughter, and her college expenses are taken care of. To work with flowers, well it's been your dream. Don't let the person who killed Willow also kill your dreams."

"Don't you see? Is my flower business a dream? Should I do the practical thing and go back to the pharmacy?"

My friend stood and fisted her hands. "No. If I'd done the practical thing, I'd be married to a man I didn't love and working as a phlebotomist in Munich. Pooh! That wasn't my heart's desire. So, I moved to Texas, where I can bake my lovely creations and see happy people."

I sank onto the edge of my bed. "I get your point. Flowers make people happy. They make me happy too."

"Precisely. Put on your big girl dungarees, and let's save your business."

"Yes, ma'am." I kicked it into high gear. Outside, I buried any doubts trying to surface. Friends had helped me through the night, and now Sophie pitched in.

If the killer was behind the devastation, he'd made his point. Back off the murder investigation.

No problemo. Only a couple of flourishing flower beds hadn't been destroyed, and I was grateful for that. The yard needed my full attention if I was going to survive as a flower farmer. Yes, I had a nest egg. It had been set aside to help me survive the lean beginning days of a new business, but not the proportion of this damage right off the bat. No more trying to solve murders.

Cowboy circled the yard before getting comfy in the shade. He moved slower than normal, but I didn't detect a limp.

Sophie cranked up country music on her portable speaker, and we walked to the shed. I handed my friend a new pair of pink garden gloves, and I slipped on my regular pair. An old Kenny Rogers tune crooned from the deck.

"I learned to speak English in school, but your country and Western music taught me American."

I bit back a smile. There were a few times it was obvious Sophie's native language wasn't English. "You should be proud of how fluently you speak."

"Thank you. Let's get working. Tell me what to do."

I led her to the back corner of the fenced-in area. It was where the intruder had hidden the night before. "Do you mind raking this raised bed while I look for any survivors?"

"I'd be happy to." She hummed with the music and moved the rake back and forth, leveling out the flower bed.

Starting at the fence, on my hands and knees, I searched clumps of dirt. If it had roots and appeared salvageable, it went in my save stack. My stomach churned at the number of dead plants. I tossed the ones beyond hope into a metal bucket.

"I think this area is ready to go. What next?" Sophie drank from her water bottle.

Standing, I stretched my back. "Looks good. Do you mind doing the same thing to the next bed?"

She nodded. "Sure."

While standing, it seemed a good time to throw the dead plants into my compost pile. As much as I longed to plant the flowers we'd saved during the night, it made more sense to continue to search for more survivors before the heat completely destroyed their chance to live.

The music transitioned to a Clint Black song, and I returned to sifting through the mess and chucking most of it.

Clink.

Cowboy appeared at my side.

"Hey, there. Whatcha doing?" I patted his side and left a dirty handprint from my glove on his golden coat. "Looks like a bath is in your future."

Sophie joined us and passed my Tervis to me. "I refilled our water bottles. What's up with Cowboy? He's been napping so contentedly."

"I think he heard a noise when I threw the last bit into my bucket." I dug through the waste. "Cowboy, you heard it too? Right?"

He barked.

"I didn't hear anything." Sophie took another swig from her water bottle.

My fingers plowed through discarded dirt and flowers until I discovered a hard object. "Here we go."

"What is it?"

I pulled out the suspicious item. "It's a green poker chip."

"You don't gamble."

"True." I studied the chip. The thing was dirty, but it didn't seem to be old. "Rusty thinks Gambler may have been involved in Willow's murder. Gamblers probably need poker chips." Goosebumps covered my arms.

"Are you okay? Your face is pale. Let's get you in the shade." Sophie reached out and touched my arm.

"Don't you see? Gambler must've torn up my yard. This is the evidence we need."

"Oh, Emma. You're not going to ignore the murder, are you? The sun must be getting to you worse than I thought. Come inside before you have a heat stroke. Or worse, before you stick your nose back into the murder investigation."

Cowboy circled us.

"You're right. I had planned to leave it alone, but I can't step away now. They've invaded my home turf, and we need to call Matt now that I have some evidence."

"What if he says it was buried a long time ago?"

"No doubt he'll argue it's not relevant, but he still needs to see this poker chip."

"Fine. You drink some of your water, and I'll call the chief of police."

I obeyed only to end her lecture. My mind raced as I sipped iced mint water. The chip was connected to the destruction of my yard, of that I had no doubt. I fanned myself with my straw cowboy hat. The next question was how, and Gambler seemed the most likely answer.

Chapter Thirty-Six

In case Chief Young laughed off my find, I took pictures of the green poker chip. Sitting in black rocking chairs on my front porch, we waited for the police chief. Cowboy snoozed near my feet, and his leash was attached to a harness. Last thing we needed was for my dog to injure himself again.

I pressed my fingers over my eyebrows, hoping for relief from a persistent headache. "Daylight's burning. What is taking him so long?"

Sophie rocked back and forth. "It's not an emergency. Do you want to get back to work?"

The pounding in my head insisted on action. "Yeah, we'll leave Matt a note to come around back."

Before the words left my mouth, the police chief pulled up in his official vehicle and backed into my driveway. He spoke into his radio communication mic before stepping out and walking toward us. "Ladies." His gaze lingered on Sophie longer than it did on me.

Interesting.

My friend smiled. "Hi, Matt."

I ushered the dog inside before facing the police chief. "Sorry to bother you again, but I found this in the yard." I passed Matt the plastic sandwich bag with the ceramic poker chip in it. "I was wearing garden gloves when I found it, so my fingerprints shouldn't be on it."

He squinted at the dirt-covered chip. "No telling how long it's been there."

"We expected you'd say that, but I've worked in the yard for years and have never seen any poker chips before. I don't believe it's a coincidence that this one shows up the day after my yard was trashed." Matt shook his head, and I rushed on. "It also strengthens my belief the person is involved in Willow's murder."

He ran a hand over his face. "How so?"

"The gambling man." Sophie's reply seemed to loosen the tense set of Matt's shoulders.

"Yeah. Remember Rusty said Gambler will do most anything to pay off his gambling debts? Even kill a person to wipe away what he owes the bad guys."

"We do have a couple of cold cases with no solid leads. As much as I doubt this will be connected to Willow's murder, we'll try to get prints off it. Anything else?"

"Oh, um, no. Thanks." His agreement surprised, scratch that, it shocked me.

"I need to shove off. See you two later."

Sophie waved. "Bye, Matt."

"See you later, Sophie." After he drove away, I faced my friend. "Are you sweet on him?"

The reddening of her face had nothing to do with the heat. "He's a customer. Nothing more."

"If you say so."

"Pooh. I'm here to help repair your yard, not discuss romantic nonsense." Sophie had lived in Lutz for over a decade and only dated casually.

Instead of making her uncomfortable, I led the way to the gate. "Despite finding a clue, we've lost time. I'll spend the next hour scouring for surviving flowers, then start planting what I can."

192

Chapter Thirty-Seven

Cosmos, bluebonnets, blue sage, and some marigolds had survived. I planted and watered all the survivors.

I trimmed the forsythia bush, and there were a few stems usable for flower arrangements. A spasm ripped across my back. It was time to call it a day, especially since I'd begun the night before.

Marigolds would be at the top of my list for new plants. There were so many festivals in Texas involving the flower, it was imperative I have plenty.

I trudged inside with Cowboy. Wasn't thirty-eight too young to feel this sore? Only a hot shower would do after a full day trying to repair damage. Afterward, I slathered arthritis cream all over my aching joints, then set out to find supper. My body needed protein and carbs. Amalfi's Pizzeria seemed like the perfect answer.

There wasn't much traffic in town, and most of the shops were closed. Not wanting my muscles to cramp, I walked. Inside the restaurant, the hostess led me to a table for two with a cheerful red-and-white checked tablecloth. The walls featured locally sourced barn wood, adding to the warm ambience.

"Is this seat taken?" Jake pointed to the empty chair across from me.

"No, and I'd love some company. Are you alone?"

He settled into the black chair. "Yes, ma'am. Celia had to leave, but I predict she'll be back sooner rather than later."

"There are three possible reasons for a quick return. To run the bookstore for Paige, spend time with you, or hang out with Brett."

He laughed. "No matter how she tries to disguise the truth, it's all about

Brett."

The waitress returned with a basket of bread, and we placed our orders.

I dipped a piece into the bowl of olive oil and balsamic vinegar. "Have you come to peace about a relationship between those two?"

"I couldn't be happier. They're good together, and I trust Brett not to break Celia's heart."

"Good for you, Jake. Be sure to tell them so they can officially date."

He shook his head. "How was your day?"

"Interesting. I even found a possible clue to the person who demolished my yard." I shared about my discovery of the poker chip.

"Kudos to Matt for following up on a lead." Jake pressed his lips together.

"Wow. Just, wow. I kinda felt the same way. Any word on a job for you with the department?"

"Nope." He reached for a piece of bread.

"Are you worried?"

"Honey, I learned years ago that worrying won't change a thing."

"That'll preach."

"Amen." He chuckled.

I laughed with him. "How long can you keep working for Brett?"

"Not sure, but there's still the option of restoring old homes. Who knows? I might decide to work on my own as a fix-it man."

"You could probably make a killing. Most construction guys only want to tackle big projects that pay big bucks. I mean, I get it, but still. Sometimes you only need somebody to replace a toilet, fix a leaky sink, or rip out old carpet and lay down new flooring."

"Touché."

"Actually, I need a person to help me repair a drip zone of my lawn sprinkler system. Whoever messed with my plants also ruined the irrigation system."

"I'll be happy to take a look."

"Oh, thanks. I wasn't hinting, just stating a fact." My face grew warm. He probably thought of me as one of those women who couldn't do anything for themselves.

"I didn't suspect you were."

The waitress appeared with a large plate of spaghetti and turkey meatballs for me. Chicken parmesan for Jake. He inhaled his dinner before I was half-finished.

Jake patted his belly. "I've pretty much settled into the apartment, but I haven't stocked up on food. I didn't realize how hungry I was until I spotted you walking this way."

"You do have a nice view of town."

Wayne Johns entered the restaurant and sat at the bar. The operations manager of the farmers' market placed an order with Ethan Tucker, the bartender, before looking at the menu.

Daniel Moore followed Wayne to the bar, but he stopped under the sign for to-go orders.

"Excuse me one minute. I want to say hi to Vince's dad." I crossed the room, then tapped the older gentleman on the shoulder. "Mr. Moore, how are you?"

He wore black slacks, and a white starched button-down shirt, and looked younger than his eighty-something age. "Emma, it's nice to see you."

"Thanks. It's good to see you, too. Are you and Mrs. Moore okay?"

"Yes, we're managing the best we can. But what about you? I heard there was an incident at your home. An invasion or something?"

How had he heard the news? I'd hardly told anyone. "All of my yard was ruined, but how did you know?"

Mr. Johns interrupted. "Emma, are you going to be able to run your booth Saturday? I got a ceramics lady from Austin who'd like it. We got to keep customers coming."

Of all the nerve. I lifted my chin. "Don't worry about me. I'll be there with flowers to sell." Hopefully, I wasn't turning into a big fat liar, but what kind of person kicked you when you were down?

"Okay. I'll see you bright and early Saturday morning." He knuckle-rolled a black poker chip with the fingers of his right hand.

Mr. Moore cleared his throat. "I go to the police station every day to check on the progress of catching Willow's killer. She was like a daughter

195

to us, and the assassin must be caught."

I stepped closer, turning my back to Mr. Johns. "Dealing with Willow's murder must be a dreadful strain on you and the family."

His graying curly hair didn't move when he nodded. "Mary keeps telling me not to bother the police. We should focus on Vince and the children, and she's correct."

"But?" Did he know his son was a possible suspect?

"Aw, dear. I can read your face. It makes sense the cops would focus on Vince, but my son is innocent. I want to make sure the police explore other suspects."

The bartender appeared with a paper bag and a receipt.

When they finished the exchange, I said, "Please tell your wife hello for me. Have a nice evening."

"Be careful, Emma. I'd hate to see anything worse happen to you." His gentle smile assured me the man wasn't making a threat. "I think of you as a friend."

"Thanks." I returned to Jake. "Mr. Moore believes Vince is innocent."

Jake propped his arms on the table and leaned forward. "I think most parents don't want to believe their child is a killer. But there are killers, and all of them had parents. They can't all be right."

"I get it. No matter how much I like Mr. Moore, Vince will remain on my list of suspects because he had the most to gain from Willow's death."

He quirked an eyebrow. "I can't help but notice you didn't mention Vince's mother."

"She's more closed off, but she does love her family. And she's protective. When Sophie and I offered to pick clothes for the burial, Mrs. Moore took Christine to another room. No matter what happens with Vince, the kids are lucky to have their grandparents around."

"What about Willow's family?"

The restaurant was filling up.

I placed my forearms on the table and leaned forward. "My theory is Willow's family believes Vince is the killer. They are probably meeting with lawyers to gain custody of the children."

CHAPTER THIRTY-SEVEN

"By staying away, they won't tip their hand."

"Yep. That's the best theory I can come up with."

"Works for me." Jake crossed his arms. "What do you say we blow this joint?"

"Sounds like a good idea." I held back a yawn. My body craved rest, and I could put more thought into the murder Monday.

Chapter Thirty-Eight

J ake walked me home and even carried my box of leftover spaghetti. He leaned against the porch's half-brick-half-white-fiberglass column while I unlocked the door.

A flash of color caught my attention. Near a black rocker sat three pots of dahlias. "Did you put these here?"

Jake shook his head. "No, I was with you."

Well, duh. "They weren't here when I left."

"There's an envelope." Jake pointed. "Do you want me to open it?"

"I must be getting paranoid." I reached for the small card. "Oh, it's from the Nelle sisters. They heard about my troubles and wanted to help. That's so sweet. They are really careful with their money, and I can't believe they brought these over."

"Those ladies are something else."

"Yes, they are." I smiled. "Would you like to come in?"

"I'd prefer to see what's going on with your sprinklers. Fixing your drip system is one less stress you need."

"Okay, come on back." I took the spaghetti and placed it in the refrigerator.

Jake walked to the backyard with the pots of dahlias, while I let Cowboy out of his crate. We joined Jake in back.

"Hey, I don't mind studying the water problem if you want to change, so you can plant those now."

"Thanks. Be right back." The sun was setting, but it wasn't dark yet. I wasted no time changing clothes, and I turned on the backyard floodlights before exiting my home. I gathered the flowers and headed to the shed, where I grabbed gloves and a hand trowel. Cowboy stood by Jake, watching his every move. "You need a dog."

"Doubt Paige will let me have one."

"Good point." I carried the three pots to one of the raised beds and went to work planting.

Jake picked up a stick and threw it for Cowboy to retrieve. "I believe I know how to fix it, but it'll require a trip to the hardware store."

"Tell me what to get, and I'll buy it."

Cowboy returned the stick to Jake and lay down.

"He seems better." Jake knelt beside my golden retriever and rubbed his side.

"I agree, but back to the hardware shopping list."

"If it's all the same to you, I'd like to explore. There could be something that works better than what I think is needed." Jake twirled the stick between his fingers before throwing it again.

Chills danced up my spine. I stood and faced Jake. "I might know who Gambler is."

His eyes widened. "Don't keep me in suspense. Who?"

"Wayne Johns. At the bar, he rolled a poker chip between his fingers. Why would he keep a chip instead of cashing it in? Same question about the man who did all the damage back here."

"Good point. Maybe they gamble so much that they don't need to cash them in." Jake stood and threw the stick for my dog again.

"Like hold on to them until the next event?"

Cowboy returned to Jake and dropped the stick at his feet.

Jake threw it again. "Yeah. It saves time if they arrive at a casino with the chips, but there aren't any casinos near Lutz. However, there are some sweet travel deals to go to Vegas for a weekend of gambling. Every casino has a unique design on their poker chips, and they won't accept anything else."

I stabbed the dirt with the hand trowel and dug a hole. "Why leave Vegas with chips if they're worthless other places?"

"You might promise yourself a return visit, and the chips are a reminder." Jake crossed his arms. "There's another possibility. There could be a secret gambling club in town or nearby. Sometimes the owners bribe cops to look the other way."

"Why?"

Cowboy dropped the stick at Jake's feet, then walked to the patio.

"It can bring money to the community. Say a woman wants to visit the weekend sales, and the husband doesn't. He might agree if he enjoys Texas Hold'em, blackjack, slots, or whatever."

I placed one bundle of dahlias in the hole and patted dirt and compost around them. "Interesting. Rusty stated Gambler will kill someone for enough money to pay off his gambling debts. If he killed Willow, why would he still be carrying around poker chips?"

"To keep him in the cycle of addiction. Kill a person, or commit various crimes, and your debt is forgiven. The person behind the crime might give Gambler a poker chip as a bonus for a job well done. Now he's got a little extra to gamble with. He can't ignore the chip, luring him back to the secret gaming room."

While processing the information, I finished transplanting the colorful flowers. "I've never heard of a secret gaming room."

Jake said, "It could be a room in the back of another business, say, the hardware store or a gas station. On the other hand, it could be in a barn or a ranch house. The key is keeping it a secret from the cops."

"Gotcha." I gathered my belongings and took them to the shed. After I put the tools away, we walked silently to the patio and sat in the bistro chairs. "We've got a murder. There are possible links to drugs and gambling. What do you think?"

"I promised to help you catch the killer, but the safest thing would be for you to walk away."

"I considered walking away more than once, but like the poker chip luring a gambler back to the table, clues keep appearing, and I'm sucked right back into the investigation."

Chapter Thirty-Nine

Sipping chamomile tea in bed that night, I reached for my murder notebook from the white wicker bedside table. Turns out I preferred writing my thoughts on paper because it allowed me to doodle. Drawing seemed to help me think better.

If I was going to catch the killer, I needed to come up with a solid motive. A reason that made sense. Was it Willow's upcoming divorce? A jealous girlfriend? Could Paige have been the target, making it a case of mistaken identity? Was it related to drugs? Gambling? Or something else?

My gut nagged me. There was a connection to gaming, even if Gambler wasn't guilty.

Besides discovering the motive, I needed to save Emma's Flowers. In some ways, it seemed much more doable. Solving a murder had never been on my radar, no matter how many mysteries I'd read.

Who was Gambler? Wayne Johns? Possibly Dave? Maybe even Kevin? Or someone I'd never met? Was the poker chip I'd found in the backyard a clue or a red herring?

Leaning back into the soft pink throw pillows, I tried to replay the conversation with Rusty in my mind about Gambler.

Local legend.

That was it. Rusty claimed Gambler was a local legend. Did that rule out Dave and Kevin? They weren't locals, and Dave had been in prison. Or was it a twist on copycat killers? The real killer could leave clues to make the police believe it was Gambler.

If Rusty hadn't mentioned Gambler, I never would be sitting here debating if the killer was local or not. Wayne Johns wouldn't have popped up on my radar either.

A squeak from outside brought me fully alert. Leaping from the bed, I reached for the baseball bat, regretting I hadn't practiced my swing yet. Still, it was my best option for a weapon.

I slipped into the kitchen. Cowboy was restless in his crate. Once I opened his door, he made a straight line to the back door and peered through the glass. My palms grew damp, holding the bat while looking out the kitchen window. *Lord, keep us safe.*

No thugs were going to destroy my yard again, but I wouldn't be stupid. It was pitch dark, and easy to get blindsided. First things first. I turned on the floodlights.

A hooded figure stood on the patio. He looked in my direction.

My heart skyrocketed to my throat.

Had he seen me? No. The kitchen lights were off. Time stopped. Cowboy panted.

Shadows and the hood prevented me from identifying the intruder. He stared in my direction for a moment, then he hightailed it out of my yard.

My legs shook like leaves. Exhaustion hit me full force. "Cowboy, you're sleeping with me tonight. We'll keep all the lights on. Inside and out. And I'll hold the phone in one hand. Baseball bat in the other hand."

Chapter Forty

Monday morning, I placed a cup of coffee and a plump blueberry muffin on Chief Young's desk. No need to insult him with a cruller because of the cliché about cops and donuts. "Good morning."

"Emma, what brings you my way this fine morning?" He reached for the coffee and removed the lid.

"Cream and two sugars. Brett assures me it's the way you like it."

"Perfect, but you dodged my question."

I sat in the chair across from his desk. "How many murders have been linked to Gambler?"

"We have a few cold cases, but we don't plan to link them to this mysterious gambler legend. Are you asking because you found a poker chip in your yard?" He kept eye contact with me as he sipped his coffee.

"Yes. I saw Wayne Johns with a poker chip last night. Does Lutz have an illegal gambling problem? Like secret casinos or anything suspicious?"

"There are always rumors of such, and I've busted up a few clandestine Texas Hold'em tournaments."

"Is that all?" His answer would not defeat me.

"Yes, ma'am. Don't worry yourself one little bit about the murder investigation. We're working on leads, and we will catch the killer."

"What about the first forty-eight-hour window of time? We're way past that."

"Emma, many crimes are solved after weeks, months, even years of investigation. Before we arrest a suspect, we need to be positive we have gathered enough evidence to convict them." He took another drink of his coffee.

"You arrested Paige."

"She's out."

My pulse leapt. "What? How?"

"A witness came forward. He was on his morning run around the same time as Paige. The man even confirmed Paige was wearing an Agatha Christie shirt." Matt set the cup on the desk. "Anything else?"

"Yeah, somebody was in my yard again last night."

The police chief hunched over his desk. "Did you report it?"

"No. He ran off after I turned on the floodlights." I explained the situation.

"Next time, call us. In fact, do you know how to avoid any more incidents?"

I nodded. "Quit looking into Willow's murder."

"Exactly."

"Okay. Thanks for your time, Matt."

He ushered me to his office door. "Okay, as in, you'll drop it?"

"I meant to step away after the goon ruined my yard, then I found the poker chip. Why is it so hard to figure out who killed Willow?"

"For starters, you're not trained. Work on your flowers, Emma."

"Thanks for your time, Matt." I left the building and hopped into Ms. Daisy. On a normal day, I would've walked to the police station to protect the environment. Today was going to be my first attempt to improve my swing at the batting cages. Lutz Park, situated on the edge of town, had baseball fields, soccer fields, a swimming pool, running paths, and a playground. There were also batting cages near the baseball diamonds. Each area was neatly separated from the others and had individual parking lots. While Lutz was a small town without a lot of big city amenities, we enjoyed sporting events.

I drove through town with the windows down, enjoying the breeze. Brett Eldredge crooned on the local country station, and I made it a duet. As long as nobody rode with me, I was happy to sing full throttle.

It didn't take long to reach my destination. Once parked in the baseball area, I grabbed a cup of quarters, my bike helmet, and my Louisville Slugger.

Not that I wanted to slug anyone, but it was time to learn to protect myself. Two nights in a row, a stranger had been in my backyard. I'd escaped harm each time, but my luck could be running out.

A father and son worked together at the first cage, so I moved to the one farthest away. I already had the wrong kind of helmet, there was no need to embarrass myself more than necessary.

I selected the softball setting, fastened my bike helmet, and took a few practice swings. Before I knew it, the ball whizzed past me. My sister and I had been forced to attend my brother Wyatt's baseball games. I adjusted my stance to the way I remembered the boys standing. The ball flew by twice more without me connecting. In fact, my allowance of pitches ended before I hit a ball.

Adding more quarters, I tried again and was thrilled at my first foul ball. When I finally hit a ball straight, er make that forward, my spirits soared.

Clapping shocked me, but I focused on the next ball coming my way. The idea of the young boy and his dad watching intimidated me to no end. When my round ended, I turned.

"Looks like you're getting better." Jake clapped.

"What are you doing here?"

"I was out for a run and saw you drive by. As much trouble as you attract, I decided to investigate."

"Were you worried I'd run into the killer?"

"It's hard to say, but I am happy you're practicing your swing."

As embarrassing as the situation was, at least Jake hadn't laughed at me. "I don't really know what I'm doing."

"Want a few pointers?"

"It couldn't hurt, but it's a Monday morning. Shouldn't you do something more important?"

"There's nothing more important than teaching you to protect yourself. Next time you try batting practice, you need to borrow my helmet. It's legit for protecting you from a flying ball." He entered the space, and the lesson commenced. First problem was the way I held my hands. My stance was another issue. The last item Jake addressed was putting strength in my swing.

After the pointers, he trotted outside the wire cage. I deposited more quarters into the machine, then stepped into the designated batter's box. A whiff, a foul, and a bunt were all progress.

"Atta girl. You've got this." Jake clapped.

I took a deep breath and swung at the next ball, hitting it as far as the cage allowed.

"Way to go, Emma."

I stepped back and smiled at him. "Thanks."

"Watch out."

I jumped out of the way of a ball and laughed. "That was close."

"Focus."

His tone sounded like my dad when he had worked with Wyatt on sports. I moved back to my position and swung at the rest of the balls with mixed results.

"Good job, Emma. Did you ever play softball?"

I stepped out of the batting cage and laughed. "No. Sports weren't my thing, but I can cheer for others who play. Let me guess. You were the high school quarterback."

"Are you thinking I was a dumb jock?"

My face grew hot. "No, I'd never think that about you. Athletes—"

"Don't blow a gasket. I was just joshing with ya."

I removed my bike helmet. "Don't make me come after you with this bat. Now that I know how to swing it, I'm a force to be reckoned with."

"Let's hope it never comes to that. Come on, I'll walk you over to Ms. Daisy." He chuckled.

I matched his pace. "Jake, there's something I need to tell you."

"Your ominous tone doesn't make me feel good. What happened?"

As we walked, I explained the incident from the night before.

"Dag gumit." His face reddened. "What do you plan to do?"

"Go to the hardware store and ask Buddy for security suggestions."

"May I come with you?"

I pointed at him. "See there? You're not a dumb jock."

"I'm not following."

"You know it's proper to say, 'may I,' instead of 'can I.'

"Or I might've gotten lucky. What do you say?" He waggled his eyebrows.

"Let's go see what we can find." I hopped in the driver's seat. When we pulled out of the parking area, Nick Jones followed us in his work truck, riding my bumper. "Jake, we've got company."

Chapter Forty-One

I drove out of the park, turning toward town and the hardware store. Nick turned his bug mobile the other way, and the tension in my shoulders disappeared. "Why would Nick be in the park so early in the morning?"

Jake drummed his fingers on his knee. "Is it possible he comes out here to pray or meditate?"

I laughed so hard I snorted. "Not a chance."

"You sound confident in your answer. So do you believe he killed Willow?"

"I don't think so. On the other hand, Tess Carranza, the librarian, believes he killed his first wife. Wait a minute. According to Rusty, Gambler is a local legend. Two men on my list who are also long-time residents are Wayne Johns and Nick."

"We need a believable motive and evidence. Although, if we can find good evidence, we won't need to figure out the motive."

"But if we determine the motive, it might be easier to find evidence. It's a vicious cycle." I parked in front of the local hardware store across the street from the bookstore. "Money is my first thought. Or the motive could be a deadly case of mistaken identity if Nick meant to kill Paige because she rejected him."

"I've never been comfortable with the mistaken identity theory. I believe Willow was the target. Money seems plausible. As far as this morning goes, Nick could've been killing time in the park between appointments because he doesn't have a full schedule. If his business is struggling, maybe he'd take money to murder Willow. It's no secret Willow worked on Fridays."

"Yep. Do you remember Paige had asked Nick to schedule enough time to spray the store and the apartment? Suppose he picked Friday, knowing it'd give him access to Willow? He could've created the perfect opportunity to be alone with her in order to kill her." I ran my hand over the steering wheel, then met Jake's gaze. "I asked Matt about cold cases this morning. He's not saying if Gambler is a suspect in any of them."

"Girl, you come off looking sweet and innocent, but underneath, you're full of grit and determination. It must've taken a good bit of nerve to question the police chief."

"I discovered my husband wasn't faithful while I was pregnant. Determined to work on my marriage, I didn't divorce him. Bo's real love was heroin, not another woman. Although there were plenty of those." I paused at the look of pity crossing Jake's face. "I'm not telling you this, so you'll feel sorry for me. I'm used to solving problems. When I became a single parent, it was time to put away foolish dreams. Instead of feeling helpless, I became a survivor and did whatever it took to provide for my daughter." I ran my hand over the steering wheel

"You should be right proud of yourself."

"Starting my flower farm was a big leap. Instead of dealing with life's blows, I decided to take some initiative. Protecting my property is one step to being proactive against intruders. Let's go see what Buddy has."

"Sounds like a plan."

Dave Smith exited the hardware store with a brown paper bag and bolt cutters. Rita sat in the passenger seat of his black Audi. The air conditioner must've been on full blast because her hair blew back while she studied her cell phone.

We entered Hewitt's Hardware Store.

Jake elbowed me. "At this rate, we're going to see all of your suspects in one morning."

"Ha, ha. Although, it makes me think I need to hurry and buy supplies to protect my home and yard."

"Lead the way, Sunshine."

Jake first picked out items for my sprinkler system. I looked around until

Buddy finished waiting on a customer. At last, the three of us discussed security systems.

Anxiety beat in my belly like a big bass drum. I agreed to what Buddy and Jake suggested. Jake assured me he could help with the installation. After seeing Nick, Dave, and Rita in the past hour, it couldn't happen fast enough.

I paid for a new lock that was near impossible to tamper with. It was perfect for the gate. Buddy suggested spikes be applied on top of my fence and gate to discourage people from jumping over it. Once more, I agreed. The men even convinced me to purchase a home security system with an app for notifications on my phone.

Jake helped me load the items into my Silverado. "If you don't mind, I'll swing by my apartment for a quick shower. My toolbox is there too, and it'll make the work easier."

"Are you sure you have time to help?"

He lifted his right eyebrow. "It's no problem. See you in a few."

The drive home was quick and easy. The sight of my gate hanging on the hinges turned my fear to anger. The lock had been cut off. No more would I play the role of cowering scaredy cat, hiding in fear. If the goons planned to get rid of me, they better be ready to fight.

Layers of protection was my plan. Locks, spikes, and a security system with cameras. In addition, I had my dog and God.

If the bad guys tried to attack again, I'd be ready.

Chapter Forty-Two

As often as I'd been to the bank with flower arrangements, there was no need to ask for directions to Rita's office. I stormed through the lobby, down the hall, and entered the room. She looked up from her desk.

"Emma, what's wrong?" Rita raised her eyebrows, but I wouldn't fall for her innocent act.

"What's wrong? What's wrong? Are you kidding me?" Fury swept through me.

Rita hustled around her desk and shut the door with a firm click. "Calm down. We can figure it out. Have a seat."

"I'd rather stand." No chance I'd give her the advantage of standing over me.

"How about some water?" She reached for a room-temperature water bottle and passed it to me. "I heard somebody ruined your yard. Are you upset about the financial setback? I'm sure the bank will assist you with a small business loan."

I twisted the top off the bottle and took a deep drink. How could Rita act so innocent? "I saw you at the hardware store with Dave. He bought bolt cutters. When I just now got home, the lock on my gate had been cut off."

"Are you suggesting that Dave cut your lock?"

"It can't be a coincidence. Why are you out to destroy me?"

"We bought the bolt cutters for Vince, er, Mr. Moore."

I took another drink and paced in the small area. "I know about your feelings for Vince. Did you kill Willow so you two could be together?"

She glared at me. "Listen up, Emma. Dave is back in my life, and Vince is too old for me."

"Don't try to fool me. I heard you talking to Vince at his house. You're in love with him."

Rita's nostrils flared. "Dave bought the bolt cutters for Vince to get into a storage unit. Vince doesn't know where Willow put the key. He's there now with Dave, and together they're trying to get in. We didn't do anything to your yard. Besides, we weren't even in town Saturday night. We went to see the Rangers play baseball."

Ah ha. "I never said when it happened."

Rita crossed her arms and leaned against her desk. "Grow up, Emma. Lutz is a small town. Most everybody knows your yard was destroyed Saturday night."

Good point, but I wasn't ready to give up. "So you and Dave didn't cut the lock off my gate before meeting Vince?"

She ran her hands over her skirt. "You know me better than that. We've worked together for years, both here and at the pharmacy. Pull yourself together, Emma." Her tone and demeanor had done a one-eighty.

I studied her expression, but my skills of reading people failed me. There was no proof she and Dave cut the lock off my gate. It was best for me to proceed with caution. If only I could pull weeds and smell the flowers, I'd calm down quicker. It wasn't an option, so I gulped the rest of my water and faced Rita. "The stress must be getting to me. Sorry."

She patted my arm and walked me to the office door. "You need to pay attention to your new puppy, your business, and that gorgeous man helping at the coffee shop. Forget about Willow's murder, and life will be easier."

"You're right. See you later." I walked home at a much slower pace, replaying the conversation in my mind. What had she meant saying my life would be easier if I ignored the murder? Was it a threat?

Goosebumps covered my arms. Rita never answered my question about killing Willow.

"Emma!"

I jumped and turned. Jake. It was only Jake. Relief flooded through my body. "Hey." My voice shook.

He met me at the street corner. "Don't 'hey' me. I about had a heart attack when I got to your place and couldn't find you."

"I'm sorry." This apology was sincere, unlike the one I'd uttered to Rita.

"Your truck is sitting in the driveway, and the gate is wide open. In fact, the lock was cut off. I tried to call, but you didn't answer."

I looked at my silenced phone. Five missed calls from Jake. Mr. Calm, Cool, and Collected must truly have been concerned. "I really am sorry. Let's finish walking home, and I'll tell you all about it."

He crossed his arms and glared at me. Ever so slowly, the frown disappeared.

"I've never seen you so upset. What happened to my easy-going friend?"

"Honey, when a friend is in danger, I shift from carefree to agitated in a heartbeat. Don't do that to me again." He gave me a gentle hug, and I hugged him back right there on the sidewalk next to the stop sign.

Chapter Forty-Three

Jake's anger calmed my distress. I believed he suffered from PTSD. Maybe all veterans did to varying degrees. How could they not if they'd put their lives on the line for our freedom?

Wearing my straw cowboy hat to shade my face, I stood on a step ladder and screwed a spike strip onto the top of my fence. Jake was installing security cameras around the back patio. We'd decided on three for the backyard, one for the side with the gate, and another camera on the front porch. It was probably overkill, but Buddy gave me a deal because a newer model had recently come out. I was a sucker for a bargain and charged the entire purchase to my credit card.

If—no when—my business expanded, I would move the fencing to allow for more growing space and adjust the safekeeping measures. As soon as we finished buffing up the security of my home, I needed to work on my gardens.

A vehicle backfired, and Cowboy barked. The dog raced to the gate, then growled.

I followed. "Cowboy, calm down." Had Jake fallen or something?

Nick Jones stood in my sideyard, staring at my puppy.

"What are you doing here? Also, what were you doing at the park this morning?"

Nick frowned. "None of your business."

"You were following me on my way out."

"If I was, it's a coincidence. Nothing more, and don't be reporting me to the cops." The pest control man stomped away.

"Are you friends with Rita Flores?"

"That's none of your business either." He turned and walked toward the road.

I watched until Nick drove away. He hadn't answered my questions. Neither had Rita. The difference was the subtlety of Rita's avoidance.

"Who are you talking to?" Jake's presence shocked me so bad I jumped.

"Nick Jones." I pointed.

Jake fisted his hands. "Was he harassing you?"

"Not as bad as last time. He said it was a coincidence we were leaving the park at the same time today. He also didn't tell me why he was here or if he's friends with Rita."

Jake's posture relaxed. "It could be a coincidence we were there at the same time. Then again, it could've been intentional." Jake looked at me with his shiny brown eyes.

"Earlier, I asked Rita if she killed Willow. She was cagey, changing the subject and never giving me an answer. It doesn't seem possible she killed Willow herself."

Jake crossed his arms, and his triceps bulged against the sleeves. "Why?"

"Rita is tiny and always wears high heels. Willow ran right out of her flat slingbacks, making me think the killer chased her. I don't see how Rita could've run in her high heels."

"Interesting point, but I've never worn heels. It probably isn't impossible."

I was five feet nine inches and didn't wear heels often. "I might try it. I've got a sweet pair of heels I bought for Abby's graduation in May."

"Hold up. Your experiment can come later. Right now, we need to finish protecting your place. We definitely need a camera on this side of the house. Can you behave if I let you out of my sight?"

"I'll go back to applying the spikes to the fence." I returned to the ladder and screwed in the next section.

Cowboy lay on the ground near me.

Jake whistled a country tune while walking away.

The disadvantage to securing my home was it lessened my chances of catching the culprit. On the other hand, staying alive was mighty important.

I pulled a screw out of my pocket and focused on the task. Solving Willow's murder could wait.

Chapter Forty-Four

After Jake and I finished securing my home, I changed into clean clothes and washed my face. Feeling fresher, Jake and I walked to town. "How do you like your apartment?"

"It'll work for now. Yesterday I bought a sound machine at the hardware store, and it helps with the noise. One day I'd like a little place in the country where it's nice and quiet. The only other downside to an apartment in town is having to park my Sequoia on the street."

I pushed my straw cowgirl hat back on my head to see Jake better. "You don't feel cramped?"

"Nah, it's good." He stopped by the bookstore. "I'll run my tools up to my apartment and meet you in the store in a bit."

"Sounds good." I entered Paige's Turn Bookshop. The place was as empty as a tomb.

Paige stepped out from behind the counter. "Hi, Emma. Please, tell me some good news."

I hugged my friend. "I'd say the best news is you're out of jail."

Paige trudged to the sitting area in front and collapsed onto the loveseat. "True, but Chief Young admitted he has lingering doubts."

I sat in the nearest chair and crossed my legs. "As long as he doesn't arrest you again, I wouldn't worry about him. After all, you've got an eyewitness."

"It'll be just my luck for the cops to give the witness an eye exam, and he'll fail."

"No way. The guy recognized you and knew what you were wearing. That's got to be a good thing."

"Even if you're right, my business is suffering. If Jake wasn't renting the apartment, I don't know what I'd do right now." She sat straighter. "If only my car hadn't broken down and needed such expensive repairs. That was the beginning of my downfall. My rainy-day emergency fund was a joke. The auto shop depleted my checking account, and I had to dip into my savings. That's why I was so desperate for a loan. Spring is here, and shoppers are returning to Lutz. I only needed enough to tide me over."

"I'm sure the timing was bad for Willow, too, with her upcoming divorce hearing. I feel certain after those proceedings, Willow would've taken over the bank and given you a loan."

"Yeah. Maybe." She fiddled with her wedding ring. "Jake's so nice. He paid me for six months upfront, and that's huge. Why did you stop by?"

"Jake really is nice." I smiled. "Can I look at the back room again? What if there's a clue we missed?"

"As long as the police kept the store closed, I can't imagine they missed a thing. But sure. Why not?" She led me to the private space for employees.

The area was well-lit and organized. "Are you up for book club tonight?"

"I don't think so. Sorry."

"It's not a problem. We'll meet next week." I studied the back room. The place was much neater than it had been the day of the murder. It was easy to identify the table where Paige opened packages of books before loading them onto the single-sided teal book cart. There was also a desk with three stacks of papers, and an Agatha Christie pencil holder full of colorful pens and markers. "Paige, do you own a gun?"

She leaned back against the table. "Yes. According to Chief Young it's the same kind of gun that was used to kill Willow. They're testing it now."

I gulped, wishing I'd used more tact. "That's a good thing, right? It'll help prove you're innocent."

"Maybe. Who knows what the cops believe?"

"Why were your tools scattered around here?"

"The night before Willow's murder, I used the hammer to adjust some shelves for a new display highlighting various Texas mystery authors. It was late when I finished, and I didn't put away the tools." Her voice grew softer with each word to the point I stepped closer to hear the words better. "I've wondered if Willow tried to use a screwdriver or hammer to defend herself?"

"Interesting. Do the police believe the initial encounter happened in here?"

"Yeah." Was I remembering correctly? "At least, I think so."

The bell over the bookstore door interrupted our conversation.

"I'll be back." She clomped away.

I surveyed the work area. How had Paige felt that Thursday night before Willow's murder? Was she exhausted from working on the shelves? I could imagine Paige finishing the project in the store and deciding to deal with her mess the next day. Knowing Willow worked the front of the store on Fridays, it made sense she could put the task off.

What if the person who murdered Willow had only come to Paige's Turn Bookshop to talk to Willow? Reason with her? Work on some kind of compromise?

It could've been Vince wanting to discuss the divorce, or it could've been anybody. Willow and the person must have argued. Willow might have refused to back down.

Nobody had reported a gunshot Friday morning. So there must've been a silencer. It didn't seem likely a person who carried a gun for protection would also have a silencer on it.

"What are you doing back here?" Jake's voice yanked me from my musings.

I jumped. "You're as stealthy as a cat."

"It's saved my life a couple times, but I'm sorry for startling you. Are you always so jumpy? Or is it from trying to solve the murder?" He'd showered, and his damp cowlick dropped over his forehead.

"Not usually." In fact, I often approached life with determination. The jitteriness was a new trait, and it was unattractive. I needed to conquer the nerves.

Jake propped his hands on his hips and looked around. "Why are you back here?"

"I'm trying to decide if the killer arrived intending to kill Willow, or did they want to reason with her. Was the murder in the heat of the moment?

We need to talk to Matt." I pulled my phone out of a pocket in my gardening short overalls and began to text the police chief.

Jake quirked one side of his mouth up. "He won't be happy, but I ain't gonna waste my breath arguing with you, Sunshine. Let's roll."

Chapter Forty-Five

Matt's terse reply to my text message left me feeling a bit anxious. **Meet me at farmers' market in five.**

Jake drove his Sequoia from the bookstore so we didn't risk being late.

"This is a sweet ride."

"Yeah. It's rugged with plenty of elbow room but smooth and quiet. I've got a little hearing loss from my time in the service, and I want to protect what's left."

"Makes sense."

Matt was parked near the entrance of the deserted market.

Jake parked, and we exited his SUV.

"What's so urgent?" Matt leaned against his car and crossed his arms.

"I was looking around at the bookstore earlier and wondering if the killer intended to murder Willow." I took a quick breath, not wanting him to cut me off. "Everyone knows Willow worked at Paige's on Fridays. It's possible he went there to have a conversation with Willow, and the conversation got out of hand."

"He or she." Jake frowned.

I met his gaze. "You're right. It could've been a woman, and I have at least one woman on my suspect—"

"Stop." Matt raised his hand. "Is that all?"

Matt wasn't going to intimidate me. "If Gambler is a hitman, should we rule him out?"

"Not so fast. Rusty said he was paid to kill Willow." Matt tilted his head.

"That doesn't exactly jive with your theory.

Like wind blowing seeds off a dandelion, Matt's argument blew away my hypothesis. "Yeah, you could be right."

"Could be?" A gruff laugh escaped from Matt.

Jake said, "Do you think the person who was behind paying for the hit changed his or her mind and decided to do the deed personally?"

I shrugged. "Maybe. When Rusty didn't commit the murder, it's possible the instigator tried to reason with Willow over whatever the conflict was."

The police chief pushed himself off his car. "I thought you had a business to focus on. The last thing we need is to solve your murder. Jake, I've decided instead of helping Emma, you should quit encouraging her. The warnings should've been enough to scare her off. If something bad happens to Emma, I'll hold you responsible."

I lifted my chin. "That's not fair. Jake's only a friend, not my keeper."

"Go visit Abby, focus on your business, go on vacation, date Jake. I don't care what you do, as long as you stay away from my investigation." Matt opened his car door. "I'm an officer of the law, and I do have crimes to solve."

Of all the nerve. How dare Matt talk to me like that? And in front of Jake, no less. My face was hot as a Texas sidewalk in July.

With a slight squeal of tires, Matt drove away.

Jake rubbed his hands together. "That was awkward."

My warm face had nothing to do with the heat of the day and everything to do with Matt's suggestion Jake, and I should start dating. "Yeah. I'll walk home. Thanks for your help today."

He glanced at his watch. "The least I can do is drop you off. I've got an interview with a guy about restoring houses around here. At the rate we're progressing, your friend Matt's not going to hire me."

"Aw, Jake, I'm sorry for dragging you into this mess."

"Hey, now, I'm a big boy. You didn't force me to do anything."

The drive to my place was short and quiet.

What was Jake thinking about? He parallel parked in front of my bungalow and walked me to the front porch. I pulled out my keys. "Thanks, Jake. See you later."

He winked. "A potential boyfriend would have asked you out to dinner. This is the least I could do. See ya' around."

No good reply came to mind, so I smiled and walked inside. Working in the yard would be a good way to get my mind off Willow's murder, or else maybe the break would help me solve the mystery of who killed Willow.

Chapter Forty-Six

The yard was still a disaster, and I didn't know where to begin. So far, my recovery efforts had been frenzied. The only rhyme or reason was to keep something alive.

"Emma, are you back here?"

I walked to the gate and opened it. "Hi, Paige. Shouldn't you be at the store?"

"Business is slow, so I closed early."

I motioned for her to follow me to the back patio. "What's up?"

Cowboy greeted her, and Paige rubbed his back. "We didn't really talk after you left the store. Did you have a revelation?"

"Not really. I keep mulling over the situation. Was the murder planned, or did the situation get out of hand? I tried to talk to Matt, but he told me to mind my own business."

Paige stood beside me on the patio and looked at my gardens. "Oh, Emma. Your yard is worse than I'd imagined. This is my fault."

"No, it's not." By agreeing to help Paige, I'd opened myself up to retaliation. Who would have believed how bad it'd be? At least I was still alive. "Chief Young warned me again today to step away from his investigation. Really though, how did I think there was any possible way I was equipped to solve a murder?"

"You read all those mysteries, and I thought you'd know what to do. Sorry." Dark circles under Paige's eyes and her sunken cheeks concerned me.

"Taking notes was about the only thing I did right."

Paige touched my arm. "Don't sell yourself short. You had a list of suspects and motives."

"I never came up with any proof. Just a lot of useless theories." Useless. Like me. Like my yard. My dream business was disappearing right along with the money I'd spent years saving. Oh, the sacrifices I'd made, and one silly promise ruined it.

"You're a good friend, and I'm releasing you from the burden of helping prove I'm innocent."

"Thanks, Paige. Chief Young is good at his job, and I'm sure he'll catch the real culprit."

"I hope you're right. Despite the eyewitness, he's likely to keep believing I'm guilty. He hasn't updated me on my gun yet. I bet he'll call me in for another talk when he knows more."

"Hey, maybe he locked you up to keep you safe."

"That doesn't feel right." She looked out over my yard and sighed. "I doubt we get to see flowers in prison."

"Aw, Paige. Have a little faith."

"I'll see you later, Emma." My friend disappeared around the corner.

After confirming the gate locked behind her, I walked the perimeter of my yard and studied the disaster. My friends had helped rescue some of the plants, but there were plenty of empty areas.

Growing flowers had always given me pleasure, and I'd been silly enough to try turning a hobby into a business.

Marrying Bo had been another ridiculous action. Sober, he'd been loving and fun. Life had never been boring with him. How had I not realized how messed up he'd been? He'd dazzled me, and I never saw through the performance. After his death, Bo's parents made an offer to buy Abby from me. Their deal would require me to give up all rights to my sweet daughter in exchange for never needing to worry about money again.

As if. No amount of money could separate me from my child.

Willow had come from money, but it hadn't made for a happy marriage. Vince's parents seemed grounded and level-headed, but they didn't appear to be rich. Had Willow's money been part of the reason Vince married her?

A divorce would've changed Vince's life in more ways than one. Faith had claimed the divorce would be ugly. Vince would lose his job and reputation. If Willow discovered he'd stolen money from the bank, he might spend time in prison. I shivered. Vince stood to gain the most from Willow's death, but did it make him a murderer?

The day Sophie and I went to Vince's house, there'd been a secret safe in his closet. I'd caught my toe on it. What was he hiding?

Better yet, how could I find out? And just like that, I was back into the investigation.

Chapter Forty-Seven

I t'd taken a lot of fast talking and dishwashing to convince Sophie we needed to go by Vince's home. She left her employee in charge of the bakery, and we went to my house and prepared dinner for the Moore family. I had enough ingredients for a Texas chicken ranch casserole.

I texted Vince. **We're bringing supper to you tonight.**

His reply was simple. **Thanks.**

Close to six o'clock, we rang the front doorbell of the Moore house.

Mr. Moore opened it. As usual, he wore nice slacks and a button-down dress shirt. "Ladies, this is so very nice of you. Mary's exhausted, and your dinner will be a real treat."

I held the chicken casserole. "If it's all right, we'll come in and work on the final preparations."

Sophie said, "We even brought paper products, so there's no cleanup for you to handle."

"Come back to the kitchen. Mary is on the way home with Blake. He had batting practice after regular practice. Sports are more complicated these days than when we raised Vince."

"I just went to the batting cage in town to practice my swing."

He paused near the dining room table. "Do you play in a softball league?"

My face warmed. "Oh, no, sir. I tried to use a bat to protect myself the other night, but it turns out I didn't know how to swing very well. Nobody ever accused me of being athletic."

"You need to be careful, dear." He resumed walking through the big house.

"I'd never aim to do real harm to someone, but it'd be nice to slow an

227

intruder long enough for me to make my escape." We followed Mr. Moore to the kitchen, and it seemed best to change the subject. "I'm sure helping Vince with the kids and looking for a new home are stressful, especially on top of Willow's death."

"Murder, dear. We can never forget." He sat on a barstool. "Some of the people around your fine town are convinced Vince did it."

Sophie placed a basket of food on the counter.

I set the oven temperature for the bread. "If my daughter was accused of murder, I'd be devastated."

He ran a hand over his face. "That describes how my wife and I feel. The marriage wasn't perfect, but we surely raised our son to know murder is a sin."

Was that a hint of doubt in his voice?

The back door swooshed open.

Lucky me. I didn't need to come up with an appropriate answer.

"I'm starved. What's for dinner?" A streak of dirt covered one of Blake's cheeks, and he looked sweaty.

Mrs. Moore followed him into the kitchen. "Why don't you take a quick shower first?"

"Maybe this will tide you over." Sophie handed Blake a cup of pretzels.

"Thanks." The teen took the snack and disappeared.

Sophie pointed to the cheese board. "Please, help yourselves. Will Vince and Christine be home for dinner?"

Mrs. Moore washed her hands, then sat beside her husband. Tonight, she wore pearls again, this time with slacks and a red blouse. "Yes. I'm surprised Vince isn't already home."

My friend had included disposable glasses, and I filled them with the ginger ale we'd brought.

Mr. Moore rolled a green grape between his fingers. "I never answered your question. We are looking for a small house. It'll be better for all of us if we live in different places. You understand?"

I nodded. "Absolutely. Even though y'all are family and love each other, it's good to have some breathing room. I'm sure you two are putting on a brave front for Vince and the kids. It must be draining. What kind of home are you looking for?"

"Three bedrooms. Two bathrooms." Mrs. Moore was a tad more abrupt than her husband. He was longer winded and a gentle soul.

"We have an agent, a friend of Vince's, who will help us look. I like the neighborhood where the Nelle sisters live." He ate the grape.

"It's a well-established area for sure. Do you think Vince and the kids will stay here?" I reached for a grape, hesitated because we were supplying dinner for them, then took one anyway and popped it in my mouth.

Mrs. Moore's shoulders hunched. "Knowing Vince, they won't make a quick change. The children need to grieve appropriately."

Vince appeared at my side, and I jumped.

"Hi, Vince. You'd make a good cat burglar the way you creep up on people."

He chuckled. "I've always been light-footed. What are we eating? Christine's talking on the phone, but I can cut her off if dinner's ready."

Sophie said, "Give me five minutes. The bread is almost ready, but help yourself to appetizers."

Vince reached toward the food, but his mom popped his hand. "Wash your hands first."

"Yes, ma'am." He chuckled but obeyed his mother.

Moments like this made it easy to see how Willow had fallen for Vince's charm.

Mrs. Moore fingered her pearl necklace. "Vince, these ladies picked out Willow's last outfit. What if we offer to pay them to clean out the closet? They can save a few things for Christine and maybe give the rest to a charity."

My pulse leapt. This could be my chance. "Oh, what a great idea. The church is collecting clothes for women to wear to job interviews, but there are other worthy organizations."

"No." Vince turned on us. His face was pale. "It's too soon."

"You're right." Mr. Moore walked over and patted his son on the shoulder. "We'll wait."

Blake entered the kitchen, looking fresh and smelling of Irish Spring. "Can we eat now?"

Vince nodded. "Call your sister in."

Sophie and I plated the food and served the family at the kitchen table.

Mr. Moore blessed the meal, and they began to eat.

"We'll head out now. I've used disposable serving dishes, so you won't need to return anything. Call me if you need a break from cooking." Sophie picked up her wicker basket.

"I'll walk you out." Mrs. Moore stood and walked us to Sophie's van. "Girls, this was such a nice treat. Thank you."

"You're welcome." Sophie smiled and patted the lady's arm.

Butterflies fluttered in my stomach. "I feel like you want to say something else."

"Well, dear. You're right. Lutz is a small town, and I heard about your trouble. Would you like to make a little extra money?"

Boy, would I. "Yes, but it must be legal. Er, not that I think you'd ask me to do anything shady. Sorry. What'd you have in mind?"

"Vince is going to Dallas tomorrow for an all-day meeting. Would you help me box Willow's clothes? He can decide later where to donate them, but at least they'll be out of sight."

"Sure. What time would you like me here?" I plucked a business card from my purse and handed it to her.

"I'll call when the coast is clear."

"Okay. See you tomorrow." We hopped into the bakery van, and Sophie drove away. "When Vince reacted to his mom's suggestion, I didn't think there'd be a chance of getting into his closet. Did you think his reaction was believable, or was it an act?"

Sophie drove around the square and parked the van behind her store. "If I didn't know about the divorce, I'd believe he was upset. He's probably a good actor, though. I mean he wasn't faithful to his wife, so he must know how to put on a good show."

"Great point. Thanks for tonight."

"No problem." She picked up her stainless-steel water bottle. "I'll drive you home in my Prius."

"I can walk."

"It will be safer for me to drive you."

I shivered. "Another great point. Thanks."

Once I got home and played with Cowboy, I settled at the French harvest table in my breakfast room with the murder notes on Nick's first wife. This time I was able to stay awake and read them. Nick may have killed Rhonda with chemicals he used for pest control, but there was nothing to make me suspect he'd murdered Willow. There was no information about guns or a relationship with Willow.

I texted Paula Jones, Nick's second wife, who'd confided in me her fears of Nick.

Hi, Paula. It's Emma Justice. Do you know if Nick owns a gun?

Cowboy whined, and I let him outside.

My phone pinged, and it was a reply from Paula.

He didn't keep one at the house when we were married. I don't know about his office.

I sent her a quick thanks and let my puppy inside. "Cowboy, it's time for bed." I hid the notes in my pantry while my dog took a drink from his water bowl. He put himself in the crate, and I gave him a treat. "Goodnight."

After brushing my teeth, I flopped into bed. If Willow had been poisoned, Nick would remain a suspect. Not having a gun moved him down my list.

Tomorrow I'd help Mrs. Moore move Willow's clothes. With a little luck, I'd find a clue to prove Vince was involved in his wife's murder. Although, for the sake of Christine and Blake, I'd like to find something to rule him out.

Chapter Forty-Eight

I carried flattened boxes from the bookstore and elbowed the doorbell at Vince's house. Funny how the cardboard slipped in my arms. I never knew it was so slick. My heartbeat quickened at the rapid clip of shoes on the hardwood floor inside.

"Good morning, Emma." Mrs. Moore smiled. The woman wore navy linen capris, black flats, a red blouse, and of course a pearl necklace. This one was a choker style. "It looks like you've come prepared."

"Preparation could be my middle name." I adjusted my faded backpack purse where I'd hidden a stethoscope in case I found the opportunity to crack the hidden safe. I'd been trained to take blood pressure at the pharmacy, and the owner had given me my own stethoscope. Early this morning, I'd watched videos online about safe cracking.

"Here, let me take some of those boxes." She lightened my load and led me upstairs. "I found some wardrobe moving boxes in the attic for hanging clothes. Willow had so many dresses and suits. Do you mind pulling them out for me? It's a walk-in attic, but they are too bulky for me to manage."

"I don't mind at all, and it sounds like a perfect solution for storing the dresses, slacks, and suits. I brought packing tape, and we can seal up Willow's belongings so they don't get buggy."

At the top of the stairs, I followed Mrs. Moore into the main bedroom, and we deposited the boxes on the floor.

"The attic is down the hall, and it won't be too hot or cold this time of year."

I followed her to the storage area and sneezed. "How nice to have the boxes still constructed. I can carry one at a time by the cut-out handles."

"Yes, that will work. After we fill one, we can bring it here and replace it with an empty wardrobe box."

I grinned. *We* probably meant *me*, so I didn't want to make it too heavy. "Mr. Moore seems focused on finding a home for you two. How do you feel?" We re-entered the main bedroom, and I dropped the big awkward box.

"He's more gung-ho than I am, but we've seen a few places. I prefer to stay with Vince and the children. It'll be more convenient to help them, but my husband insists we need our own space." She entered the main closet. I formed the flattened cardboard into boxes, taping the bottoms while Mrs. Moore brought out stacks of gorgeous garments. "Willow had an extensive wardrobe." Her critical tone surprised me.

It wasn't my place to speak ill of the dead. "I still believe auctioning them off could really help a charity."

"Unfortunately, Vince isn't ready, my dear."

My face grew warm. "Sure, whenever he's ready, is what I meant. I didn't intend to push, but one day he'll decide it's time, and Willow's classic style will always be popular." I folded a stack of blouses and kept my mouth shut. I was here to be helpful and find potential clues. There was no judgment from me on Vince's grieving period, but if he'd been the killer, would he mourn the loss of his wife? The thought continually nagged me.

"Willow grew up accustomed to money, and buying expensive outfits never fazed her." A jazzy ringtone ended the conversation. Mrs. Moore glanced at her phone. "Excuse me, please."

"Would you mind bringing me some water on your way back?"

She nodded, then swiped her phone as she exited the room. "Hello, darling."

I grabbed my stethoscope and dashed to the other closet. Vince still hadn't filled it with his clothing. Where was he staying? It didn't matter, at least for now. I knelt down and felt around the floor until my fingers snagged on the carpet. With a tug, a false floor lifted and revealed a gray safe.

I tried turning the handle. No luck. After a quick glance over my shoulder,

I put the earpieces in my ears and placed the diaphragm on the door. I turned the dial left and listened for a click. Twelve. Now right. Around and around until another click. Fifty-eight. Left again. I strained to hear. Maybe seven? Once more to the right. The dial grew tighter at fifteen. I stopped rotating the combination lock and turned the handle. It didn't budge.

Why not? I'd heard the clicks.

Sweat beaded my forehead. I looked around the space for possible numbers written on the baseboard or a shelf.

"Emma, how's it going?"

I raced to the bedroom and beat Mrs. Moore by mere seconds. "I'm making progress."

"Darling, you look hot, and I forgot your water. Be right back."

I darted back into the closet and shut the door. An empty tie-rack rattled. I studied it. There. Right below the wood was faint writing. 12-56-4-15. Close to what I'd tried but not exact. I repeated the numbers to myself and dropped to the floor. My heart raced. I turned the dial back and forth, stopping at the appropriate numbers.

Click.

I tried the handle, and it moved. Lifting the lid, I discovered manilla envelopes and memory sticks. My heart leapt. No clue what was important, so I grabbed one of each, then returned everything else to the proper order. No. I reached for one more envelope and closed the safe, then placed the carpet square over it. I grasped the stethoscope and hustled back to the bedroom, stuffing all the items into my bag.

Breathless, I returned to folding Willow's tops, hoping to look normal by the time Vince's mother returned. She'd already questioned why I was perspiring. It was a good thing she couldn't hear my racing heart.

Mrs. Moore appeared and handed me a water bottle. "Here you go."

"Thanks."

"You're welcome." Her gaze darted around the room before landing on me. "I thought you'd be farther along by now."

I gulped the water, then screwed the lid on securely. "Sorry, Mrs. Moore. I didn't realize I was slow. Do you want me to keep helping?"

"Yes, and please call me Mary." She disappeared into the main closet, and I breathed easier.

"Mary, it is." I wrote on the outside of the box what it contained. "Is Vince living in this room, or did he take a guest room?"

She returned, carrying two spring dresses. "What are you implying?" The harshness of her tone startled me.

"Oh, you know. It might be hard to sleep in the same bed without Willow."

She nodded. "I've had friends avoid their bedrooms after their husbands died. After five years of her husband's passing, one of my dear friends still sleeps in the family room recliner with the TV on."

"Aw, that's so sad. Is that what Vince is doing?"

"Why do you care?"

I shrugged, knowing I couldn't accuse him of murdering his wife. "We're moving Willow's clothes to the attic. Is there more to be done? Like hire somebody to redecorate the bedroom and closets?"

"That's a good idea, as long as he decides to keep the house." Mary hung the dresses in the cardboard wardrobe. "This one is ready to be taped shut."

"Yes, ma'am." I secured the box and labeled it before trying to lift it. "Ugh, this is too heavy for me. Is it possible Mr. Moore or Vince can help move it back to the attic? Maybe even Blake?"

"No." Her shoulders drooped. "Daniel will accuse me of interfering, and there's no need to upset Vince or Blake. Let's try together."

We each took one side and half-carried and half-dragged the full wardrobe to the attic.

I laughed. "You're much stronger than you appear, Mary."

"Don't tell my husband." She held a manicured finger to her lips. "He enjoys taking care of me."

"That's very sweet. You're secret's safe with me." I smiled. Mary probably had no clue what was involved in a bad marriage. How had Vince kept the secret of his failing marriage from his parents all these years?

Chapter Forty-Nine

Late that afternoon, I took Cowboy for a walk and ambled through town. My poor puppy had been cooped up in his crate too long while I'd helped Mary box up Willow's belongings. After we completed the job, I couldn't wait to discover what the documents and memory stick might reveal. There were duties needing my attention first, though. I'd watered my plants, and Cowboy needed to burn off some energy. The information could come later.

We walked up the street and turned onto the square, bumping into Mary and Rita. "Hi, ladies." I tightened my grip on the dog leash. "Sit, Cowboy."

Mary's eyes widened. She'd changed into linen slacks and a purple blouse.

Rita said, "Emma, I meant to call you earlier. I need to order flowers for, er, a special event."

"Sure. How about I come by the bank tomorrow and we can discuss your needs?" I hoped it would be possible to help despite my meager supply of surviving flowers.

"Perfect." Rita ran a hand over her black skirt. "See you then."

"Mary, it's good to see you again. I'd love to stay and chat, but my dog needs his exercise."

Mary's face cleared. "Good to see you too, dear." The women walked in the direction of the bank, and I headed the opposite way.

Jake turned off the coffee shop lights and stepped outside. "Emma, how's it going?"

"Fine. I just bumped into Rita and Mrs. Moore. Were they in the coffee shop, and why are you closing up?"

"Brett had an appointment, and I volunteered to work. As for your other question, they've been here over an hour. I would've closed earlier, but they were deep in conversation. Why?"

Cowboy tugged on the leash. I said, "Do you mind if we walk and talk?"

"No problem." He did a final jiggle of the door before touching my arm. "Lead the way."

I walked toward Paige's store. "Who was doing most of the talking?"

Jake swiped a hand over his chin. "Why?"

"They seem an unlikely duo. Rita is in love with Vince, and Mary led me to believe she thought Vince and Willow had a good marriage."

"Mary? As in Vince's mom?"

"Yeah. Sorry. She asked me to call her by her given name this morning when I helped her with a project."

"Okay, well she seemed to be in control."

"Really?"

"Yeah, she did most of the talking, and Rita did a lot of nodding."

"Interesting." I paused while Cowboy sniffed a parking meter. "Mary and I boxed up Willow's clothes and jewelry without Vince's permission today. By the way, I found a bunch of hidden documents and memory sticks. I snuck out with a couple." I detailed the time I'd spent with Mary.

"If I was working for the police department, I might have to arrest you for stealing. What you did was both dangerous and illegal."

"Are you curious, though?"

"Yeah, I gotta admit that I am. Would you like help going over what you found?"

"Sure, but I left them at home." Dark clouds filled the sky. "How'd your job interview go?" I encouraged Cowboy to continue walking with a gentle pull on his leash.

"Better than trying to get hired by Matt."

"Aw, that's good in one way, but I'm sorry about Matt. Have you considered applying at other police departments?"

"Sure, but Lutz isn't far from my sister, and I can help Brett with the shop if I stay here."

"You two are good friends."

"We've been through a lot together. He's like a brother to me."

"I understand. Sophie and I have had our share of struggles too. She stood by me when my husband died, and I supported her through the process of becoming a United States citizen. Even though I have a birthsister, Sophie and I are as close as siblings. Maybe closer." Thunder rumbled in the distance, and I led the dog in the direction of home.

Jake said, "I get it. What about Vince? Who is he close to?"

"Willow was close to Faith Meier, but Vince and Zig aren't exactly friends. According to Zig, they've never called each other to hang out." The wind picked up, and I fastened my hair into a ponytail.

"Understood. Who does that leave?"

"Some might say his girlfriend, although nobody knows who that is. To be honest, the girlfriend could be a rumor. Vince's parents are helping with the kids, but I'm not sure they grasp the life Vince has led. Zig says Vince runs with a fast crowd, but that doesn't mean those men are his friends."

"Like those uppity women pretending to be Willow's friends."

"Exactly." We walked down Main Street in silence until reaching my house. I unlocked the door. Cowboy raced through the house and stopped at his water bowl. I followed at a much slower pace. "Can I get you something to drink, Jake?"

"Sure. Let's look over your findings."

I pointed to the large kitchen table. "It's all right there. How about a Dr. Pepper?"

He was at the table surveying what I'd spread out. "Yeah."

After refilling Cowboy's water bowl, I fixed drinks for Jake and me, then joined him at the table.

Jake had opened one envelope and was going through a stack of papers.

I reached for the other one and pulled out a pile of spreadsheets. "Oh, dear. Why couldn't it be a journal of Vince's thoughts and feelings?"

"Vince doesn't strike me as the poetic type who records his emotions."

"Hmm." I'd taken a few business courses at night and hoped to make sense of the numbers. Except for Cowboy panting at my feet, we worked in silence.

"Ooh-wee." Jake held up a page. "Offshore bank accounts. In Belize. It'll take a bit more digging to prove the money was stolen."

My pulse leapt. "Vince and Willow went to Belize a few years ago. If I remember correctly, she went shopping and was supposed to meet him. He turned up hours later, and she'd been so worried she called the local police. Willow thought he'd been kidnapped or something."

"Nothing in this file makes me think he was spending money on a mistress. There are no entries for jewelry stores. Actually, I don't know what kind of receipts would be here to prove he was having an affair."

"What if his secretiveness had nothing to do with another woman and everything to do with stealing from the bank?"

Thunder rumbled in the distance.

"Rumors are not facts. I'd guess most gossip is the exact opposite of truth. So, unless we've got a witness claiming to see Vince with another woman, perhaps we should rule out the affair angle."

"Okay." I shrugged. "Strike infidelity as a motive, and he rebuffed Rita when she made a play for him. We've got proof Vince was stealing money from the bank and hiding it in other countries."

"Let's play with this new theory." Jake popped his knuckles. "If Vince planned to steal the money and move, my guess is he might change his identity. The fewer people involved in his scheme, the easier it'd be not to get caught."

Cowboy barked, then whined at the back door.

"I wonder if Willow suspected. After all, she slept a few feet away from the evidence." I moved to the door and let the dog out.

"Don't forget Rita. She might have picked up on something from working so closely with Vince."

I yawned. "True, and I'm going to see her tomorrow. I'll try to pump her for information. I'm really curious about her connection with Mary Moore."

"It's possible Rita and Mary are the two women who love Vince the most. Emma, you need to be cautious. If they believe you're trying to prove he murdered his wife, they might try to stop your investigation."

I nodded. "I'll be careful."

My phone vibrated on the table with a text message from Rita. **I'm working late on a project. Can you come to the bank now?**

"Oh no."

Jake said, "What's wrong?"

"This isn't good. Rita wants to see me now." Butterflies swirled in my stomach.

Cowboy scratched on the door, and I let him inside.

Jake tightened his lips into a flat line. He paced the short distance between the table and where I stood at the back door. "Something's hinky. I don't trust her."

"If I refuse, she'll become suspicious."

"She could already suspect you know something. It hasn't been a secret that you've been investigating Willow's death."

My phone vibrated again. **Emma, did you get my message?**

"I've got to give her an answer." I stared at the phone.

Jake crossed his arms. "I'm going with you."

Lightning flashed, and Cowboy howled.

"No. I'll convince her to stick to our original arrangement. Why don't you take the memory stick and see what else you can discover about Vince and his schemes? I'll come by Anytime Coffee tomorrow, and we can discuss it." I placed the device in his warm hand.

"Why don't I believe you?"

"Watch." I reached for my phone. **Tomorrow is better for me. I'm dealing with my dog right now.** "Happy?"

His gaze met mine. "I won't go straight to happy, but I'll meet you at the coffee shop when it opens, unless it's too early."

"Sounds good to me." I walked him to the door. "Have a good night, Jake."

"You, be careful." He squeezed my hand before walking away.

My ringtone sounded, and Rita's name appeared.

"Hi, Rita."

"Emma, tomorrow my schedule is packed. I need you to come over tonight. Get your dog settled, and text me when you get here."

Ugh. Jake wouldn't be happy, but I needed answers. "Sure. It might take a few minutes, though. He must feel the storm coming."

"I'll be here." Rita disconnected about the same time more thunder popped.

"Cowboy, where are you?" I walked through the rooms and found my puppy hiding in the back corner of my closet. "What's the matter? Are you scared?"

He whined.

"If it makes you feel better, I'm scared too. Different reasons, but I'm still scared. Can I catch Willow's killer? Will my business fail? See? You're not the only one with fears."

I secured Cowboy in a special shirt designed to help dogs not be afraid during storms. "I'm sorry to leave you, but I'll be back soon."

The rain had begun. Walking would leave me drenched, so I texted Rita I was driving and would arrive soon.

Chapter Fifty

The rain transitioned to a downpour with frequent rumbles and flashes of lightning. It was easy to find a parking place on the square. I turned off the truck and looked around. This dark, stormy night had the makings of a scary poem.

I verified my phone settings. Sophie and Abby were my emergency contacts, and they could look up my location if I disappeared.

I flipped up the hood of my rain jacket and rushed to the front door of the bank.

No sign of Rita, so I pounded on the glass door. Rain sluiced down my body, and my tennis shoes were soaked.

Rita appeared and let me inside. "Hi, Emma. Thanks for coming tonight."

Like there had been a choice. I entered the cool interior and shivered. "Sure. What do you need me to do?"

"Heidi Bauer turns forty tomorrow, and I'd like to throw a little impromptu party. There's been a lot of stress around here lately, and I thought we were due some fun."

"What'd you have in mind?" I removed my jacket and hung it on the back of a chair in the sitting area.

"Let's discuss it in my office." She turned on the toe of her high heel and clip-clopped away on the stone floor.

Not wanting to slip on the slick floor, I followed at a much slower pace. My wet shoes squished and squeaked with every step.

Tonight, Rita's office was organized. Even the stacks of paper on her desk appeared orderly. She said, "How's your investigation going?"

"You should ask Chief Young for updates, because he told me to mind my own business." On the way over, I had imagined if Rita was going to ask my thoughts, she'd lead up to it. This was way more direct than I'd anticipated.

"I heard Paige Booker has been arrested. What do you think about that?" One penciled eyebrow lifted in challenge.

I shrugged, trying to look nonchalant. "Paige is a friend, and I believe she's innocent. She's also out of jail."

"What?" Rita's voice squeaked.

"Yeah, an eyewitness came forward."

"Oh, I guess that's good." She wrung her hands. "Excuse my manners. Have a seat, Emma. Can I get you something to drink?"

"I'm not thirsty, but thanks. I'd really like to hear what you need for Heidi, then go home and slip into my yoga pants and a sweatshirt. The rain gave me a chill." Or the frightening vibe rolling off Rita. A shiver shot up my back. "Hot tea is what I'll go for when I get home."

"Okay. I'll keep this brief."

I sat in the chair nearest the door and pulled out my phone. "If you don't mind, I like to take notes on my phone."

"No need to pull out your phone." She emitted a humorless laugh. "It's so simple, really. Maybe a rose at her teller station and a bouquet in the break room. Heidi can take it all home tomorrow night."

"Okay. Let my just close my note app." Was my response convincing? My cold fingers trembled. I switched to the camera app and pushed the video button. It would at least record our conversation. Better than nothing, and I hoped it could be found on the cloud if I was harmed by Rita. "Sounds easy enough."

"Yes. Easy peasy for sure."

A crash sounded in Vince's office, and I jumped in my chair. "What was that?"

Rita's face paled. "Um, uh, I better check."

"Wait, what if a burglar snuck in? Don't you want to call the police?"

"No. It's probably nothing to worry about. When was our last earthquake?"

"We're not known for big earthquakes in Texas. I really think you should call for help."

Rita breezed past me and headed toward Vince's office.

I stopped the video and sent a text to Jake. **It might be a good time for our date. I'm at the bank. Please, hurry.** I'd apologize later.

Another chill ripped up my spine.

Rita stood behind me. "So, you've got a date? Let me guess? The handsome barista who's helping Brett."

I leapt from my chair, turning to face the woman. The back of my thighs pressed against her desk. "It's none of your business."

"I disagree. You're supposed to be discussing a job with me. Not texting your boyfriend."

With my thumb, I swiped the audio button on the text message. "Rita, you left the room, giving me the opportunity to confirm my date with Jake. I didn't think you'd mind."

"What happened to getting cozy home alone because of the rain?" She narrowed her eyes.

Fear twisted in my belly like a Texas tornado. "I'm going to leave now. Tomorrow, I'll return with your order."

Mary Moore appeared in the office doorway. "Emma, I'd hoped it didn't have to come to this. Go into the lobby. I'll be right behind you, so don't try anything stupid."

I didn't have any personal experience with firearms, but I recognized the fact Mary was pointing a gun straight at me.

Chapter Fifty-One

Cell reception wasn't the best in Lutz, and the storm probably made it worse. The wind howled, and rain splattered against the bank windows. Where was Jake? Had the bad weather prevented him from receiving my message? The point of the text had been for him to rescue me.

No, I was capable of talking my way out of this situation. I didn't need somebody to save me. Wait, Mary had a weapon. This was beyond my skill set.

"Hurry up." Mary kept the gun pointed at me.

With slow steps I entered the dim lobby.

Rita disappeared down a semi-dark hallway.

"Mary, I don't understand." My words came out breathy. "What's going on?"

"Humph." She stood straight as an arrow, pointing her firearm at me. "Daniel and Vince coddle me. Neither one believes I'm strong."

I cleared my throat. "I know you're a woman of strength. You worked hard today and conquered a task your son wasn't ready to handle. You're strong mentally and physically."

"Darn right."

"Why'd you murder your daughter-in-law?" Had she taken Willow by surprise?

"I knew Willow was trouble with a capital T the day Vince brought her to meet us. You can't marry a person with that much money and expect to be happy."

I didn't believe her ridiculous assumption, but this wasn't the time to argue. Mary needed to believe I was on her side. That way she'd be less inclined to murder me. Maybe. Hopefully. "So what'd you do?"

"I couldn't prevent the wedding, but the day I met Rita, we bonded. We both love my son, and she'd make him a good wife. On my last visit, I noticed how far the marriage had deteriorated. Rita verified the truth and told me Willow had filed for divorce. There was no way on this sweet earth I'd let her get away with divorcing Vince. I tried different ways to stop the proceedings."

"Like what?" I'd slipped my phone into my pocket earlier, but I couldn't send a message without drawing Mary's attention.

"I started rumors about Willow, and when that didn't work, I tried to talk her out of it myself. Suffice it to say, nothing I did made a difference. As the trial date approached, I grew desperate."

"Is that where Rita came into the picture?"

"Yes. I was aware her ex-fiancé had a nefarious background. As luck would have it, he was recently released from prison. I offered him money to knock off Willow." Mary looked in the direction of the offices. "What's taking her so long?"

We stood by ourselves in the bank's well-furnished lobby. "I'll wait here if you want to look for her."

"How dumb do you think I am?" Her frown was so deep her eyebrows almost touched. Black eyebrows. No doubt she died them to match her hair.

"Sorry. I only wanted to help." I gave her the best smile I could muster in these circumstances.

Mary took three steps toward the hall leading to the offices, but the gun remained aimed at me. "Rita, where are you?"

I needed a weapon in the worst way, but I couldn't have snuck my baseball bat into the bank earlier. Time to improvise. There was a bank counter with deposit slips. The pen was chained to the top, so it wouldn't do any good. What else could be used for a weapon? Hurling a chair wouldn't work because she'd be able to shoot me before I threw the piece of furniture. My biggest fear was Mary looked older and too frail to fight. Could I focus on the danger she presented and ignore her grandmotherly appearance? It'd be the smart thing. The brave action, even. But I'd feel like a big bully. Still, she was the one pointing a gun at me. *Please, Lord, let my survival instincts kick in.*

Chapter Fifty-Two

I edged behind the public bank counter and leaned on it while slipping the phone out of my pocket. It was hidden from Mary's view by a box of deposit slips. The screen was blank.

"What are you doing?" The gun quivered.

"My legs are shaking so hard, I'm afraid they won't hold me much longer. Please, let me prop up here for a minute." I gave her a weak smile. "You understand? We worked hard today. Frankly, you amaze me. Your stamina is stronger than mine."

"Humph." Mary frowned. "I'd think you'd be stronger. After all, you're a flower farmer."

I shrugged. "What can I say?"

Rita's footsteps sounded, and Mary turned in the direction of the sound.

I swiped my phone and called Jake, muting my side in order not to alert my captors.

"What were you doing?" Mary hissed at Rita.

"Sorry. Dave called, and I told him we've got trouble that needs to be handled."

"Is he willing to off her?"

Rita sniffed. "He's contacting Gambler."

Ah-ha. "Are you saying Gambler killed Willow?"

Both women turned and stared at me.

"Uh, that's what you said, right? I mean, why not tell me? Satisfy my curiosity before you kill me. Please."

Mary said, "I don't see how it can hurt. There won't be anyone for you

248

to tell. We asked Dave to do the job, but he was too much of a coward to murder my daughter-in-law."

I nodded and slipped my phone back into the pocket of my jeans, hoping, like all git-out, Jake would be able to hear us.

"Why are you so far away?" Rita walked toward me and grabbed my arm.

"Sorry. I was feeling weak." We passed the velvet ropes hung between brass stanchions. The posts looked sturdy. In fact, I'd often seen children swinging on the velvet. It might be my best choice of weapons, but I needed to attack while it was only the three of us. All bets would be off when Gambler arrived. Bets? Oh, dear. I better pull myself together. "Rusty told me he'd been paid to kill Willow."

"Yeah. I don't know what Dave was thinking. The kid's a dopehead." Rita led me to Mary, and we stood in a loose circle. "That's when we thought of Gambler."

"Who is Gambler?"

"I'm surprised you didn't figure it out. It's Kevin Anderson."

"But he's not a local." I'd seen him the morning of Willow's murder as he entered the coffee shop. He'd tried to conceal his face then, and Jake remembered him ordering two cups of coffee.

Rita said, "He's lived in the area for years, but he keeps a low profile."

Whoa. "Then the rumors are true? He'll kill in order to pay off gambling debts?"

"You betcha. He's done it for years." Rita's phone rang, and she walked away to take the call.

Back to only Mary and me. This would be my best opportunity to escape. "How do you plan to leave with me? Someone is bound to see us. What about the security cameras?"

"Rita can rig the system. There won't be any recording of you being here."

"I told my friend about meeting Rita tonight."

"She'll say you never showed up."

Rita appeared before I could take action. "It's all set."

Now what was I going to do?

Mary said, "What's the plan?"

Rita eyed me. "Give me the keys to your truck."

"They're in my raincoat." I walked over and pulled the keys out of the pocket.

"Mary, take her truck to the farmers' market. Leave it in a shadowy area. I need to get money to pay Kevin, and we'll meet you there."

The older woman took the keys, then snatched my jacket. "You don't mind, do you, dear?"

"Help yourself." A little rain wouldn't hurt me, and Mary was the one with a gun. Who was I to argue?

Rita unlocked the heavy glass door. Mary passed her the gun and slipped away. Rita locked the door with a loud click.

I gazed into the dark, rainy night. Where was Jake? Was it possible Sophie was working at the bakery? Had she noticed any unusual activity over here? Would she be suspicious and call the police? No, it was too late for her to be in the bakery. She was probably already home in bed.

"Follow me." Rita took me to Vince's office. She opened the modern davenport, where a small safe hid. She tapped in eight numbers and turned the handle.

Lucky Rita. She didn't have to spin a safe like the one Vince had in his house. "I heard Gambler will kill a person for five hundred dollars."

"Unfortunately, he doubled the price for you." Rita shrugged. "He went to Vegas and lost, and I'm paying the price." She counted out ten bills.

"It sounds like you and Mary are close. Whose idea was it to kill Willow?"

"We grew close over our concern for Vince. Willow never appreciated him the way we do." Rita locked the safe and stuffed the money into the pocket of her black skirt.

"I found proof Vince has stolen money from the bank. He's planning to leave the country. I bet he'll change his identity. Has he asked you to join him?"

Rita's eyes widened. "You're lying."

"No, I'm not. The proof is hiding in a fireproof combination safe in his bedroom closet."

"I don't believe you. If he was planning an elaborate heist, I'd know about it. We discuss everything related to the bank."

"Vince wouldn't have shared his plan with you if he wanted to cover his tracks."

Her complexion turned pale. "Let's go."

I hurried out of the office, but Rita had to lock the door. Her high heels would slow her ability to keep up with me, but she probably wasn't worried. She'd locked us in the building.

I ran to the lobby and dove behind a teller's window. Where was the emergency switch? I crawled as fast as possible. There. I spotted the panic button. It was under the ledge of a teller station. I mashed it with my finger.

"Emma, we don't have time for theatrics. You may not have noticed, but Mary gave me her gun on the way out. Just because we hired Gambler, it doesn't mean I won't shoot you myself. After all the lies you told me about Vince, it won't take much for me to pull the trigger."

I crawled to the next teller's station and pushed the panic button. "How do I know you won't shoot me if I come out?"

"It'll be much easier to shoot you in the country than figure out how to move your dead body, and cleaning up the blood will be another unpleasant task."

"All right. I give up." My heart raced. I scurried forward and punched one more panic button. There. I'd pressed every alarm I could find. With shaky knees, I stood.

"Good girl. Let's go."

I walked as slow as possible around the teller stations, then across the lobby. When Rita turned her back on me, I grabbed a stanchion and swung, aiming for the back of her shoulders.

She turned and tried to dodge me.

The base of the brass post glanced off her shoulder and hit her jaw, knocking her to the hard floor.

Ack.

The keys skittered across the marble floor.

The gun fired.

I ducked behind a chair with my fingers still clenching my weapon of choice.

Rita's eyes opened and closed. She appeared to fight for consciousness.

I duckwalked to Rita and eased the gun from her fingers.

Somebody pounded on the door.

With a stanchion in one hand and Rita's gun in the other, I ran to the door to see who it was.

Jake and Sophie stood in the rain.

I yelled, "Let me get the keys."

"Are you okay?" Jake's voice carried through the thick glass doors.

"Yes. Call the police." I moved away, then returned to them. "And we need an ambulance for Rita."

Sophie pulled out her phone.

I placed the gun on the nearest desk and dropped the stanchion before hunting for the keys. They were under a chair in the waiting area. I bent down and snatched them.

Rita turned on her side and spoke. Her words came out garbled.

"You may want to lay still in case you have a concussion." Her head had hit the floor and probably caused more damage than the pole. I fled to the door and tried several keys. The longer it took, the more my hands trembled. I kept glancing at Rita to confirm she wouldn't get the drop on me. The other woman looked dazed. Her mouth opened and closed, but no intelligible words came out.

I returned to inserting wrong keys. At last, one thick silver key went into the lock and turned. Hallelujah.

Sirens sounded.

Jake pulled the door open, and I ran out of the bank and into the rain and safety.

Sophie hugged me. "You scared us to death."

"I can't believe you're awake. Thanks for coming." I hugged her. "Y'all, Mary Moore is behind Willow's murder, but Gambler is the killer."

Jake squeezed my shoulder. "Who's Gambler?"

"Kevin Anderson."

"Two black coffees. Hoodie guy. I can see it." Jake nodded.

CHAPTER FIFTY-TWO

Sophie gasped. "He's always so nice when he comes into the bakery."

"Oh yeah, you know him." I wiped at the wetness on my face, unsure if it was rain or tears of relief.

"Breakfast croissant and jelly-filled donut every Saturday morning. He's usually my first customer of the day."

How did I not realize?

Chief Young screeched to a halt, parked cattywampus, and ran to where we stood on the sidewalk. "What's going on? The bank's security company called, reporting several of the silent alarms triggered even though the bank is closed."

I raised my hand. "That was me."

"What's happening?" His right hand hovered over his gun, and he looked both ways.

"Rita's hurt, but she's one of the conspirators behind Willow's murder. Also, Mary Moore, Vince's mother, appears to be the mastermind behind the deadly deed. She's in my truck somewhere at the farmers' market."

Matt's eyes bulged. "Don't go anywhere. I've got a whole heap of questions for ya."

"Okay, but I need to sit down." My legs quivered.

"Fine, but don't touch anything involved in the events that went down here tonight." Matt stalked to the curb and barked orders into his cellphone.

Sophie patted my shoulder. "Let's go sit in one of the comfy chairs they provide for loan customers."

I turned, but my noodle legs wobbled. "Oh no."

Jake slipped one arm around my shoulders and steadied me. "It's probably the shock. Lean against me."

The three of us walked into the bank. I pointed to the black leather chairs. "We never touched that area."

More sirens sounded.

We settled into the chairs. Local cops and deputies walked back and forth. Rita was hauled off in the back of an ambulance and followed by a sheriff's vehicle.

Jake said, "May as well get comfortable. It's probably going to be a long night."

Sophie huffed. "I'll be back." She turned on her toe and headed in Matt's direction.

Jake lifted his eyebrows. "What's that about?"

"Knowing Sophie, she'll be back with coffee for the authorities and comfort food for us." My stomach growled. Besides the comfort of friends and food, I took time to call my daughter. She needed to hear I was safe before rumors reached her, and I needed to hear her voice. It'd been a long day, and the night wouldn't end anytime soon.

Chapter Fifty-Three

The next morning, Cowboy's barking woke me up. Sun streamed through the bedroom window, and my phone display showed it was close to eight.

Upon standing, I fought off a dizzy spell. It'd been a short night, and I never functioned well when sleep deprived. Once the room quit spinning, I headed to the kitchen. "Good morning." I opened the crate and rubbed the growing retriever's head. "Is it time to let you sleep in the bedroom with me? Or after weeks of roaming, do you like the security of your crate?"

Cowboy licked my face, then trotted to the back door.

I walked outside with him, wearing a faded blue daisy T-shirt and shorts.

Now that I'd helped catch Willow's killer, what did my future hold? I'd dreamed of working with plants for most of my life. My journey of proving Paige's innocence had cost me dearly. Yet if I'd had to do it all over again, I'd still stand up for my friend.

If I humbled myself, was it possible to get back my old job at the pharmacy? Even if it didn't fill me with joy, it paid the bills.

"Anybody home?" One of the Nelle sisters called out from the side of the house.

"I'm coming."

Cowboy raced me to the gate.

Ruby, Gaby, and Rosalita all stood wearing grins as big as Texas. Each one held a planter of flowers.

Rosalita said, "Don't just stand there, Emma. These are heavy."

My dog barked, then ran the perimeter.

I opened the gate and took the containers. "What are y'all doing?"

"You're our friend, and you need help. So, here we are." Ruby leaned close. "You might want to fix yourself up. There are men coming too."

"Men?" My voice squeaked.

Ruby nodded. "You're one of us, and we're fixing to help you out of this jam. First, get changed."

I set the flowers in the shade. "Do you mind if the dog stays with you? Or would you prefer to come inside?"

Gaby pointed to my patio table and chairs. "We'll sit right there, and the dog won't bother us."

"Okay, thanks." I dashed inside. For the love of daffodils, the sisters were up to something. It didn't take me long to wash up and slip on more appropriate clothing. I grabbed my straw cowgirl hat and headed to the door. On my way out, Cowboy darted inside.

Jake and Celia stood on the patio deep in conversation, and I joined them. "Hi, Celia. Jake, can you explain what's going on?"

He reached for a cup on the patio table and handed it to me. "Hot tea sweetened with local honey. As for the rest, the sisters called the locals together. The plan is to replant your gardens with starts, I think they called it. They don't want you slowed down by planting seeds again."

I sipped my tea and gazed at my crowded yard. Tess Carranza, Faith and Zig Meier, Buddy Hewitt, Tyler Legend, Katie Paxson, Wayne Johns, Dr. Bushy Erb, and Sophie. Why wasn't she at the bakery?

There were even a few people I didn't recognize. I pinched my lips to stop their trembling. Nobody wanted to see me cry.

Sophie hurried over to me. "We need some guidance from you on where the different plants need to go."

"Why are you here?"

She shrugged. "That's what friends are for. I put a note on the bakery door, telling people to come over and lend a hand."

"Oh, my goodness. Thanks." I gave her a quick hug, then gathered my sketches from the garden shed. Whatever my friends and neighbors had brought over would be perfect, even if they weren't what I'd originally planned to plant.

By late afternoon, the crowd had dwindled to Jake and me.

I pointed toward the patio. "Let's have a seat. I think there's some lemonade left."

"Sounds like a plan."

"Hello, Emma?" A familiar masculine voice called out from the sideyard.

"We're on the patio."

Matt appeared. "I heard you had quite the crowd here earlier."

"Sure did." I was too emotional to express my appreciation, so I changed the subject. "Help yourself to a cookie or whatever is left."

He took three cookies and a can of Dr. Pepper, then sat in a patio chair. "Thanks. It's been a long day."

"Did you get any sleep?"

"Nope. But it's worth it to be able to report our progress to you."

"How soon until I get Ms. Daisy back?"

"Give me a couple of days for the lab techs to finish going over it. Or should I say her?" He bit into a chocolate chip cookie.

It was easier to be patient with the police chief now that I knew he'd made some arrests.

Jake winked at me.

Matt wiped his mouth with the back of his hand. "Mary Moore convinced Rita Flores the answer to all of Vince's problems would be to get rid of Willow. They knew a divorce would ruin Vince, so they had to act fast. Mary convinced Rita to ask Dave to kill Willow. Mary also provided the money to pay Rusty. When that didn't work, they tried to find Gambler, otherwise known as Kevin Anderson. Time was running out before the divorce hearing, so Rita went to talk to Willow. She asked her to take it easy on Vince. Willow wouldn't agree. The women argued, and Rita left in a rage. She called Mary and told her the hit was on. Gambler was ready and waiting."

"Whoa, talk about the worst mother-in-law in history. What about Nick?"

"Gambler waited for him to leave the store before approaching Willow. There wasn't time for him to snatch her and take her to some remote region.

Instead, he killed her there and tried to make it look like Paige did it."

Jake cleared his throat.

I spoke up, "Vince was the first person I thought of."

Jake rubbed his hands together. "Speaking of Vince, did you have time to look at the files we gave you?"

"We did, and we contacted the FBI. They have an agent questioning Vince now. Rita Flores, Dave Smith, Kevin Anderson, and Mary Moore are also being questioned by my officers. Jake, we may have an opening for you sooner than I expected."

I said, "Who wrecked my yard?"

"Best I can tell, it was Kevin. That slimeball will pretty much do anything for a buck, especially if he's not doing well at the poker table."

"The poker chip made me think it was him. What about Vince's father?"

"Daniel Moore had nothing to do with the murder or anything else bad. He's innocent."

"That's good to hear." I sighed. "He's awful nice. Do you believe he'll return to Baltimore?"

"My best hunch is he'll remain in Lutz for the sake of Christine and Blake. Willow's family is actively involved now too."

"Matt, do you think Nick killed his first wife?"

"That happened before I became the chief of police. Give me time to wrap up Willow's murder, then one of us will take a look at her case." Matt stood. "I need to hit the road. There's more to do before I can call it a day."

"Matt, thanks for the updates."

"No problem. I'll see myself out." He moseyed away.

Jake smiled. "I'm surprised he didn't offer you a job."

"Even though I'd like to see justice for Rhonda Johns, I don't want to be a cop. This is where I belong. Growing flowers." I motioned toward the gardens. The town had stood by me today, and they'd restored my faith in people.

"If it hadn't been for your tenacity to prove Paige was innocent, I'm not positive Matt would've solved the crime. Leastways not as fast as he did."

"I appreciate the compliment, but the only mysteries I plan to solve in the future will be the fictional ones I read for book club."

"Good to know." Jake stood. "I'll see you around, Emma."

"You betcha." I walked him to the gate. "Take care of yourself."

"You too, Sunshine." He kissed my forehead and disappeared before I could respond.

Goosebumps danced up my spine in a delightful Texas two-step, and I smiled. Hopefully, Jake would stick around town.

I walked through my restored gardens. My daughter and Emma's Flowers were my top priorities. It was time to trust myself to make my business work. It was time to trust men. They weren't all like my husband and Vince. Jake had turned out to be one of the good guys.

The time had come to open my eyes to all the possibilities life had to offer. I'd start as soon I recovered from solving my first homicide.

Kentucky Hot Brown Sliders

Ingredients:

- 12-ct. pkg. small sweet Hawaiian rolls
- 6 Slices Gruyère cheese, divided
- ½ pound thinly sliced deli turkey
- 1 small tomato, cut into ¼-inch slices
- Cook 6 slices thick-cut bacon then cut into 2-inch pieces
- ¼ cup shredded Parmesan cheese
- ¾ cup melted butter, melted
- 1 tablespoon Dijon
- 1 ½ teaspoons Worcestershire sauce
- 1 teaspoon light brown sugar

Directions:

1. Preheat oven to 350°F. Lightly spray an 11- x 7-inch baking dish with cooking spray. Horizontally cut rolls and place in the baking dish.
2. Cut 3 slices Gruyère cheese and place on rolls. Add turkey slices on top of cheese. Add tomato slices on turkey, then add bacon pieces. Add remaining cheese slices on top of bacon. Sprinkle with Parmesan cheese and add roll tops.
3. Stir together melted butter, Dijon mustard, Worcestershire, and brown sugar. Carefully pour over rolls and allow it to soak into rolls. Cover dish with foil, and bake until cheese is melted, approximately 15 minutes. Uncover, and bake until the tops are golden brown and crisp,

probably eight to ten minutes. Allow to stand 5 minutes before serving.

Gardening Tips from Emma Justice

When starting your garden, don't mix light and water needs. It's important to pay attention to the light and water needs of your plants. Mixing plants with different needs can lead to over- or under- watering. Some flowers thrive in the shade while others thrive in direct sunlight. So, you can see why it's important to plant your flowers where they have the best chance to grow.

If your soil is too tough to work with, consider raised beds. Include a weed barrier on the bottom, cover it with good loam topsoil and compost and fill the bed. Raised beds are good for flowers and vegetables.

Happy gardening!

About the Author

Jackie Layton is the author of cozy mysteries with Spunky Southern Sleuths. Her stories are set in Texas, Georgia, and South Carolina. She lives on the coast of South Carolina where she enjoys walks on the beach and golf cart rides around the marsh. Reading, gardening, and traveling are some of her favorite hobbies. She always keeps a notebook handy to write down ideas for future stories. Be careful what you say around her, because it might end up in a book.

SOCIAL MEDIA HANDLES:
https://www.facebook.com/JackieLaytonAuthor
https://www.facebook.com/Joyfuljel
https://www.pinterest.com/jackielaytonauthor/
https://twitter.com/joyfuljel

AUTHOR WEBSITE:
https://jackielaytoncozyauthor.com/

Also by Jackie Layton

A Low Country Dog Walker Mystery Series:
Bite the Dust
Dog-Gone Dead
Bag of Bones
Caught and Collared
A Killer Unleashed